Praise for *Tough Luck*

'From the first page of this noir thriller, you know things are only going to get worse, but you can't stop reading.'

Newsweek

'Jason Starr's *Tough Luck* (is) the kind of book you read with a wince, but you read it straight through because you can't put it down. Starr (is) a terrifically taut writer.'

Baltimore Sun

'A wild ride through a mob-saturated Italian-American community in 1980s New York, keeping the surprises coming up to the last sentence.'

Publisher's Weekly

Praise for *Hard Feelings*

'a tale that reads like James M Cain modernised by Bret Easton Ellis ...'

Maxim Jakubowski, *Guardian Unlimited*

'... In his psychological thriller *Hard Feelings* ... Starr has plumbed the shallows of his brittle characters and their selfish lives, depicting them in a hard-edged style that is clean, cold and extremely chilling ...'

New York Times Book Review

'... Jason Starr is the first writer of his generation to convincingly update the modern crime novel by giving it provocative new spins and *Hard Feelings* is his most accomplished thriller yet. It might be new-school noir but like the classics of the genre it has a brutal escalation of tension, pungent dialogue, a hardboiled simplicity and grace. It's also darkly funny and a pure pleasure to read. As you race through it you realize that Jim Thompson has just moved to Manhattan ...'

Bret Easton Ellis,

'... a gripping novel of paranoia and obsession that's damn near impossible to put down ...'

Jim Driver, *Time Out*

"... a powerfully written, thoroughly involving novel of paranoia, obsession and revenge ...'

Brian Ritterspak, *Crime Time*

'... Convincing and entertaining ... *Hard Feelings* dances a mesmerizing tango between reality and its menacing shadow ...'

Time Out New York

Praise for *Fake I.D.*

'Bang up-to-date, but reminiscent of David Goodis and Jim Thompson, *Fake 'I.D.'* is a powerful novel of the American Dream turning into the American Nightmare that marks Starr out as a writer to follow.'

Time Out

Praise for *Nothing Personal*

'... Original modern noir tale reminiscent of Jim Thompson or David Goodis ...'

The Irish Times

'... Diabolically well-plotted noir thriller ... Gentle readers should take heed ...'

'... Wholly satisfying. *Nothing Personal* is a fast, well-paced and well-plotted domestic crime thriller ...'

'... The King of Noir is back. It doesn't get any darker or funnier than this ... The best novel of the year ...'

Praise for *Cold Caller*

'... Well crafted and very scary ...'

'... Cool, deadpan, a rollercoaster ride to hell ...'

'... Tough, composed and about as noir as you can go. Starr is a worthy successor to Charles Willeford ...'

'... Tough, dark, elegant, pure 90s noir ...'

'... At the cutting edge of the revival of classic American noir fiction ...'

TWISTED CITY
JASON STARR

Also by Jason Starr

JASON STARR

TWISTED CITY

NO EXIT PRESS

This edition published in March 2005 by No Exit Press,
P.O.Box 394, Harpenden, Herts, AL5 1XJ
www.noexit.co.uk

A CIP catalogue record for this book is available from the British
Library.

ISBN 1 84243 132 3

2 4 6 8 10 9 7 5 3 1

Typeset by Avocet Typeset, Typeset, Chilton, Aylesbury, Bucks
Printed and bound in Great Britain by Cox & Wyman, Reading

For Sandy and Chynna

1

LEAVING THE INTERVIEW with Robert Lipton, the CEO of Byron Technologies, I wrote the lead to my article in my head:

After Byron Technologies' dismal first half performance, analysts will search for signs of life in the company's third quarter earnings report, but the bottom line could be the end of the line for this floundering tech start-up.

Actually, I could've gone either way on Byron. While the company had decent quarter-to-quarter revenue growth and showed increasing sales, their cash-burn rate was out of control and they were losing a ton of money.

Lipton seemed like a good guy and I would've liked to write an article with a positive spin, but Jeff Sherman, the wonderful editor-in-chief of *Manhattan Business* magazine, had a rule—no more than three positive articles in a row. Since my last three articles had been favorable, this one had to be a bashing.

Waiting for the elevator on the twenty-ninth floor of the Seventh Avenue office building, I noticed a woman standing to my right. She was a few years younger than me, maybe thirty-two, with short, stylishly cut red hair and pale, lightly freckled skin. She had a slender, attractive build and was wearing a black designer business suit. Something about her appearance reminded me of my sister, Barbara.

I wasn't planning on saying anything to the woman, but she caught me staring at her and I smiled instinctively. When she smiled back I said, "Hi, how's it going?"

"Good," she said. "Thanks."

We both looked up at the digital numbers indicating the building's floors. I continued to look over at her, still thinking about my sister. When we made eye contact again I said, "Long day, huh?"

"Yeah," she said, blushing.

There was another awkward silence as I noticed that the ring finger on her left hand was bare. When she looked at me again I said, "Do you want to go for a drink?"

I wasn't usually impulsive, and the question surprised me as much as it did her. She hesitated for a few seconds, sizing me up. I guess I didn't look like a serial killer, because she said, "Okay. Sure."

We got on the elevator together and talked some more. Her name was Heather. She was a marketing exec at an ad agency. When I told her I was a reporter for *Manhattan Business* she seemed surprisingly interested, asking me a lot of questions about my job. We left the building and headed downtown on Seventh Avenue. It was starting to get dark.

"So where are we going?" Heather asked me.

"There's this Scottish bar on Forty-fourth," I said.

"Okay," she said.

We continued talking, mostly about our jobs. Our arms brushed a few times and she didn't seem to mind. Waiting for a traffic light to change, we stood face-to-face for a few seconds. She had light blue eyes that went well with her hair. I decided she was Irish, or part Irish. I realized she looked nothing like my sister, who had dark, wavy hair and dark eyes like me.

The front of St. Andrews was smoky and noisy. It seemed like an office party was going on, because everyone was in business suits and seemed to know each other. We wove our way to the back and settled onto two available stools at the bar. A bartender wearing a dark-green-and-navy-plaid kilt took our drink order—a pint of Guinness for me, a bottle of Corona for her.

"So where're you from?" Heather asked.

"Originally, Long Island," I said. "You?"

"Westchester," she said.

"Really. What part?"

"Ever heard of Hartsdale?"

"Sure," I said. "I went to school with a couple guys from around there. You know Mike Goldberg?"

"No."

"Stu Fox?"

"No."

"Oh, well."

The bartender brought our drinks. I gave him fifteen bucks and told him to keep the change.

I sipped my beer, then said, "You know what's funny? When I first saw you, you reminded me of my sister."

"Really?"

"Yeah," I said, "but the thing is you look nothing like her."

"I guess it's just one of those things," she said, smiling. She took a sip of beer, crossing her slender legs, then said, "So does your sister live in the city?"

"Yeah," I said. "I mean, no. I mean, she used to live in the city. She died fourteen months ago."

"I'm sorry."

"It's okay."

I sipped my beer, realizing that my palms were sweaty.

"You know what I think?" she said. "I think when people die they stay with the people they loved for eternity."

"You mean like ghosts?"

"Or spirits. Or just an energy. I don't believe there's any such thing as dying."

"I like that idea," I said.

14

We looked into each other's eyes for a few seconds, then laughed nervously at the same time. I liked Heather and I could tell she liked me too.

We finished our beers and ordered another round. Over half an hour went by and the conversation was still lively. I didn't want to hit on her too hard, but I also didn't want to give her the idea I wasn't interested. So at an appropriate time, after she said something funny and I laughed, I casually rested my right hand on her left leg. Right away I knew I'd blown it. She immediately crossed her legs, rotated away from me on her bar stool, and checked her watch. I tried to make more conversation, pretend nothing had happened, but she stopped talking. A few minutes later she said she had forgotten that her cousin was coming over to her apartment tonight and she had to meet her. I tried to talk her into staying, but she thanked me for the drinks and left the bar quickly.

Finishing my second pint alone, I felt like a moron. A nice girl like Heather probably dated guys ten times before sleeping with them, and I had started pawing at her like a horny teenager. If I'd just played it cool, maybe asked for her number or suggested meeting for lunch sometime, maybe it could have led to something.

I ordered another pint, feeling like even more of a jerk.

I had a deadline at two P.M. tomorrow for my article, but I wasn't ready to leave the bar. As I was nursing my third Guinness, the drunk-looking guy with long, stringy brown hair who had sat on Heather's vacated bar stool stuck out his big sweaty hand and said, "Eddie. Eddie Lomack."

15

Normally I hated when drunks talked to me at bars, and I would have ignored Eddie, but my own good drunk feeling was starting to set in, so I had more patience than usual.

"David," I said without shaking his hand.

"David," he said. "That's a good name. Simple, anyway. Don't gotta spell it out for people a lot."

"That's true," I said, wishing I'd kept my mouth shut.

"People don't ask me to spell my name either," Eddie slurred. "I just say my name's Eddie and that's good enough for them." He laughed. "So what happened with that girl you were talkin' to?"

"Girl?"

"The hot little redhead who was just here."

"There was a hot little redhead here?"

"Come on, I saw you walk in together; then she got up and left. What the hell happened?"

"Oh, *her*," I said. "She was late for an appointment."

Eddie gave me a long, drunken stare, his eyes looking like they weren't firm in their sockets, and then he said, "Late for an appointment, my ass. She ran out on you, didn't she?"

"Let's just say there was no love connection," I said.

Eddie laughed, more than necessary. I shifted my stool away from him to avoid being hit by saliva, and then I looked at my half-full pint, deciding I'd leave as soon as it was gone.

"Who needs her?" Eddie said when he was through laughing. "You can do better than that, my man. Hey, you wanna see a picture of my girlfriend?"

Eddie leaned back, wobbling so much he almost fell off the stool. After he steadied himself, he reached into his pocket and took out his wallet. He opened it to a picture of a naked blond centerfold.

"Pretty good-lookin', huh?" he said. Then he said, "Oh, and here's my other girlfriend."

He opened his wallet to a picture of another naked blonde.

I smiled and took another gulp of my beer; then I put the glass down on the bar, deciding that I'd had enough. I reached into my right pocket to leave a tip for the bartender when I realized my wallet was gone. I felt my other pockets, but the wallet wasn't there either. I checked all my pockets again, then looked around on the floor near my bar stool.

"What's wrong?" Eddie asked.

"I can't find my wallet," I said.

Eddie started looking around too as I stood up, feeling my pockets again. Then the realization set in that I had been pickpocketed. I suddenly felt hot all over and I became even more frantic.

One of the Scottish bartenders came over and asked me what was wrong.

"Somebody stole my wallet," I said.

"You sure?" he asked.

"Yes, I'm sure!" I shouted.

Now other people nearby were looking over, and a couple of college-age guys started searching on the floor.

Eddie was still looking around too, and then it hit me what had happened.

"Give me my wallet back," I said to Eddie.

He gave me a drunken stare, then said, "The fuck you talkin' about?"

"Come on, I know you took it," I said, "or you were working with somebody who took it." I looked around, but there was no one suspicious-looking nearby. I turned back to Eddie and said, "Give me my fucking wallet back."

A big surly-looking guy with a blond crew cut and bulging muscles squeezed into a tight black T-shirt came over. I figured he was the bouncer. "There a problem here?" he said.

"Yeah, there's a fuckin' problem here," I said. "This guy stole my wallet."

"I didn't steal nobody's wallet," Eddie said.

"He's lying," I said.

Eddie started taking things out of his pockets—his keys, change, crumpled up bills, his own wallet.

"See?" Eddie said. "Where do you think I got his wallet, up my ass?"

"Why do you think he took your wallet?" the bouncer said to me.

"Maybe he didn't take it, but someone else did," I said, "somebody he was working with. He was distracting me while his friend took my wallet."

"I wasn't distracting nobody," Eddie said. "I was just sitting here, minding my own, then he starts screaming I took his wallet."

18

"Did you see him with a friend in the bar?" the bouncer asked me.

"No, I didn't see him," I said, "but that's what happened. Can't you call the cops or something?"

Eddie stood up off his bar stool.

"Hey, enough'a this shit, all right?" he said. "I didn't take your fuckin' wallet."

"Yes you did," I said.

"You callin' me a fuckin' liar?"

"Yes."

"Fuck you, asshole."

I pushed Eddie, not hard, but hard enough to knock him back a few steps. But he was so drunk—or faking drunk— that he fell backward, knocking over the bar stool and spilling his beer onto the woman to his right. The woman's boyfriend started shouting at Eddie, and the bouncer grabbed my arm and pulled me through the crowd toward the front of the bar.

"What the hell're you doing?" I said. "Let go of me."

He didn't let go until we were outside.

"The guy took my wallet," I said, "I'm telling you."

"I don't give a shit about your wallet," the bouncer said. "There's no fightin' in the bar. Now get the hell outta here 'fore I call the cops!"

The bouncer went back inside. A couple of seconds later Eddie came out. He looked at me, then headed away toward Sixth Avenue.

"Please," I said, walking next to him, "I don't want to fight with you, okay, and I don't want to call the cops either—I just want my wallet back. You can keep the money, all right? I just want my credit cards and ID and everything else."

Eddie stopped and turned to face me.

"For the last fuckin' time, I don't have your fuckin' wallet," he said, spraying spit in my face with each *F* sound, "so just leave me the fuck alone."

Watching Eddie walk away, I tried to decide what to do. I could call the cops on my cell phone, but by the time they came Eddie would be gone. Besides, from the position he'd been sitting, Eddie couldn't have taken the wallet himself—his partner had to have taken it, and by now his partner was probably long gone.

Then there was the chance that I was wrong about Eddie altogether—that he'd had nothing to do with it.

I decided that calling the cops would be a waste of time. I'd spend the whole night filling out forms for nothing, because they wouldn't make any effort to catch a pickpocket. I walked to the corner and checked the garbage can, figuring that the thief might have taken the cash and dumped everything else nearby. My wallet wasn't in the top layer of garbage in any of the garbage cans around the intersection of Forty-fourth Street and Sixth Avenue. I walked around the block, checking other garbage cans, finding nothing. Finally, I decided it was hopeless. The pickpocket could have dumped my wallet down a sewer, or anywhere.

I only had forty-five cents on me, so I couldn't take a bus or the subway. Walking home along Seventh Avenue,

I took out my cell phone and got the numbers for my bank and credit card companies, and then I started closing my accounts.

2

DURING THE HALF-HOUR-OR-SO walk to my apartment on West Eighty-first Street, I froze my bank account and closed my credit card accounts, relieved to find out that nothing had been charged on any of my cards. I'd heard horror stories about identity theft, so later I'd have to call the credit bureaus and report that my wallet had been stolen. Then, tomorrow, I'd try to replace my more minor cards—Blockbuster, United Health Care, the New York Public Library, Duane Reade Dollar Rewards Club—and deal with the headache of replacing my Social Security card and driver's license.

As usual, when I entered my apartment hip-hop music was blasting and the living room reeked of pot. I was slightly surprised, because Rebecca had said she was going to be out for the night.

"I'm home!" I called down the hallway, toward the bedroom, but I doubted she could hear me over the pulsing music.

I went into the narrow kitchen. There had been a six pack of Amstel in the fridge this morning, but now there was just an empty carton.

"Sorry, yo, we got thirsty."

I looked over and saw Ray, one of Rebecca's dancing friends, standing there, smiling by the entrance to the kitchen. Ray was a clean-cut Latino guy and he was dressed in tight pants and a tight, ribbed, Ricky Martin-style T-shirt, showing off his lean, ripped body. Rebecca claimed Ray was gay, but I hoped she was lying. If she left me for Ray or somebody else it would've solved a lot of problems.

"It's okay," I said. "I probably shouldn't drink any more tonight anyway."

"*You* out partying?" Ray said, his eyes glassy from the pot he'd smoked. "Say it ain't so."

"I just had a couple beers," I said.

"Still," Ray said. "We should call Eyewitness News down here to do a story. David Miller gets fucked up— details at eleven."

I was used to being the butt of jokes for Ray and Rebecca's other friends; because I held a steady job and didn't drink a lot or do drugs they treated me like I was Mr. Rogers.

As Ray laughed, I took out a carton of orange juice from

the fridge and gulped some from the spout.

"Seriously," Ray said, "sorry about the beer, yo, but we needed to get a buzz on for tonight. But don't worry 'bout it—next time I come by I'll bring you another sixer."

Whenever Ray came over he drank my beer or ate food from the fridge and always promised to replace it, but never did. At this point it was like a running joke.

I was still guzzling orange juice when Rebecca sashayed into the kitchen. She was twenty-four, and there was no doubt she was hot. She had wavy brown hair that went halfway down her back, a fit, slender body, and small, doll-like features. Whenever people asked her what she did for a living she always answered, "I'm a modern dancer," which used to impress me, until I saw her dance. A few weeks after we met, I went to a showcase that she and her friends were putting on at a space they rented out downtown, and I was surprised by how awkward and ungraceful she was. After that night, it became painful to hear her talk about her dancing, taking it so seriously, when I knew she was deluding herself. She blew off most of her dance classes and auditions, sleeping through the alarm clock, or just not bothering to show up. The only dancing she did on a regular basis was when she went out to clubs and partied with her friends four or five nights a week.

"I thought I heard your voice," she said. "What up, yo?"

Rebecca was originally from Duncanville, Texas, then she lived in L.A. for several years before moving to New York. She had a faint Texas accent and spoke in Southern

Californian, slash Manhattan, slash twenty-something "upspeak," making the ends of most of her sentences sound like questions. She also used a lot of pseudo hip-hop slang, which most of the time sounded forced and stupid—a white girl from down south trying too hard to fit in in the big city. I used to think her style of speaking was cute; now, like a lot of other things about her, it just annoyed the hell out of me.

But, I had to admit, she looked especially hot tonight in skintight jeans, a pink halter top, and matching pink sandals. I had never seen the sandals before and I realized why my Visa card had a $124 charge on it from a purchase made this afternoon at Wheels of London, a shoe store on Eighth Street.

She came over and kissed me on the lips, slipping her studded-tongue into my mouth for a second or two. She tasted like a bong hit.

Then she pulled back and said, "How was your day, cutie?"

"All right," I said.

"The business writer was out lettin' his hair down tonight," Ray said.

Rebecca looked at me with an intrigued smile. "Are you *drunk*?"

"No, I just had a couple beers with the CEO I was interviewing."

"Oh, how did that go?"

"It went okay," I said. "I mean, I think I got all the information I need for my article."

"Good, I'm *so* happy for you," she said.

"So what's this about a party tonight?" I asked.

"Oh, it was kind of a last-minute thing. Rachel told me about it this afternoon. Her manager's friend is this, like, famous clothing designer or something? Anyway, he's having this big party at this new club in Soho tonight—it should be slammin'. Wanna come?"

I knew she didn't really want me to go—if she did I wouldn't have had to basically invite myself—but I wouldn't've gone if she begged me. When Rebecca and I first met and I was excited about dating her, I used to go out clubbing and barhopping with her and her friends all the time. It was fun the first couple of times—dressing up like an MTV groupie in FUBU jerseys, Snoop Dogg jeans, and other clothes Rebecca bought for me. But after a while I started feeling ridiculous—the old guy in his mid-thirties out with a bunch of kids in their early twenties—and Rebecca started going out without me.

"I'd love to," I said, "but I have a deadline for tomorrow afternoon."

"Blow it off," Rebecca said, acting disappointed.

"Sorry, can't," I said.

"Well, I'm gonna miss you." She kissed me again, making out with me for a few seconds. When she broke away she said to Ray, "Ready to go, cuz?"

"After you, baby," Ray said, smiling widely as he put his arm around her waist.

As Rebecca was leaving the kitchen, I said, "By the way, your credit cards won't work tonight."

Rebecca stopped and turned around, suddenly panicked. "Why not?"

"I got pickpocketed."

"You did?" she said, sounding more concerned about her credit cards than the fact that I had been robbed.

"Yeah, it must've happened in an elevator or something," I said. "I thought I felt something, but when I realized what had happened it was too late—my wallet was gone."

"That sucks," Rebecca said, still probably thinking about her credit cards. "Did you call the police?"

"For what?"

"I don't know. Just to report it?"

"They won't do anything."

"You sure?"

"He's right," Ray said. "The police won't do shit about a wallet."

"So why won't *my* credit cards work?" she asked.

"Well, I had to close the accounts, didn't I?" I said.

"I guess that was smart," she said. "You think you can, like, lend me some money tonight?"

Lend, I thought. That was a good one.

"The only money I have is in the dresser in the bedroom," I said. "I can't get any more until I open my bank accounts tomorrow."

Rebecca pouted. I wanted to say, "Too bad," but I guess if I had the ability to turn her down I wouldn't have let her have access to my money and credit cards in the first place.

"How much do you need?" I asked weakly.

"How much do you have?" she asked.

"I don't know. Maybe twenty bucks."

"That's *it*?"

"Sorry."

It felt good to put my foot down with Rebecca for once, but of course in this case it helped that I had no choice.

"Hey, I know," Rebecca said, brightening. "You keep your Discover card in the top drawer of your dresser? So that card must still work, right?"

I'd forgotten about the Discover card. I rarely used it, but Rebecca had one in her name too.

"Yeah, it works," I said.

"Slammin'!" Rebecca said. She started out of the kitchen with Ray, then turned back to me and said, "Hey, you sure you don't want to come out with us?"

"Next time," I said.

"I shouldn't be home *too* late," Rebecca said. "Two or three. I have my cell if you need me."

"You mean *my* cell," I said.

"What?" she asked, confused.

"Have a great time," I said, smiling.

When Rebecca and Ray were gone I scavenged the fridge, eating some leftover burrito from the other night and a yogurt, and then I went to the alcove in the living room and booted up my computer. The Windows wallpaper came on—a picture of my sister Barbara and me, taken at Syracuse. She was a senior and I was a sophomore and we were in front of my dorm—me in jeans and an Orangemen basketball jersey and her in a Lands' End sweater, a knapsack over one shoulder. She looked good in the picture, but it didn't really do her justice. She had pale skin, but the picture made it ruddier, especially around her cheeks, and she must've been having a bad hair day, because her hair looked much frizzier than it really was. I tried to remember who had taken the picture—maybe Aunt Helen or a friend of Barbara's— then I became distracted by the scent of Glow by J. Lo that Rebecca had left in her wake.

I opened a file in Word and worked on my article for a while, but I couldn't concentrate, thinking about the last time I saw Barbara, at Sloan-Kettering.

"You can't even look at me anymore," she said. "I disgust you."

She looked so awful—half-bald from the chemo, her skin ghostly gray. It was hard to believe the tumor in her brain had been discovered only three weeks earlier.

"What're you talking about?" I said. "That's crazy."

"See? You can't even look at me right now."

I turned toward her, realizing she was crying.

"Come on, stop it," I said, getting up to find her a tissue.

"Get the hell out of here!" she screamed. "Just go!"

"Calm down, I didn't mean—"

"I hate you, you son of a bitch! Just get the fuck out of here!"

I started working again, writing a line I'd insert somewhere in the story about how Byron Technologies would likely have to seek equity financing later in the year, but I couldn't focus, remembering the awful, hollow sounds the shovelfuls of dirt made against Barbara's coffin. I had been in shock during the entire funeral, unable to cry or show any emotion, and for weeks afterward I remained in a zombielike state, unwilling to accept the fact that she was dead. I stopped showing up for my job as a technology reporter at the *Wall Street Journal*, without giving any explanation. Eventually the paper's personnel department informed me that I had been terminated, but I didn't care. I spent most of my time in bed, lying on the couch, or wandering the streets, confronted by memories of Barbara wherever I went. Just standing on a street corner would remind me of a time we had been on that corner, and I'd remember snippets of conversations we'd had, things we'd laughed about, and the memories would be so vivid that the idea that she was dead, that I couldn't call her up on my cell phone or drop by her place to hang out, would seem incomprehensible.

I remembered one Saturday afternoon, taking one of my usual long, aimless walks through Central Park. The park had as many memories as the streets, but it was a beautiful, early spring day and I needed to get on with my life. I walked to the East Side, then back through the winding paths of the Ramble, exiting onto the wooden footbridge. I'd taken a picture of Barbara on the bridge once. Holding the camera vertically, I'd knelt, shooting up at Barbara, who was posing like a fashion model with a hand on one hip and her windblown hair pushed over to one side, her image perfectly framed by the midtown skyscrapers in the distance. I continued along the path adjacent to the West Drive, and stopped for a moment past the boat landing, where people were lounging on the grass, listening to a scruffy guy playing old folk songs on an acoustic guitar. During "Moon Shadow," I remembered how Barbara had a few old, scratched-up Cat Stevens albums that I'd donated to a thrift shop with most of her other things. The memories were getting too painful, and I was about to leave when I spotted a girl on a blanket on the lawn.

The girl was wearing denim cutoffs and a red bikini top, her head tilted to the left slightly, toward the sun. She looked young, in her early twenties, and the way she was lounging, looking so relaxed and content, reminded me of all the afternoons Barbara and I had spent in the park.

I was going to walk away when the woman looked at me and smiled widely and waved. I thought it was cute—the way she seemed so spontaneous and comfortable with herself, like a child almost. I smiled, realizing it was probably the first time I'd smiled in days, or even weeks. I also realized that I needed someone else in my life, that I couldn't take being alone anymore.

Without giving it any more thought, I approached the girl, figuring I'd say, *Hey, don't I know you from somewhere?* I knew it was a lame opening, but it had worked for me several times before, and besides, I wasn't the type of guy who could think of great, spontaneous pickup lines.

But, as it turned out, I didn't have to use any line,

because the girl spoke to me first.

"Hi, I'm Rebecca."

She smiled again, and I noticed the silver stud glistening on her tongue. I'd never understood why people pierced their tongues, or any other parts of their bodies other than their earlobes, but I had to admit there was something sexy about it. She also had wide, eager eyes and a friendly smile. I stared at her for a few seconds before I said, "Oh, I'm David," and we started talking. The conversation wasn't exactly riveting—we discussed how great the weather had been so far this spring, and how pretty the lake was—but I could tell she liked me. Then the scruffy guy finished "Moon Shadow" and started "Stairway to Heaven."

"Nobody can play it like Jimmy Page," I said.

"Who?" she asked.

Okay, so there was a generation gap, but there was something intriguing about her, and at least I wasn't thinking about Barbara.

After a few minutes, she invited me to join her on her blanket. I happily accepted, and I tried my best to keep the conversation going. Every guy has a repertoire of a few stories that he uses in an attempt to woo women, and I was no exception. I told her about the trip Barbara and I had taken to Europe one summer during college, the time a frying pan started an oil fire in my kitchen and I barely got out of my apartment alive, about the boating accident that had killed my parents when I was five, and then I went on my usual rant about how crowded Central Park was getting and how Riverside Park was much hipper. After I was through with my monologue, my mouth dry from talking so much, she told me all about the trauma of her parents' divorce and how she'd moved to California the summer after high school graduation. After living in L.A. for several years, trying to make it as a modern dancer, she moved to New York, and she was currently living on a friend's couch in Brooklyn. Although, as I spoke, she said "wow" and "awesome" at appropriate times, I knew she was barely paying attention. I wasn't offended, though, because I wasn't really listening to her either. I guess we were at that awkward, beginning stage of a relationship when you're too concerned with trying to impress the other person to really care about anything else.

I walked her out of the park, to the subway on Seventy-ninth, and asked her for her phone number. She wrote her number in eyeliner on my forearm, which I thought was cute and sexy. The next night we went out to dinner at the Cajun in Chelsea. Afterward, we went out to a club called Aria, which she obviously frequented, because all of the bouncers and bartenders called her "Becky." We danced for a couple of hours, then went back to my place and had sex. She liked to take control in bed, getting on top and pinning me down hard, and I was also really turned on by the big dragonfly tattoo just above her ass.

Over the next couple of weeks, I didn't obsess about Barbara as much, and I was able to live a normal, functional life again. I couldn't get my job back at the

Journal, so I started applying for other jobs, and tried to do some freelance work on the side. Rebecca and I went out sometimes, but most nights she just came over to my place, usually late in the evening or early in the morning, to have sex. Most of my past girlfriends had been conservative in bed, so it was refreshing to be with Rebecca, who loved to bite me and talk dirty. Once in a while, she tied me up to the bedposts and spanked me.

After we'd been seeing each other for about a month, the friend whose couch Rebecca had been crashing on lost her lease, leaving Rebecca with no place to live. Figuring that she and I were practically living together anyway, I suggested she move her things over to my place until she found another apartment. I made it clear to her that I couldn't see us getting seriously involved, and she agreed that we were "just having fun." As long as we both had the same minimal expectations, I figured I had nothing to worry about.

When we'd met, Rebecca was working part-time at a coffee bar in Soho. She got fired from her job after showing up late three mornings in a row—each time, she'd been wasted or had a hangover and slept through the alarm clock—so I started lending her money while she tried to find something else. We kept a tab of how much she owed me, but it was only a few hundred dollars, and I didn't really care if she paid me back.

One night, after Rebecca and I had been living together for a few weeks or so, I took her out with me to a party at my friend Keith's, a guy I knew from Syracuse. Keith and my other friends acted weird all night, and I figured they were just jealous because Rebecca was much better looking than their dates. About a week later, after work one night, I went to Ruby Foo's on Broadway to meet Keith and Mike, another friend, for dinner. When I approached the table I was surprised to see Keith and Mike seated with several of my friends, some with their wives and girlfriends. It was June and my birthday was in October, so I knew this wasn't a surprise party.

I joined them at the table and said, smiling, "Hey, what's going on?"

Everyone was friendly, but no one would explain why they were all there.

"Come on, what's this all about?" I asked.

People looked at each other, then turned to Keith for leadership. Keith stared at me for a few seconds, then said, "We're worried about you, man."

"Worried about what?" I said. I had no idea what he was talking about.

"We don't think Rebecca's right for you," he said.

I didn't know what to do, so I smiled. Everybody else remained very serious.

"You gotta be kidding me," I said. "Why isn't she right for me?"

"We think she's dangerous," Keith said.

I laughed. Rebecca was ditzy, shallow, a little on the wild side, but dangerous?

"Dangerous?" I said.

I looked at my friend Joe, who'd brought his wife,

Sharon. Then I turned toward Phil, with his girlfriend, Jane, and looked over at Tom, and Stu, and Mark, and Rob, but no one would crack a smile.

"So what is this," I said, "some kind of intervention?"

"We're doing it for your own good, my brother," Phil said.

Since Phil had gotten a job in the marketing department at Jive Records he had started calling everybody "my brother."

"Look, I'm sorry if you guys didn't hit it off with Rebecca," I said, "but I really don't think it's any of your business."

"She's psycho," Joe said.

"Psycho?" I said. "How is she psycho?"

"Didn't you hear what she said to me the other night?" Sharon said.

I remembered how at the party Rebecca had had a few too many and had argued with Sharon, calling her "a dumb, ugly bitch."

"So her drinking gets a little out of hand sometimes," I said.

"She said she wanted to slit my throat," Sharon said.

"She didn't mean it," I said. "Come on, you guys have never gotten drunk?"

I was looking in particular at Tom, infamous for drinking sixteen bottles of Rolling Rock one night freshman year.

"I saw her doing coke in the bathroom," Keith said.

"So what's a little coke?" I said. "Come on, Keith, man.

I remember in college, you used to make runs into the city all the time for coke and 'shrooms."

"That was the eighties," Keith said, as if that explained everything.

"We're doing this for your own good," Mike said. "We think the girl's got some serious problems and you're gonna get hurt."

"You have no idea what you're talking about," I said.

"You're hiding from yourself emotionally," Jane said.

Phil and Jane had been going out for about six months, and I barely knew her. She was going for her Ph.D. in psychology at the New School, so of course she thought she had all the answers.

"Oh, am I?" I said.

"You haven't fully dealt with your emotions about your sister's death," she continued. "You're only in this relationship with Rebecca because it's a convenient place to hide. You're very vulnerable right now, and you're probably not even aware of what you're doing."

"You don't even know me," I said. "Who the fuck do you think you are?"

"Chill, my brother," Phil said.

"I appreciate your concern," I said to everyone, "but I think you're all a bunch of assholes."

I stormed out of the restaurant. The next day, Keith left a message for me at work, apologizing for organizing the intervention, but reminding me that it was for my own good. I didn't bother returning the call.

Over the next couple of months, I fell out of touch with

most of my friends, but I stayed with Rebecca. Freelancing wasn't working out, and supporting Rebecca was seriously depleting my bank account, so when I was offered a job at *Manhattan Business* for roughly half of what I'd been making at the *Journal*, I had no choice but to take it. Rebecca went about her routine—shopping during the day and going out with her friends at night, and I went about mine—working during the day and into the early evening, and hanging out in my apartment the rest of the time, or occasionally going to a movie alone. Once in a while, Rebecca and I went out to dinner together or hung out in the living room, watching TV, but otherwise the only times we saw each other were when we were having sex. Our romps became even wilder and more adventurous. Sometimes she left me tied up to the bedposts for hours while she went out shopping, and I often wound up with cuts and bruises.

Occasionally, after one of our early-morning sessions, Rebecca got very intense and melodramatic, telling me about how traumatic it was for her when her father left her mother—just packing up one day and leaving without any warning—and how she'd always been terrified of men abandoning her. Whenever Rebecca talked like this I couldn't help feeling trapped. I knew that Rebecca and I had no future together, and I began to dread the inevitable day when I would tell her it was over.

Then, one night in bed, Rebecca started nibbling on my ear playfully and asked me if I could see the two of us getting married someday. Of course the answer was definitely no, but, caught off guard, I changed the subject. The next day, she didn't mention marriage again, but I decided that things were starting to get a little too serious and it was time to call it quits.

When I came home from work, I told her there was something important we needed to discuss.

"What?" she asked.

In gym shorts and a sports bra, doing crunches on the living room floor, she looked especially hot. As usual, rap was blasting on the stereo.

When I turned down the throbbing music she said, "Hey, that was my boy Jay-Z."

"Last night," I said, trying to avoid eye contact, "you said something about us getting married."

"I *did*?" she said, acting surprised.

"Yeah, you did," I said.

"That's so funny, I was probably half-asleep." She held up her head and chest off the floor, her face turning pink as she tightened her abs for several seconds, and then she relaxed.

"What I'm trying to say," I said, "is at this point in my life I don't think I'm really ready to—"

"Don't worry, I didn't mean it," she said.

"You didn't?"

"Of course not. Why would I want to be somebody's wife?" She made the idea sound ridiculous.

"Oh," I said, "because last night you—"

"You shouldn't believe everything I tell you," she said.

We continued to live together and nothing really changed. She went out to hip-hop clubs and bars at least a few nights a week and we hardly spent any time together. She made more passing comments about marriage—usually when she was drunk or on whatever drug was fashionable that week, but sometimes she was completely sober. Whenever I confronted her about it she always claimed that she didn't remember saying it or that she didn't really mean it.

Then, one night, I overheard Rebecca in the living room bragging to her friend Monique about how I was "a little puppy dog," and how well she had trained me. She said she could get me to do anything, even paint her toenails, and she predicted that by next year we'd be engaged with a joint bank account and her name on the lease.

I felt like an idiot for letting Rebecca use me and take advantage of me for all of these months. When Monique left, I marched into the living room, prepared to tell Rebecca to move the hell out. But when I was about to speak, I imagined what it would be like if she left—I'd be alone again, wandering the streets.

Rebecca asked me what was wrong and I said, "Nothing. Coming to bed soon?" And a few days later I was ordering her credit cards in her name.

* * *

I typed the first sentence of my Byron Technologies article and continued outlining the rest of it. In the opening, I'd describe Robert Lipton, the CEO, as "desperate" and describe how he had "irresponsibly deceived investors by pursuing an unrealistic business plan." Then I'd go on about how the company had been rapidly losing market share and was likely to file for Chapter Eleven by year's end.

While the article wouldn't be totally inaccurate—Byron did have some major financial problems, and I had some serious doubts about the long-term viability of the company—it still bothered me that I couldn't write a fair story, outlining the negatives and positives and letting the readers reach their own conclusions. But Jeff Sherman hated lukewarm articles and insisted that in order for the magazine to stay "edgy," reporters had to write strongly opinionated articles no matter what. The other day, when he'd called me into his office and reminded me that I'd written three "puff pieces" in a row and that my Byron Technologies article had to be negative, I told him that I didn't think, in this case, a negative article was justified. He told me, "You don't like the rules? Maybe you'd be happier working someplace else." I would've loved to tell him to go fuck himself, but the job market was tight and, especially with the way Rebecca had been spending my money lately, I couldn't afford to be unemployed.

I was typing so hard my wrists hurt. I took a break, flexing my hands, and then patted my front pants pocket where my wallet had been. A sudden, sickening emptiness overtook me, and I rushed down the hallway to the bedroom. I spilled out the contents of the top drawer of my dresser onto the bed and searched through everything, hoping by some crazy chance it would be there. But after looking through the stuff for the second and third times I realized I was just deluding myself—my favorite picture of Barbara, that I'd taken when she was sixteen, was gone.

I started crying. Not just crying—bawling. Everything—the stress of the whole night, my screwed up relationship with Rebecca, missing Barbara more than I had in months—was hitting me at once. As I sat on the bed, sobbing, taking short, erratic breaths, I imagined that Barbara was with me. She was sitting next to me on the bed, putting an arm around my shoulders, telling me, *Don't worry, Davey. Everything's gonna be okay*.

Then I remembered what Heather had said to me in the bar about spirits. I didn't really believe in any of that metaphysical crap, but, figuring I had nothing to lose, I said to the empty space to my left, "I just want you to know how much I miss you. I think about you a lot, all the time actually, and I wanted to tell you how sorry I am for not saying good-bye to you that day at the hospital, and for acting like such a dick the whole time you were there. But I think you know how much you really meant to me. If you didn't know it, I hope you know it now. I loved you, Barb. I thought you were the greatest sister in the world. I hope you can hear me now, that I'm not just talking to myself. But you're not fucking here, are you?"

I stood up and swatted everything from the bed onto the floor and screamed, "Damn it!" Then, looking down among the contents of the dumped-out dresser drawer, I noticed a snapshot of Rebecca taken in front of the fireplace in the living room. She was standing sideways to the camera in cutoffs and a little-boy T-shirt, her hair flung over to the left side, her lips pursed in an I'm-better-than-you way. The flash had reddened her eyes, giving her a devilish quality.

I left the apartment, not even bothering to take a jacket, and headed toward Central Park. I entered at Eighty-first Street and veered left along the path through the woods. I might have passed an occasional jogger or a body sprawled on a bench, but the park was dark and empty. Then I noticed two young guys—one black, one white or Puerto Rican—walking about twenty yards behind me. I didn't want to look back over my shoulder again, but I sensed they were following me. I started walking faster, but their footsteps were getting louder and I could hear their breathing, so I knew they had gained on me. I started to run as fast as I could, my heart pounding and my adrenaline flowing. I thought about veering off into the woods, but I stayed on the path, and around the next bend I reached a playground and saw streetlights ahead of me. I exited the park at Eighty-fifth Street and Central Park West and walked downtown a block, looking back over my shoulder, relieved to see that the kids weren't following.

I reduced my pace to fast walking, gasping, still looking back after every few strides. I crossed Central Park West at the next light and walked quickly along Eighty-fourth Street. I was angry at myself for getting into a potentially dangerous situation. Normally I had better instincts, avoiding all places in Manhattan that were quiet and unpopulated, especially at night. At Columbus Avenue, my pulse and breathing returned to normal and I started seeing the humor in the situation. If the kids had tried to steal my wallet, I would've had nothing to give them.

Back at my apartment, I cleaned up the mess in the bedroom, then showered. Afterward I felt refreshed and clearheaded, and I decided that tonight I'd finally break up with Rebecca. All I had to say was, *It's over*, and I could go on with my life.

It sounded so simple.

It was after ten o'clock. I returned to my computer, hoping to at least finish a rough draft of my article. I connected my headset to a little digital tape recorder and started transcribing the interview I'd had earlier with Robert Lipton. As I listened to Lipton go on in his upbeat voice about his company's prospects, I kept rehearsing in my head what I'd say to Rebecca. I had trouble concentrating. I mistyped words and sentences and I had to replay parts of the recording, sometimes three or four times. As I was working, I realized that I'd forgotten to contact the credit bureaus about my wallet. I went online and did a search for "what to do if your wallet is stolen" and found all the information I needed. After I called the credit bureaus and put fraud alerts on my accounts, I remembered that I hadn't canceled one card from my wallet—an Emigrant Savings Bank ATM card that I rarely used.

After nearly an hour on the phone, getting put on hold and talking to two customer service reps, I was finally able to close the account. I tried to get back to work, but I was starting to feel the way I had right after I discovered my wallet had been lifted. I felt like a sucker, like I'd been violated. I couldn't believe I'd let it happen. I hadn't been drunk, so I couldn't use that as an excuse. I remembered how Eddie had distracted me, showing me the pictures of the naked women, and how I had leaned forward slightly on my stool to see the first one. At that moment, anyone behind me could have had access to my front pocket and easily swiped my wallet.

I finished outlining the article at about one o'clock. I was exhausted, but I wanted to stay up to have it out with Rebecca. I was afraid that if I waited until the morning, I'd lose my edge and wouldn't be able to go through with it.

I turned on the TV in the living room for some background noise and lay on the couch. I dozed for a while, then woke up and checked my watch. It was past three. I realized that tonight could be one of the nights that Rebecca didn't come home. Sometimes when she went out she didn't return until the next afternoon, claiming that it had gotten late and she was wasted so she'd "crashed" at some friend's place. Of course, I often wondered if she was cheating on me. I hoped she was in bed right now with Ray, or some other guy, and that they were having great sex, or better yet, falling in love.

I got up from the couch and was about to head toward the bedroom when I heard the lock in the door turning. A few seconds later, Rebecca entered. She was obviously wasted—standing unsteadily, her eyes glassy and bloodshot—and when she saw me in the living room facing her she reacted as if she had entered the wrong apartment. Then her confused expression morphed into a drunken smile and she said, "Hey, what up, yo? ... I mean, what up besides you?"

She tossed the Gucci pocketbook that she'd bought last week on my Visa onto a chair, then wobbled over and kissed me on the lips, giving me a whiff of alcohol.

"I had the bestest time tonight," she slurred. "That new club blew, but Chaos was hype, yo. I met this choreographer guy? I forget his name—Mike or Mick or Mel something-or-other. I have his card in my pocketbook." She reached toward her side, slow to realize that she had already put her pocketbook down. She went on: "Anyway, I had such a bitchin' time talking to him. He has this, like, company, you know, a dance company, and he wants me in this, like, show? It's some kind of modern jazz-like show or something or other. Who knows? Next year at this time I might be dancing at Lincoln Center. Don't worry; I'll still talk to you when I'm famous."

She started laughing, as if she'd made an hilarious joke, and then she undressed. First her top came off, and then she wiggled out of her jeans and kicked away her sandals.

"It's over," I said.

Rebecca stared at me, half smiling. My words didn't have the cathartic effect that I'd thought they would.

"What's over?" she finally asked.

"Us," I said. "I want you to move out."

She continued to stare at me ambiguously, then started to laugh.

"Very funny," she said. "I almost thought you were serious for a second."

"I am serious," I said. "We both know we're totally wrong for each other and that this isn't going anywhere. We probably should've broken up months ago, but we should just be mature adults now and—"

"Come on, let's go to bed," she said, coming up to me and taking my hand. "I've been thinking about your hot, studly body all night."

"I'm serious," I said, letting go of her. "I think you'd be a lot happier with somebody else, somebody your own age, somebody you have more in common with."

She came up to me again and put her arms around my waist, pressing her tiny, firm breasts up against my chest, and then she began to run her studded tongue gently along the outline of my lips in a slow, circular motion. I hated that I was getting turned on.

When she started to kiss me I was finally able to pull away and say, "Stop it," although not with much conviction.

"Ooh, you're ready for me, I see," she said, reaching into my gym shorts and starting to kiss me again.

"Stop it," I said again. This time I took a few steps backward, creating several feet between us.

"God, what's wrong with you?" she said. "Wait, I know, it's your wallet, right? You're still bumming about that."

"It's not my wallet," I said. "Look, I know this isn't the best time to talk about this. I mean, you're obviously wasted—"

"I am not wasted," she said defensively. "I didn't even smoke tonight. I just had some E, a few drinks, and one teensy-weensy little line of coke." She held up her thumb and forefinger about an inch apart, as if measuring.

"Whatever," I said. "I just wanted to let you know I made a decision."

She stared at me for a long time with her mouth sagging open in exaggerated disbelief, then said, "Decision? What *decision*? You're making *decisions* about my life, telling me I'm fucking *wasted*? I am not fucking wasted, and you are not fucking breaking up with me."

"Seriously," I said. "I want you to pack your things and move out as soon as possible. Let's not make this any more difficult than it is."

I started toward the hallway leading to the bedroom, proud of myself for expressing my feelings so well, when a large object soared by my head. I ducked, then heard the crash. I looked up and saw that the vase of fake orchids from Pottery Barn had smashed onto the floor, shattering glass all over the hallway.

I turned back toward Rebecca and said, "Are you out of your fucking—" then I had to duck again as another vase—this one ceramic—came at my head. It missed, crashing against the wall behind me, and then I charged her. She was reaching toward the mantel above the fireplace for more breakable objects. As she grabbed a small ceramic pitcher in one hand and a glass candlestick in the other, I held her arms from behind, trying to restrain her.

"Get off!" she screamed. She swung her arms and kicked violently, as if I were trying to strap her into an electric chair.

"Calm down," I said, "just calm the fuck down," but I knew I was just wasting my breath.

I managed to push her back against the brick wall adjacent to the fireplace. Her face was bright pink and she was trying to bite my arm.

"Come on," I said, then groaned as she kneed me in the balls. I keeled over for a moment and she was able to break free. With her right hand she swept everything off the fireplace mantel onto the floor. More glass shattered. She headed toward the kitchen and I went after her. I was about to grab her when she turned and slapped me in the face. It was a real slap—it stung—and before I could do or say anything she slapped me again, harder than the first time. When she came at me with both hands, fingers extended like claws, ready to scratch my eyes out, I finally snapped into action. I managed to get hold of her wrists and I forced her back into the living room, pinning her down on the couch.

"I've had it with this shit," I said. "Tomorrow you're out of here, got that? You're out of here!"

She spat at me, and started screaming again, when someone knocked on the front door. I put my hand over her mouth, but she was still able to scream.

"Is everything okay in there?"

It was Carmen, the old Italian woman who lived across the hall from us.

"Fine, thank you," I said.

"It's not fucking fi—" Rebecca said, and I pressed my hand down harder, muffling her words.

"Are you sure everything's okay?" Carmen said.

"It's all right," I said. "Thank you!"

I held my hand over Rebecca's mouth for about a minute, until I was sure Carmen was gone, and then I said, "What the hell's wrong with you? Are you out of your mind? Huh? Are you out of your mind?"

Rebecca had started to calm down, breathing normally, and I moved my hand away. I realized I'd been pressing down with more force than I'd thought, because her lower lip was bleeding. It must have gotten cut on her bottom teeth.

I moved to the other end of the couch and sat with my head in my hands. Then I heard sobbing noises and I looked over and saw that Rebecca had started crying. I sat there, letting her cry, figuring it was better than letting her go on a rampage, breaking things.

Finally she said, "I'm not a bad person, right? I'm not a bad person, am I?"

Her mascara was running and blood was collecting on her lower lip.

"I know I'm not a bad person," she said. "I'm a good person. I have problems, but everybody has problems, right? I'm not a bad person. Please don't tell me I'm bad.

Please don't tell me I'm bad."

"I never said you were bad," I said, hating myself.

"I won't be bad anymore," she said. "I promise. Just don't leave me. I couldn't handle it if you left me."

She started kissing my neck and my chest, then my stomach, then lower. I tried to push her off me, and when I tried again it was too late.

"Sit back and watch me," she said.

3

WHEN THE ALARM clock blared I couldn't get out of bed. I had to hit the snooze button four or five times before I managed to make it into the shower. I got dressed lethargically, wishing I were still asleep. I said good-bye to Rebecca, but she couldn't hear me. She was snoring, drooling onto her pillow.

Heading toward the subway station along Seventy-ninth Street, lost in thought, I stepped onto a huge pile of dogshit. Cursing, I looked around for a puddle to dunk my shoe into, but it hadn't rained in days, so I had to scrape the sole against the edge of the curb to get off as much of the shit as I could. People rushing by smiled at me smugly or gave me look-at-that-stupid-idiot-who-stepped-in-shit looks, and I glared back at them, wishing they'd mind their own fucking business.

Continuing along the block, still cursing under my breath, I decided that my real problem was New York. I was sick of the crowds, the pollution, the noise, the smells, the traffic jams, and the dog shit. And I was sick of rushing everywhere and feeling stressed-out and angry twenty-four fucking hours a day. I didn't know why I even lived in New York anymore. I never went to the theater, or clubs, or museums, and I hardly ever went out to restaurants or bars. Actually, aside from going to work, I rarely went below Seventy-second Street or above Eighty-sixth, or ventured farther east than the sliver of Central Park between the northern end of the Sheep Meadow and the southern end of the Great Lawn. Despite living in one of the biggest, supposedly greatest, most culturally diverse cities in the world, I spent about eighty percent of my time in roughly a half-mile radius of my apartment.

If I left New York, I could start my life over again. With my *Wall Street Journal* experience alone I could move to a smaller city and get a job at a newspaper. I could be the big-shot reporter from New York; everybody would look up to me and respect me. Maybe I could meet a woman, someone I really liked, and I could have a normal, happy life. We'd have a big house and kids—a boy and a girl—and we'd have a backyard and a swimming pool. I tried to imagine myself and my happy family living in California or Florida—someplace sunny—as I descended the steep, dirty steps to the subway.

I rode the jam-packed 1 train to Fiftieth Street, then

walked uptown on Broadway. *Manhattan Business*'s publisher was a cheap shit, and, although the magazine had been at the same location on Fifty-second Street for years, the office had been designed and decorated as though it were a temporary location. Except for the executive offices at the far end of the cavernous space, there were no walls. The office was divided by rows of closely aligned room dividers to give us a sense of "privacy." The floors weren't carpeted, and the old floorboards were corroding in spots. The walls had chunks missing, and the place desperately needed a paint job. The windows were filthy, the ceilings were cracked, and the air-conditioning and heat never seemed to work.

I was heading down the corridor toward my office, really a large cubicle, when I heard Peter Lyons, the associate editor, call out my name. I turned around and saw him approaching behind me. Peter was very tall, maybe six-five, and had a small, balding head.

"Just the man I was looking for," he said.

Although Peter was American, from Westport, Connecticut, he spoke with a British accent, which, rumor had it, he'd picked up after spending his junior year abroad in London. He also wrote in a pseudo-British style, which was especially annoying when he "edited" my stories, adding unnecessary adverbs and words he'd obviously pulled from a thesaurus. He was five years younger than me ,with three years less experience, and he didn't have a financial background *or* a journalism background. He'd majored in creative writing at

Wesleyan, for Christ's sake, and it was humiliating to have to listen to his editorial critiques of my work when he had no idea what he was talking about.

"Morning," I said, forcing a smile.

"I was expecting to see your article yesterday," he said. "Remind me again of its subject matter?"

"It's a company report on Byron Technologies."

"Ah, yes, Byron Technologies," he said. "And what's their story?"

"Silicon Alley tech company, provide communication and remote-access solutions as well as support for various applications along multiple product lines. Lost two-forty a share last quarter, preadjusted EBIDTA. Pro forma earnings were a loss of seventy-six cents a share, missing the Street's whisper of a loss of sixty-eight cents a share, but the gross revenue number of six point two million was point four million more than what most analysts had expected. The company's burning cash and will have to raise money in the fourth quarter—maybe sell some equity, possibly through a secondary offering, although in the current climate the prospect of this seems unlikely. On a positive note, the company has cut spending over the last few quarters, mainly by reducing payroll on their sales and marketing staffs and focusing more on the support side of the business, where their margins are much higher. The company's long-term viability depends upon their ability to reduce spending while maintaining their growth rate, as well as lowering their cash-burn rate, but the company is an unlikely takeover candidate because of all the debt on their balance sheet and because a great deal of consolidation has already taken place in their industry."

I'd said all this talking as fast as I could, barely pausing for breath, and Peter looked lost, his eyes glazing over.

"Sounds compelling," he said. "I certainly look forward to reading it. Send it to me asap."

"Love to," I said, "but I didn't write it yet."

"Really?" he said, locking his jaw and exposing his lower teeth. "And why exactly is that?"

"My deadline's not till this afternoon."

"Those deadlines are for me, not for you. Didn't you see the memo I sent you about that last week?"

I always deleted Peter's memos without reading them.

"Must've missed that one."

"Well, it spelled out the deadline situation in great detail. In the future you need to deliver your stories to me twenty-four hours in advance of your ultimate deadline so I have adequate time to edit them."

"Gotcha," I said, fake-smiling.

"Very well then," he said. "Carry on."

In my office, cursing out Peter under my breath, I got to work, transcribing Robert Lipton's interview and outlining my article. There was no way Jeff Sherman could call this one a puff piece. Adding to what I'd come up with last night, I'd write a paragraph questioning Byron Technologies' business model, calling it "unrealistic" and "a throwback to the Internet mania of the late nineties," and I'd call the company's decision to market its products in Canada and Mexico "a fatal error."

I started writing the actual article, banging it out at my usual forty-five-word-a-minute speed, when Angie Lerner entered my office.

Angie was a reporter who worked in the office next door to me. She was very cute, with straight brown hair and a great smile. Although she was slightly overweight, especially below the waist, she was confident about her appearance and not afraid to wear sleeveless shirts and tight pants, which made her even sexier. Although she was only twenty-six, she had a mature, level-headed way about her that made her seem closer to thirty.

Usually I tried to find things wrong with women, noticing and amplifying every fault, but there was nothing wrong with Angie Lerner. She was perfect wife material—stable, down to earth, intelligent. It was easy to insert her into my fantasy of the house in the suburbs, a two-car garage, weekends on the golf course, two cute kids. But for some reason I always avoided the women who were perfect for me, going after the ones with FUCKED UP flashing on their foreheads instead.

"Working?" she asked.

"What?" I said, lost for a moment, staring at her. Then I said, "Yeah."

"What on?" she said, glancing at my monitor.

"Don't ask," I said.

Angie shook her head knowingly; we complained to each other about Jeff and Peter all the time.

"You know what Jeff told me the other day?" Angie

said. "I'm in his office and he goes, 'Your articles aren't nasty enough.' He said I need to grow a backbone, stop being so wishy-washy."

"Why do we even work here?"

"For our great salaries."

"We could deliver pizzas or flowers, answer phones somewhere. At least we'd have our integrity."

"Do what I do—just hand in the stories, and don't think about it. The most important thing is to get your bylines."

"Yeah, if Peter doesn't fuck them up first. Headhunters always ask me why my *Journal* articles were so much better written than my *Manhattan Business* ones. I try to explain it, but I get the sense they never believe me. It's like a convicted criminal swearing he's innocent."

Angie plopped down in the seat next to my desk. I asked her what else was going on and she started whispering to me about the latest office gossip—Simone, who worked in Accounting, and Brad, who worked in Marketing, had gotten drunk two nights ago and had sex, which was especially juicy because Brad had recently gotten engaged. I was listening to every word Angie said, but got distracted, thinking about Rebecca, frustrated that I hadn't gotten rid of her yet. Angie must have noticed my agitation, because she said in a suddenly concerned voice, "Is something wrong?"

"What do you mean?" I asked.

"I don't know. You just seem out of it."

"It's my story. I just want to get it out of the way."

I knew this explanation didn't hack it. We always had

deadlines, and it had never stopped me from killing time with Angie until the eleventh hour.

"I'll go bug somebody else," she said, getting up.

"I'm not trying to blow you off," I said.

"Sure, you're not." Then, smiling, making it into a joke, she said, "See you later."

I watched her leave, feeling bad for acting so cold. She knew I was living with Rebecca, but I had never talked to her about the relationship, and I wondered if I should. She was very rational and supportive, the type of person who always took your side in a fight, and maybe what I needed was for somebody like her to tell me that I had to dump Rebecca's ass and get on with my life.

I picked up my phone to call Angie and apologize when the light on my extension lit up, indicating that I had an incoming call. I was going to let my voice mail answer, but then I decided to pick up, figuring it might be a last-minute contact calling me back about my article.

"David Miller."

"Hello?"

The woman's voice was meek and high-pitched; I had to strain to hear her.

"Yes?" I said.

"Are you David Miller?"

"Speaking."

There was silence for a couple of seconds, and then the woman said, "I have your wallet."

I straightened up in my chair and smiled. "Wow, that's great—wow. Where'd you find it?"

The line was silent again. I wondered if she'd hung up or the connection was lost.

"Hello?" I said.

"Yeah," she said.

"I said where'd you find my—"

"The bus," she said. "The First Avenue bus."

"Really?" I said. "Jesus, I wonder how it wound up there. I was pickpocketed in this bar in midtown last night. How'd you get my work number?"

"It was on a business card."

"Wow," I said. "Thank you so much for calling—this'll really save me a big headache. I thought I'd have to get a new Social Security card and go to the DMV, stand in one of those ridiculous lines—"

"So do you want it back or not?"

Suddenly the woman sounded rushed.

"Of course," I said. "How can I get it from you?"

"I live downtown," she said, "on Avenue B and Sixth."

"Okay," I said, finding a pen and piece of paper to write on. "You want me to meet you someplace near your apartment, or—"

"You can come to my place to get it," she said.

"Fine," I said. "No problem. What time?"

"How's right now?"

I glanced at the time on my PC—11:18. I could zip downtown and make it back up in plenty of time to finish my story before the two o'clock deadline.

"Sounds great," I said. "What's your address?"

She gave me the address and told me her name—Sue.

"Okay," I said. "I'll be there in twenty minutes, a half hour. Thanks so much for calling."

I typed a quick couple of paragraphs, then grabbed my jacket and headed down the corridor toward the front of the office. On the way out, I leaned into Angie's cubicle. She was on the phone, so I whispered, "Sorry." Without speaking she mouthed, *It's okay*, and smiled.

I took the subway downtown instead of taking a cab, figuring it would be faster at this time of day. After exiting the Eighth Street station on Broadway, I headed east along St. Marks. I hadn't been to the East Village in a long time, and I'd been to Alphabet City only once or twice, when I first moved to the city after college. I'd heard about all of the gentrification that had taken place east of First Avenue, but the changes weren't as dramatic as I expected. Internet cafes, trendy macrobiotic restaurants, and hip clothing stores had replaced many of the bodegas, dive bars, and hole-in-the-wall record stores, but the streets were still crowded with plenty of self-important, pseudo-Bohemian wannabes and burnouts, and there were still lots of seedy-looking bars and stores selling what looked like garbage—they had to be fronts for something.

Avenue A had definitely improved over the past decade, looking as yuppified as Amsterdam Avenue in my neighborhood, and Tompkins Square Park wasn't the drug-infested hellhole it used to be. There were actually kids in the playground and normal-looking people walking along the paths and sitting on benches. But the area hadn't been entirely cleaned up. Outside the park there were still plenty of drug-addict types huddled on street corners and milling around phone booths.

I headed down Sixth Street and found Sue's building, near Avenue B. It was a nice block, but the five-story tenement where Sue lived had definitely missed out on the neighborhood's renaissance. The facade was dilapidated, with crumbling concrete, and at least a couple of apartments were burned out, the windows boarded up with plywood. Along the front of the building there was a waist-high fence, with several overflowing garbage cans beyond it. The door to the building had a small window, about one foot by one foot, too high to see inside, as if it were designed to give push-in rapists privacy.

Two very thin, junkie-looking guys with dirty faces and filthy clothes were hanging out on the sidewalk in front of the fence. They'd been having a hushed conversation, but they stopped talking and stared at me as I approached.

I had a bad feeling about going inside the building, and I considered forgetting about the wallet and returning to my office. I actually turned around and took a few steps back toward Avenue A, when I thought about the picture of Barbara tucked behind my driver's license. It was just an old Polaroid, trimmed down to wallet size, but I'd kept it in my wallet for years and it meant a lot to me.

I walked by the two junkies, who were still watching me, and entered the building. Garbage littered the floor of the vestibule—some of it was sticking to my feet—and there was a strong, nauseating smell of urine that reminded me of the way Manhattan streets smell in August. I held my breath as I pressed the buzzer to apartment fourteen. A few seconds later a staticky, barely audible voice said something I couldn't understand.

"Sue?" I said, but the loud static came back on as I spoke.

"It's me," I said. "David Miller ... the wallet guy."

More static came on. The odor in the vestibule was so bad I had to hold my shirt up over my face to breathe. I was about to go outside when the buzzer sounded, opening the inside door. I thought it was weird that she'd buzz a total stranger up to her apartment, but she probably figured that a guy who worked at a financial magazine wouldn't chop her into pieces.

The interior of the building was as run-down as the exterior. There was an old, rickety looking staircase to the left and overflowing garbage—some bagged, some not—piled up next to it. As I headed up the four steep flights of stairs, my shirt still covering half my face, I heard a TV blasting *The Price Is Right*, and a guy screaming with an Indian accent—I made out the words "piece of shit"—and I saw several huge, fearless roaches on the walls. It got warmer on each floor until it became downright hot. Again, I considered turning back, but then I thought about the picture. I'd had it for about twenty years, and it would suck if I couldn't get it back, especially after coming this far to get it.

I heard a door open on the floor above me and I continued up the stairs.

4

SUE WAS WAITING for me on the fifth floor, peering out of the partially opened door of apartment fourteen. When I arrived on the landing, I could see only a sliver of her face and body.

As I approached the apartment, the door opened wider and Sue poked her head into the hallway. She was even shorter than I'd expected—about five feet tall—and very thin. She had brown hair, cut in a boyish style around her ears, and pale skin.

"Come in," she said in her mousy voice, which sounded even higher and squeakier than it had on the phone.

"Thanks," I said hesitantly.

I entered the small, cluttered apartment, or really a rectangular-shaped room. The place was maybe two hundred square feet, *maybe*, and had a rusty sink, a tiny stove, and an old refrigerator, probably from the sixties, at one end, and a wide-open window at the other. A small, beat-up drop leaf table and two large, antique-looking chairs, partially covered in peeling white paint, were near the brick wall. Near the other wall, a futon lay on the floor with a small, old Turkish rug in front of it. A mish-mash of paintings, photographs, and posters hung around the apartment, including old framed posters of Van Gogh's self portrait and that famous picture of the Flatiron Building, and what looked like an original oil painting of an overweight nude woman. While the apartment had obviously been decorated with things purchased at thrift shops, or maybe even found on the street, everything had been arranged with a well-thought-out, maybe shabby-chic sense of style.

I stood in the center of the room as Sue knelt down for a moment near the futon. The apartment was as hot as the stairwell, and I was sweating through my shirt. Sue stood up, probably noticing how uncomfortable I looked, because she said, "The fan broke."

I glanced at the old, dusty fan in the corner, wondering when was the last time any air had circulated in this room.

"Yeah, it is kind of hot in here, huh?" I said.

"It's the tar roof," she said. "Anytime the sun's out it gets boiling in here."

I took my first good look at Sue, double-taking at how thin her arms were. She was wearing old, ripped khaki shorts and a tanktop, and she was much thinner than I'd thought. Her face was gaunt, with her cheeks sunken in, and her body reminded me of the photos of Auschwitz victims. Her skin was more than pale—it had a worn-out, ghostly appearance—and her eyes were as lost and vacant as Barbara's had been during her final days in the hospital.

I stood there for several seconds, broiling in the heat, wanting to leave and get the hell back to my air-conditioned office.

"So," I said, "my wallet …"

"I have it," she said, not moving. I noticed how her mouth moved in a strange way when she talked, as if her jaw were misaligned.

"Great," I said. I waited a few seconds, then said, "So … can I have it back?"

"Sure," she said, "but you're gonna give me a reward, right?"

I don't know why I didn't expect her to ask for money or why this question offended me so much. Of course, I didn't mind giving her something as a token of thanks, but I guess I felt like she should have been up front about it on the phone.

"I don't have a lot of cash on me," I said, reaching into my pocket and taking out some crumpled bills. "My wallet was stolen last night and I didn't have a chance to go to the bank yet." I found a twenty and said, "How's this?"

"Not enough," she said, staring at my hand, suddenly seeming very agitated, wiping her nose repeatedly with the back of her hand.

I reached into my pocket. I had a ten and a few singles.

"Thirty-three's all I have," I said.

"I want three," she said.

"Excuse me?"

"Hundred," she added.

"*What?*"

"I want three hundred bucks."

"That's crazy," I said. "I already canceled most of my cards anyway. I just wanted the wallet back to save me some inconvenience—"

"Three hundred's the price," she said.

"I'm not giving you three hundred dollars," I said.

"Then I'm not giving you your wallet," she said.

We stood there in the sweltering apartment, staring at each other. Sue had a serious, unyielding expression, but I still felt sorry for her. She looked very nervous and agitated and I realized she was probably a junkie.

I would've left right then if it weren't for that picture of Barbara. I still knew I wasn't being entirely rational about it, but I felt like if I didn't get it back, I'd always regret it.

"Look, I'm trying to be reasonable," I said. "I appreciate that you called me and I want to give you a reward, but three hundred's crazy. I have an idea. How about you can keep the money that was in the wallet too—there must be fifty, sixty bucks in it—"

"The wallet was empty when I found it," she said. "Your cards and everything were in it, but there was no money."

Her dark, lifeless eyes were focused straight ahead at my chest; by the way she was avoiding eye contact, I was positive she was lying about something. Either she'd stolen the money herself or she was working with Eddie Lomack, the drunk who'd distracted me in the bar last night. Suddenly I could picture her and Eddie meeting last night, after Eddie had walked away. They'd probably split the money from my wallet and then tried to figure out how they could soak me for more.

"I don't have any more cash on me," I said. "I don't know what you expect me to do."

"Go to an ATM," she said.

"With what?" I said. "I don't have a cash card."

"I'll give it back to you."

"I canceled it already."

"Go to any Chase branch," she said. "They'll give you a new temporary card, or you can take out money right away with picture ID."

She spoke with such assurance about banking policy that I wondered how many other wallets she'd held for ransom. I was also irritated by how she knew that I had an account at Chase. Obviously she'd gone through my wallet pretty carefully.

"Did you steal my wallet last night?" I asked.

"What do you mean?" she said, overly defensive. "I found it on the train."

"You told me it was the bus."

"That's what I meant—the bus, the First Avenue bus."

"Look," I said, "I know you're trying to make some money off me, but it's not gonna happen. I have my driver's license in that wallet and some personal things that I'd like to have back, but I'm not paying you three hundred dollars. If you won't give it back to me I guess I'll just have to live without it."

I turned to leave when she said, "Two hundred."

Without turning back toward her I said, "No."

"One-fifty," she said.

I opened the door.

"A hundred bucks," she said, "but that's as low as I'm going. I don't care—I'll throw the fuckin' wallet away."

"Deal," I said.

She held out her hand to shake; I saw the track marks on her arm—some looked fresh—and I kept my hand right where it was, by my side.

"You got picture ID on you, right?" she said.

Because I'd been planning to go to my bank during lunch today, I had my passport with me.

"Yeah," I said.

"Good," she said.

I headed back down the stairs, holding my breath most of the way and breathing under the collar of my shirt when I had to. When I left the building I took a series of deep breaths, as if I'd been working in a coal mine all day.

I remembered seeing a Chase branch on Broadway and Eighth Street when I'd gotten off the subway. I walked there as fast as I could. It was almost twelve-thirty, and the deadline for my article was two o'clock. I could have handed the article in late and it probably wouldn't have been a big deal, but I didn't want to have to get into it with Peter.

At the bank, two of the three bank officers were taking breaks, and there were two people ahead of me, waiting to see the other officer. After waiting for more than half an hour, one of the other officers returned from his break and helped me. His name was Stanley Carmichael. He was a squat, balding guy with very thick glasses, and he had to be the slowest bank officer in New York. It would have taken an average person a few minutes to reactivate my account and issue me a temporary banking card, but it took Stanley Carmichael nearly half an hour. It was excruciating to watch this guy squinting at the computer monitor, typing with one finger, and calling other bank workers over to help him input information. Finally, I had my new ATM card and I withdrew three hundred dollars—one for Sue and two for myself.

It was almost one o'clock when I left the bank and started jogging back to the apartment building on Sixth Street. I rang Sue's apartment, hoping she would come down to meet me this time, but naturally she buzzed me up and I had to climb the four flights of stairs. When I reached the top floor, the door to apartment fourteen was ajar, but Sue wasn't standing there waiting. I knocked two times, then went inside and said, "Hello?"

Sue was walking toward me, coming from the direction of the futon. There was a funny burning odor in the apartment.

"Did you get the money?" she asked, seeming much more relaxed than she had before.

I reached into my pocket and handed her the one

hundred dollars in twenties. As she counted the bills, I glanced beyond her and saw a syringe on the futon. Adjacent to the futon, on the floor, there was a small frying pan.

"So can I have my wallet?" I asked.

"I want another hundred," she said.

"*What*?" I said.

"You heard me."

"We made a deal."

"I changed my mind."

"I don't have any more money on me," I said, feeling my face getting warmer.

"Yeah, right," she said. "You had your wallet stolen last night and you just went to the bank. You must've taken out another hundred at least."

"Look, I've had it," I said. "I just ran to Broadway and back to get you your hundred bucks and now you're gonna give me my fucking wallet."

"Fifty," she said.

"Maybe I should just call the cops right now," I said.

"I didn't have to call you, you know," she said. "I could've thrown the wallet away when I found it."

"You mean stole it."

"I didn't steal it."

I was tired of arguing and haggling. Another fifty bucks to get my wallet back and go on with my life seemed worth it.

"All right," I said, "give me my wallet and I'll give you the money."

She lifted the futon and picked up my wallet. She handed it to me and I was giving her the fifty bucks when the door opened behind me.

"What the fuck's this shit?"

I turned around toward the door and saw a short, unshaven Latino guy in a black leather vest and nothing underneath. His eyes were glazed over and bloodshot, and he was sweating more than I was.

"It's nothing," Sue said, suddenly very nervous. "He just works for the landlord."

"Landlord, huh?" the guy said. "So now you fuckin' his friends too?" Then he said to me, "You fuckin' my lady?"

"It's not like that," Sue said. "He's just somebody I—"

The guy pushed her aside, almost knocking her down, and said to me, "You fuckin' my lady? Huh? You fuckin' her?"

"No," I said, backing away. "Of course not."

"Bullshit you ain't," he said. "Why you got money out?"

"It's not like you think," Sue said. "He's just—"

The guy pushed Sue away and she fell onto the floor. Then he came closer to me and opened a switchblade.

"You fuckin' my lady, bitch?"

"Relax," I said. "Just calm down, all right?"

Holding the blade in front of him, he closed in on me, looking as crazed as a death-row psychopath. He was between me and the door so I had nowhere to run.

"Take it easy," I said. "Just—"

"You fuck my lady," he said, "maybe you wanna fuck

this." Then he lunged at me with the blade. He would have stabbed me in the chest if I hadn't moved to my left at the last moment. He still got my right arm below the shoulder, but before I could feel any pain he was coming again, this time toward my face. I grabbed his right forearm with both of my hands and we struggled. The blade, a few inches in front of my eyes, looked like a sword. Sue was screaming for him to leave me alone, but he was relentless. I squeezed his forearm harder, knowing that if I let go that would be it. He swung his left fist and punched me in my face, getting my lower lip, but I didn't let go of his forearm.

"I didn't fuck her," I managed to say, but I knew it would be impossible to get through to him; he was out of his mind, probably whacked-out on drugs, and he wouldn't calm down until I was dead.

Sue grabbed him from behind, trying to pull him off me.

"Stop it!" she screamed. "Stop it!"

"Fuckin' cunt," the guy said. "I'm gonna cut your fuckin' tits off." He straight-armed her in the chest and she fell back against the wall.

I was trying to wrestle the switchblade away, without making much progress. Sue came up behind the guy and jumped on his back, but she was so weak and slight that he continued to struggle with me, unaffected. I hoped someone in the building would hear all the commotion and call the police.

Sue put her hands over the guy's face, scratching at his eyes.

"Fuckin' cunt ... fuckin' ho," the guy said. "I'm gonna fuckin' kill you too, bitch!"

The guy backed up, ramming Sue hard against the front door until she finally let go of his face. He brought back his hand and turned, about to stab her, when I grabbed him from behind. I watched for the blade, knowing that at any moment he could wheel around and jab it into me.

The guy turned, breaking free, and I saw the blade coming toward the side of my face. I backed away, turning my head, and the cold metal and the guy's rough fist brushed past my right cheek. He screamed something in Spanish—the only word I could make out was *puta*—and came at me again. This time I was ready. I grabbed his arm with the switchblade before he could bring it forward, and I held it steady. With my other hand I tried to work the blade free, but he wouldn't let go. I was using all of my strength, determined not to let this crazy asshole kill me. I have no idea how long we struggled—it could've been a few seconds or a few minutes. I was staring into the guy's wild eyes, knowing I probably looked just as wild, as Sue screamed, trying to pull us apart. Then, somehow, I managed to work the blade free and it clanged onto the floor. Sue picked it up and the guy and I continued to struggle. I twisted his arm back and he pulled my hair. Then he elbowed me in the gut, and that's when I really lost it. I grabbed him around the neck, getting him in a headlock. Then I kicked a chair out of the way and rammed his head as hard as I could against the steel door. I guess I could've stopped right then, because he wasn't fighting back anymore, but I didn't want to. I started kicking him, again and again. I don't know how many times I kicked him, but it was more than five and less than twenty, and then, after giving him one final kick in the ribs, I backed away.

I stood there in front of him for a long time, panting like an animal. He was still curled up on his side, not moving at all.

Sue kneeled down over him, crying, shaking him, saying, "Ricky, oh, my God, Ricky. Wake up, baby. Come on, wake up … Come on, just open your eyes—just open them … Don't die—don't die on me, baby. Don't die!"

She said other things too, but all of the noise faded to nothing.

Finally Sue stopped crying and turned to me and said, "You killed him."

The apartment seemed twenty degrees warmer and it was spinning.

"What the hell're you talking about?" I said. "We'll call an ambulance. He just got knocked out, that's all."

"Look at him, you fuckin' idiot," she said. "He stopped breathing, he doesn't have a pulse. He's dead."

As I looked down at his perfectly still body, panic set in. I was shaking so badly I could barely speak.

"I didn't mean it," I said. "You know that, right? I was just trying to stop him, to keep him from … I mean, he would've killed you, or both of us, or he would've … It was an accident, damn it!"

"It doesn't matter," she said. "You still killed him."

I was so dizzy I could barely stand as Sue remained on her knees, sobbing next to the body.

"Come on, you saw what happened," I said. "It was self-defense, he was out of his mind, he …" I stopped and stared at the body for several seconds, still in disbelief, then said, "Come on, he's not really dead. How can he be dead?"

"You must've crushed his skull or something," Sue said. She was still crying.

"That's impossible," I said. "We'll get an ambulance, they'll work on him—"

"Just shut up!" she screamed. "Just shut the fuck up!"

I stared at the body.

"Why the hell did he come after me like that anyway?" I said. "What the hell was wrong with him?"

Still sobbing, Sue caught her breath and managed to say, "He was just jealous."

"Jealous?" I said. "Jealous of what? What the hell are you talking about?"

"He wanted me to stop bringing guys back up here," she said. "He said he wanted to get married. 'It's just gonna be me and you, baby. Just me and you.' That's what he always said."

For several seconds I stood there, staring. Then I got a hold of myself and slapped the side of my leg, fumbling around, finally finding my front pants pocket. I took out my cell phone when Sue said, "What're you doing?"

"Calling the police," I said.

I'd inputted 911 and pressed enter when Sue said,

"Don't do that."

"Why not?"

"Just don't."

I ended the call.

"It's okay," she said. "You can go. I'll call the cops."

"What the hell're you talking about?"

"Just gimme a thousand bucks and I'll take the rap," she said.

I stared at her, then said, "Are you out of your mind?"

"It'll save you a lot of trouble," she said, "and you won't go to jail."

"Why would I go to jail?" I said. "It was an accident— you saw the whole thing, the way he came in here like a maniac. I'll just tell the cops the truth."

"It wasn't an accident," she said. "You went crazy and killed him."

"Bullshit," I said. "It was self-defense. He tried to stab me in the face. If I let him go he would've gone for the switchblade again."

"You know how hard you rammed his head into that door?" she said. "Then all those times you kicked him, probably busting his ribs? That doesn't sound like self-defense to me."

"But you'll be here," I said. "You can tell them what really happened, how he was still coming after me, how …" I stopped myself, knowing it was pointless. I couldn't count on her to back up my story, especially when I wasn't even sure about the story myself.

"Trust me, it'll be a lot easier if I say I did it," she said.

"Ricky used to beat on me all the time—he even busted my jaw once. I've called the cops on him tons of times—they know all about us. I'll say I snapped—I couldn't take it anymore. He came after me and I just grabbed him and went crazy on him."

I stared at the body—on its side, facing away from me. I knew the logical thing to do was call the police, but I wasn't thinking logically. I was sweating and shaking and I couldn't concentrate. Like a hit-and-run driver, I just wanted to get away.

Don't be an idiot, I thought. *Call the cops.*

I input the 9 in 911 when Sue said, "*Stop,*" in a way that told me that she meant it. I stopped dialing.

"Call the cops, I'll lie my ass off," she said. "I'll tell them I picked you up in the park and brought you back here. We were gonna fuck, but you didn't have enough money, so you had to go to the bank. See, it all fits. Then, when you came back here, Ricky walked in on us. You two started fighting, then you flipped out and killed him."

"They won't believe you," I said.

"Bullshit they won't," she said. "Besides, it's against the law to go to hookers. You want that getting out?"

I looked at the cell phone, then at the door, then back toward Sue.

"I'm calling the cops," I said, "and I don't care what you tell them."

"If you call the cops you're going to jail," she said, "but do whatever you want."

I dialed the first 1.

"I'll say you were fucking me," she said. "I'll swear my ass up and down till they believe it. Go ahead—make the call. I dare you."

I waited a few seconds, my thumb on the 1 button, thinking that the police could easily believe Sue's story over mine.

I pressed end and stood there for a while, trying to think it through some more, but my thoughts were jumbled.

"A thousand's nuts," I finally said.

"That's the price."

"Five hundred."

"A thousand."

I shook my head, glancing at the body briefly and feeling nauseous.

"What if somebody heard something?" I said. "Your neighbors. What if somebody heard us fighting, or heard my voice—"

"People in this building never hear anything," Sue said.

"But why should I trust you?" I said. "How do I know you'll really tell the cops you did it?"

"Because I want my money, that's why."

"But how do I know you'll keep your story straight?"

"I can't change my story," she said. "Once I tell the cops I did it, that's it."

I hesitated again. Everything was blurry and my hand holding the cell phone was sweating. Then a voice inside me screamed, *Leave*! and I said, "Fine," and headed toward the door.

"Meet me with the money tomorrow night at seven,"

Sue said. "Starbucks on Astor. You're not there, I'm turning you in. I'm not fucking around."

I stepped by her and around the body and left the apartment.

The relief of being back outside, breathing in the cool, Manhattan air, was even greater than before. I walked up the block as fast as I could, at a pace equal to jogging. At the intersection of Avenue A and Seventh Street, there was a Don't Walk sign; rather than waiting for it to change, I walked alongside the traffic, then jaywalked diagonally across A, telling myself that I had to keep moving no matter what.

At Tenth Street, I cut over a couple of blocks to Second Avenue and headed uptown. People were giving me funny looks, and I realized that, in addition to my lower lip, which was still bleeding, my shirt was torn below the shoulder and some blood was seeping through. A few minutes later, as I continued up Second, I feared that I'd made a huge mistake. Ricky wasn't much taller than Sue, but he was stronger and had to weigh at least fifty pounds more than her; the police would never believe that she'd overpowered him.

In the crosswalk of Second and Fourteenth, I stopped, ready to turn back, but I decided it was too late. Sue had probably called the police already. They could be at her apartment right now, questioning her. She wouldn't be able to handle the pressure; she'd break down and tell them that I'd killed Ricky. I'd try to explain that I'd acted in self-defense, but after leaving the apartment that would be even harder to prove.

I leaned against a lamppost to steady myself, feeling helpless and stupid, when I had an epiphany.

Maybe it didn't happen.

I hadn't checked for Ricky's pulse or heartbeat. He'd looked dead, but it could have all been staged. I knew I'd banged his head pretty hard, but was it hard enough to kill him? They could all have been working together—Sue, Ricky, and Eddie Lomack, the drunk from the bar. Maybe this was how they operated—pick a guy's wallet, then see how far they could take it. If they could get the guy to think he killed somebody, they'd soak him for even more.

As I continued walking up Second Avenue, I became even more convinced that the whole thing was a scam. I felt like a real sucker and I decided I'd never tell anyone what had happened.

At the next corner, I stopped walking and took out my wallet. The picture of Barbara was still there, tucked in the window behind my driver's license. I slid it out and stared at it for a while, then replaced it behind the license and hailed a cab to midtown.

5

WHEN I ARRIVED at work, I went right to the bathroom and washed up at the sink. My face looked worse than I'd thought. My lower lip was swollen to about twice the size of the upper, and there was a small cut in it, making me resemble a boxer during a post-fight interview. The cut on my upper arm was superficial, though, barely piercing my skin. I cleaned up the best I could, then headed toward my office. Along the way I passed Amy Shumsky, who worked in Payroll, and Jenny Shaw, the personnel director. They asked me what happened, and I told them that I'd fallen but that it wasn't as bad as it looked. I purposely kept walking so they couldn't ask me any more questions, and then I turned along the corridor leading to the editorial department.

I sat at my desk and got right to work on my story. I always seemed to work best under deadline and I started writing as fast as my fingers could press the keys. After everything that had happened at Sue's apartment, I was very pissed off, and it came out in my writing. I blasted Byron Technologies' management, calling them "deceitful," and characterizing their accounting practices as "Enronesque." In reality, the company's management had been up front with investors, and a minor accounting error regarding the reporting of last quarter's pro forma earnings had been quickly and publicly corrected. But I was on a roll, and the negative ideas kept flowing. I used a portion of a quote—taken out of context—from Kevin DuBois, an analyst who covered Byron's stock. DuBois had told me that "I wouldn't be surprised if the company has to raise cash later in the year, perhaps with a secondary offering, but they have a great product and outstanding management and I'm still quite bullish on the future." In my story, I wrote a paragraph, stating that Byron Technologies had "an alarming cash-burn rate" that could lead to bankruptcy by year's end, and I'd ended the paragraph with DuBois stating, "The company has to raise cash."

In about fifteen minutes, I'd finished a rough draft of the article; then I went back through it, rearranging sentences, changing words, correcting typos, inserting quips. As I was working, I saw Angie enter my office in my peripheral vision. She waited for me to pause from typing, then said, "Where've you been?"

"The bank," I said.

"All day?"

"I had some other errands to run too."

"I thought you had to work on your story."

"I do."

I stayed facing the computer monitor, partly because I wanted to finish my story and partly because I didn't want Angie to see my fat lip.

"Hey, what's that?" she said.

She came up alongside me to my right and reached onto my desk for a copy of *People* with Tom Cruise on the cover. As she turned pages of the magazine, it was hard to keep facing away from her without raising suspicion. I noticed she was wearing the same perfume she always wore, the one that I'd never liked on other women, but that always smelled great on her.

"I didn't see this issue yet," she said. "Mind if I borrow it?"

"Sure."

"Thanks ... God, what *happened* to you?"

She had turned to look at my face.

"I tripped," I said.

"Tripped?" she said. "Where?"

"Outside the bank."

"How?"

"Shoelace. It was pretty embarrassing. I fell right on my face on the sidewalk. I felt like a total idiot."

"You should sue."

The word *sue* made me cringe.

Angie must've noticed, because she said, "Are you sure you're okay?"

"I'm fine," I said.

"Your shirt's ripped."

I looked down at the tear in my shirt, as if noticing it for the first time.

"Huh," I said, acting dumbfounded. "I guess it must've ripped when I fell."

Angie was squinting at my shirt, looking unconvinced.

"It's nothing—really," I said.

Now she was staring at my face again.

"You look like you were in a fight," she said.

"I know," I said. "It's crazy, isn't it?"

"You want me to get you some ice or something?"

"No, I'm fine, thanks. I just have to finish this story."

"No problem," she said. "Stop by later and say hi."

"I will," I said.

I returned to work on the article and finished it at a few minutes after two o'clock. After proofreading it quickly on the monitor, I sent the file to Peter Lyons. He'd fuck it up with Britishisms, then send it back to me; then I'd forward it to Jeff for some final idiotic input before it went to Copyediting.

Relieved to get my article out of the way, I ordered in a smoked turkey on rye for lunch, and then I spent most of the rest of the afternoon on the phone, setting up interviews for my next story. At around four-thirty, I went down the corridor to Angie's office. She was laughing, sitting across from Mike O'Hara, a recent college grad, who worked in the marketing department.

"How's it going?" I said.

They both gave me looks, as if I were intruding. Then Mike said, "Dude, what happened to your face?"

"Fell," I said. "It's no big deal. I guess I'll come by later."

"That's okay, dude," Mike said. "I gotta take off anyway. I'll call you tonight, Ang, okay?"

"Okay," Angie said.

Mike put his hand on Angie's shoulder and she put hers over it for a second or two, and then he left the office.

"Ouch," I said.

"Shut up," Angie said, blushing.

"So what's the deal with you guys? Are you a couple now or what?"

"Why do you care?"

"No reason. You know me—I just like to get the latest dish."

"We went out a couple of nights ago," she said.

"Really?" I said, surprised by how jealous I felt.

"I had a pretty good time," she said smugly. "We went to this little Italian place in the Village; then we went to a bar and had a few drinks. It was fun."

"Isn't he a little young for you?"

"He's twenty-two."

"Exactly. You're what, four years older than him?"

"Jesus, who're you, my father?"

I could tell she was enjoying making me jealous.

"Sorry," I said. "He seems like a nice guy. You two make a great couple."

"I don't know if I'd consider us a *couple*."

"Whatever you want to call it."

I hung out with Angie for a while, talking about office minutiae—Mitchell in Accounting's ugly shirts, rumors about looming staff cuts, speculation about who kept leaving dirty dishes in the kitchen—but there was tension between us and I felt awkward. Eventually I made an excuse and left.

Walking home rather than taking the subway, I decided that tonight I was going to really break up with Rebecca. I belonged in a normal relationship with someone like Angie, and as soon as I dumped Rebecca I could get my life back on track.

Passing the Time Warner buildings at Columbus Circle, I rehearsed possible breakup lines. I could use the standard, "It's not you, it's me," or "I think we should start seeing other people." Or, taking the self-deprecating angle, I could say, "I'm not good enough for you—you deserve someone better." But I knew those stock lines wouldn't work with Rebecca. She'd think I wasn't serious, and then she'd come on to me, and before I knew it, I'd be back in bed with her.

Maybe I didn't have to say anything—just give her the silent treatment. Or maybe I should take the opposite tactic—barge into the apartment like a total psycho, screaming, "Pack your things and get the fuck out, you crazy bitch!" Maybe to get through to a psycho, you had to become psycho.

I shuddered, remembering bashing Ricky's head into the steel door.

Continuing up Broadway, I managed to forget about Ricky but was suddenly bombarded by memories of Barbara on practically every block. I remembered reading magazines at Barnes & Noble, eating shrimp dumplings at Ollie's, arguing about the ending of some movie while having spicy tuna rolls at Dan.

Then I veered over to Columbus, passing Banana Republic.

"So do I look like a rock star?"

I was outside the dressing room, modeling a red leather jacket and a pair of black jeans.

"You look gay," Barbara said.

"Gay, rock star, what's the difference?" I said.

Looking into the mirror, I squinted, furrowing my eyebrows, trying to look hip.

"Eh, I guess you're right," I said. "Guess I'll just buy the jeans and those two sweaters. You think I should just get the blue one, or the gray and the blue?"

"I'm moving in with Jay," she said.

I turned around toward her, half smiling, hoping she was joking. "Yeah, right."

"I wanted to tell you before; I was just waiting for the right time."

"And this is the right time?"

"See? I knew you'd get like this."

"Jay's such a dick."

"I love him."

"You don't love him."

"Yes, I do."

"Come on, Barb, you can do so much better than that loser. I mean, the guy's so fuckin' pompous. And he puts you down all the time, makes all those passive-aggressive comments ..."

"I shouldn't've told you."

"I'm not letting you do this."

"You don't own me."

On the corner of Columbus and Seventieth, I bumped into an old woman pushing a wagon filled with groceries.

"Watch it," she said, but I kept walking.

When I arrived at my apartment building I tried to get psyched again for breaking up with Rebecca, but I'd lost my edge. I didn't think I could pull off the psycho act, so I decided I'd be Mr. Sensitive Guy instead. Maybe if she saw how much pain she was causing me, and if I even shed a few tears, she would get the point.

In the hallway outside my apartment I heard rap music blasting and I smelled pot, so I figured Rebecca was having a party. She often had parties—without bothering to tell me in advance, of course—inviting ten or so friends over to the apartment to eat, smoke, drink, and do drugs, and they wouldn't leave until the middle of the night, or sometimes the next day. It wasn't unusual for me to encounter a few bodies sprawled on the couch or on the living room floor as I was leaving for work in the morning.

I went into the apartment, surprised to see no one around. Maybe the party hadn't started yet.

I turned down the pulsing music.

"What up, yo!" Rebecca called from the kitchen.

I left the foyer and saw Rebecca by the stove, stirring a pot of spaghetti. She looked incredible, almost elegant, in a strapless black dress, high heels, her hair up, but I promised myself that I wouldn't let anything sway me.

"I thought you'd be home later," she said. "I wanted to have everything ready. What happened to your face?"

"Tripped," I said, sick of hearing myself say it.

"Shut up! Where?"

"Outside a bank."

"What bank?"

"Chase."

"Oh, shit."

"It's all right."

"You wanna put frozen peas on it?"

"It's too late for that."

"You sure?"

"What're you doing?"

"What do you mean?"

I jutted my chin toward the stove.

"Oh, just cooking you up some dinner," she said. "Why don't you go chill, change into the outfit I laid out for you—that sexy Johnny Blaze shirt I bought you and those tight jeans that show off your package?"

I stood there for several seconds, unable to come up with the words I wanted to say, and then I continued down the hallway.

I washed my face in the bathroom, resolving to just go

out there and do it, damn it—tell her she had two days to move out.

I left the bathroom, noticing that the rest of the apartment was dark. I made my way to the dining alcove, where Rebecca was seated at the table set for two, a single candle burning in the center. She was holding a glass of wine and there was another glassful across from her.

"You didn't change," she said. Then she must've noticed my tense expression, because she said, "Come on, have some wine. The guy at the liquor store recommended it."

I didn't move.

"Are you, like, pissed at me for something?" she asked. "Because I just want you to know, I have, like, no idea what happened last night. I remember going out with Ray and everything else is foggy. I know we met people at Chaos and I was dancing with this guy Ramon or Raul who had these really cool dreads? Last thing I remember—me, Ray, and these two old guys started drinking. I mixed champagne and vodka. Stupid, right? Then I took a pill and somebody bought me more drinks and I have no idea what happened after that."

"So you really don't remember anything about last night?" I said.

"No, why?" she said. "I didn't do something bad, did I?" She tried to look worried.

"Not really," I said. "Unless you consider throwing a vase at my head bad."

"Shut up! I threw a vase at your head?"

"Only a couple of times."

"Oh, God—I'm so sorry."

"You also broke everything from the fireplace mantel."

"I was wondering where everything went."

"I cleaned up the mess this morning."

"I can't believe I did that. I'm really sorry."

"It's too late for sorries. Just pack up and move out tonight."

I tried to walk away but she grabbed my arm, pleading.

"Come on," she said. "I said I'm sorry. I'll pay for everything I broke."

"Pay for it with what?" I said. "You know how much you owe me so far? You have no intention of paying me back and you know it. Can you let go of my arm, please?"

Still holding on to me, she said, "Look, I know I'm not perfect, all right? I party too much and I go crazy with money and sometimes I, like, lose control. I admit all that, okay? But I swear I'm gonna change. I'll get a job, you can cut up my credit cards. I'll chill out on the clubbing and the partying and I'll stop buying new clothes. I'll go to thrift shops, and no more Sephora—I'll buy my makeup at Duane Reade. I won't take cabs anymore, I'll—"

I freed myself and continued past her, saying, "Nothing you say is going to change my mind."

Following me, she said, "Is this because of last night? Because whatever happened, whatever I said or did, I swear to God it'll never happen again."

"It's over," I said. "Just pack your things and move out."

"What do you mean, over?" she said, as if she were hearing me for the first time.

"You have to leave," I said. "I'm sure you can stay with Ray or one of your other friends for a few nights, until you find someplace permanent."

She grabbed my arm—harder this time.

"Come on, let's just chill and talk," she said.

"There's nothing to talk about," I said, wriggling my arm free. "I told you from the beginning this wasn't serious, and you agreed. Remember? You said we were just having fun."

"We were having fun," she said. "Then I fell in love with you."

I laughed, hoping she'd laugh too, but she didn't.

"Come on, you know that's ridiculous," I said. "You love my apartment and my money. You don't love me."

"You really mean that?" she said. "You really think that's, like, what kind of person I am?"

"I heard you talking to your friend Monique."

"Monique? When was I talking to Monique?"

"I don't know, couple of months ago, whenever. I heard what you said, how I'm your puppy dog, how you just want me for my apartment and money."

"I never said that."

"I know what I heard."

"I can't believe this is happening," she said, starting to cry.

"Look," I said, "I admit I was at fault here too. I know I invited you to move in with me and I started lending you money, but that's because I was in a very vulnerable position, because my sister had just died and ... Look, none of that is important right now. What's important is that we both have to move on."

Rebecca was staring at me as if in disbelief, a few fake tears dripping down her cheeks.

"I can't believe that's what you really think of me," she said. "I mean, why would I, like, gold dig off you? I mean, you're just like some reporter, making forty-two a year. If I wanted to gold dig, I would've gone after a doctor or a lawyer or an investment banker—somebody with real money."

"So maybe you should think about doing that," I said.

I turned around and headed back into the dining area.

"Okay, stop it!" she screamed. "Just fucking stop it!"

I looked back and saw her glaring at me with her hands over her ears, as if to block out the sound of her own screeching voice. I'd seen Rebecca lose it plenty of times, but I'd never seen her act quite like this. She seemed like she was having some kind of breakdown.

"Look," I said. "I really think we should both—"

"Stop saying 'look,'" she said. "I hate it when you say 'look.'"

"Okay, I think I know what this is all about now," I said. "It's about your past, isn't it?"

"What about my past?"

"The issues you have. Your father leaving and men abandoning you and all that. I know it's not easy for you to let go, but if we both work through this together—"

"You don't know me! You have no idea who I am!"

"I'm not saying I *know* you," I said. "I'm just saying I know what's going on inside your head. I mean, I have trouble letting go myself sometimes; that's why I think if you just move out, without making a big deal—"

"There're things about me you don't know," Rebecca said. "If you knew them you wouldn't do this. You'd understand why you *can't* do this."

I had no idea what she was talking about. I was afraid she was going to have another fit, start throwing things at me again.

"Okay, let's just relax now," I said, "take deep breaths—"

"You think I'm this, like, nice, innocent person," she went on, "but I'm not. I'm not like that at all."

"Look—"

"Stop saying 'look!'" she screamed.

Great, I thought. Now she'd attack me again and Carmen would come to the door, complaining, and we'd have a replay of last night.

"Let's just cool it, all right?" I said. "I'm not trying to get into some he-said, she-said blaming match with you. What I mean is … I mean, it's not me, it's you … I mean, it's me, not you … It's my fault."

"I was married once," she said.

"You were married," I said as a statement.

"Yes, I was married. See, you don't know anything about me. You just think you do."

Rebecca still looked unstable, and I didn't want to say anything to upset her any more.

"His name was David," she added.

"David, huh?"

"Yes, David," she said. "When I met you, I thought it was, like, an omen. I thought that God had brought another David into my life to give me a chance to do things right, to, like, prove I could have a normal relationship? See, things with David and me got fucked-up. Like, really fucked up."

"Did this 'other David' live in New York?" I asked, convinced she was making this whole story up.

"No, this was when I was living in L.A.," she said. "He owned this bar I used to hang out at in Venice. You know my snake tattoo?" She stuck out her shoulder to show me the tattoo of the coiled python. "David had the same one on the back of his leg—he didn't have any more room on his arms. Anyway, he was a lot older than me—I was twenty-two; he was forty-two? I guess I was, like, looking for a father figure or something?"

I was staring at her, trying to look like I was believing her.

"Anyway," she said, "after we were going out for, like, a month he was, like, 'Let's get married.' The wedding was nothing fancy—we got in his car and drove to Vegas. We were both drunk during the ceremony—it was a blast—but when we drove back to L.A. the party was over. I remember the first time he hit me. I couldn't believe it—I just stood there, staring at him, my nose gushing blood. After that things started getting bad—like, really bad." She was crying. "Finally, I couldn't take it anymore. I mean all that abuse every day. I knew I had to end it somehow, so one day I just ..." Her voice faded, overtaken by sobbing. She couldn't answer for several seconds, and then she said, "I ended it. One day I just ended it."

I knew she was making the whole story up. It was just a lame, desperate, last-ditch attempt to get sympathy from me, and it wasn't going to work.

"Look, I'm very sorry your marriage didn't work out, but—"

"Stop saying 'look,'" she said, clenching her fists.

"All right, look," I said. "I mean, not look. I mean, I think you're a really great person. I'm sure you'll land on your feet, and some guy's gonna be lucky to—"

"You still don't get it, do you?" she said. "I don't want 'some guy'—I want you. Before I met you I didn't think I'd ever have a normal relationship with a guy again. I mean, I thought I was, like, cursed or something. Then I met you and fell in love. I know you don't think I care about you, that I'm just into partying and all that? But it's not true. I care about you a lot—more than anything in the world. I just have a hard time showing it sometimes, that's all."

She started crying again. She suddenly seemed harmless and innocent, and I had to remind myself that she was insane.

"I'm really sorry about this," I said, "but it's over, so you can just forget about trying to—"

She started kissing me. I was trying not to kiss her back,

but it was hard to stop myself. Then the phone started ringing.

Holding on to my shoulders, she said, "Let it ring."

"I'll be right back," I said, wriggling free.

I went into the kitchen and picked up.

"David, is that you?"

Shit. I was hoping I'd never hear that annoying, mousy voice again.

"Yes," I said, trying to act natural because Rebecca could overhear us.

"I couldn't do it," Sue said. "The body's still up in my apartment."

Rebecca was looking over, trying to eavesdrop. She was about ten feet away, though, and I hoped she couldn't hear the voice on the other end.

"Oh, hi, Steve," I said, deciding I'd pretend to have a conversation with Steve Pinkus, who worked in Copyediting.

"Steve?" Sue said. "Who the fuck's Steve?"

"No way," I said, smiling.

"Stop dicking around, you stupid asshole," Sue said. "We're in big trouble now, really big trouble, and I wanna know what the hell you're gonna do about it."

"What exactly is the problem?" I asked, looking at Rebecca, who was still watching me.

"I told you the problem, you fuckin' jerk-off—I didn't call the cops, so you better get your ass over here right now and do something."

I pictured Ricky, or whatever his real name was, sitting

next to Sue, maybe with an ice pack on his head. They must've thought they'd found a real sucker.

"I'm sorry about that," I said, glancing at Rebecca again, who was still listening in.

"Sorry about what?" Sue said. "What're you talking about?"

"Can I send you a new file in the morning?"

"*What*?"

"That sounds great."

"I'm gonna call the cops right now—I'm not playing around, dickhead."

"Okey dokey. Bye-bye."

I hung up the phone and returned to the dining area.

"Something wrong?" Rebecca asked.

"No, that was just Steve Pinkus in Copyediting. Look, it's nothing personal. I've had some great times with you and I think you're a great person and all that, but I really think we should—"

The phone started ringing again.

"Let the machine pick up," Rebecca said in a raspy, sexy voice that usually turned me on.

The phone was still ringing.

"I'll take it in the bedroom," I said.

When I picked up, the answering machine had already answered—Ja Rule rapping in the background with Rebecca's voice saying, "We're out having fun right now, but if you leave us a message—"

"Hello," I said.

"Hang up on me again and I'm gonna—"

"Look, I know what you two are doing," I said in a hushed tone, "and it's not gonna work. So you better go out and find yourself a new sucker, because—"

"What're you talking about?" she said. "Ricky's dead, and you better get your stupid ass over here and do something about it."

Sue sounded truly panicked. Maybe it was all a scam—Ricky was sitting right next to her, coaching her on what to say—and this was all part of the setup.

Or maybe it wasn't.

I took a deep breath, shaking my head, then said, "Gimme half an hour," and hung up.

I remained in the bedroom for a few minutes, trying to pull myself together. Finally I changed into jeans, a sweatshirt, and sneakers, and then I returned to the dining alcove, where Rebecca was still seated, waiting for me.

"Gotta go," I said.

"What do you mean?" she said, frowning.

"Problem with the file for my story," I said. "Gotta go to the office and resend it."

"Can't you do that from here?"

"I didn't back it up on disk."

"Come *on*."

"Sorry."

"When are you coming back?"

"Hour or so."

"Why so long?"

"I might have to stick around while they copyedit it."

"What about dinner?" She bit down gently on her lip

and looked me up and down. "I had a really great dessert planned too."

"Let me know how it was," I said.

I hailed a cab on Columbus and had to say, "Avenue B and Sixth Street," five times, the fifth time practically screaming, before the Russian driver understood what I was saying. As we pulled away, I noticed that the cab reeked of cigarettes. I cranked open the window, letting in bus exhaust and street noise. We passed Spazzia, where Barbara and I used to go for brunch sometimes on Sundays.

"Me and Jay are breaking up," Barbara said to me at a table near the window. She was drinking her second Bloody Mary, her hair cut short to shoulder length.

"I'm sorry," I said, "but I can't say I'm not happy about it."

I reached across the table and touched her wrist; then she yanked her arm away as if I had cooties.

Glaring at me, she said, "You fucked up my whole life," loud enough that a couple at a nearby table looked over. She took a big gulp of her Bloody Mary, almost finishing it, and I wondered if she was drunk.

"Me?" I said. "What did I do?"

"Dr. Kellerman says you're the reason I can't have a functional relationship with a guy."

"I don't know why you pay some guy one-fifty an hour to insult you."

"He said we spend too much time together."

"You're basically the only family I have in the world, so,

what, we can't hang out together? Is that some kind of crime?"

"*I hate you so much right now.*"

The cab was stuck in traffic near Seventy-second Street, cars and buses all around us honking their horns. I realized the cabdriver was talking to me.

"What?" I said.

"You want me to take East Side?" he said with his Russian accent.

"Yeah, fine, whatever," I said, staring out the window.

When the cab turned onto Avenue A, I was so certain that Ricky wouldn't be in the apartment I almost considered telling the driver to turn around and head back uptown. Then I remembered how believably desperate Sue had sounded on the phone, and I decided that since I'd come all the way down here I might as well make sure.

I got out at the corner of Sixth and A and headed down the block toward Sue's building. I remembered how relieved I'd felt this afternoon when I'd left there, and it was hard for me to believe that I was going back.

I went into the vestibule and rang apartment fourteen. She buzzed me in and I headed up the stairs. Near the third floor, a thin, light-skinned black guy in an army jacket passed me on the stairs, pushing me hard with his shoulder.

"Hey," I said, but the guy kept going.

I hated New Yorkers; I hated people. I wanted to move to the country, deep into Vermont or New Hampshire or—

better yet—Canada. Saskatchewan. I'd live in a cabin with no TV, never see a human face again.

When I reached Sue's floor I caught my breath, then rang the bell to her apartment. I heard footsteps going back and forth. It sounded like one person was in there, but I wondered if Ricky was there too, maybe scrambling to hide.

I rang the bell several times in succession, upset that so much of my time was being wasted, and then Sue opened the door. I noticed that she was shivering as she moved to the side to let me into the apartment.

I entered the foyer and, as I expected, the body wasn't there.

"Look," I said, pointing my index finger, as if scolding a delinquent child, "I've had it with this bullshit. Stay the hell away from me or I'm calling the cops, and I mean it. I don't care what story you have, either—the second I hear your voice I'm gonna—"

I noticed that Sue wasn't looking at me—her gaze was focused to my right and down slightly. I looked over my right shoulder and saw Ricky on his back—the lower part of his body inside the bathroom, the upper part in the main part of the apartment a few feet away from me. His eyes were half-open, but perfectly still and glazed over, and his light brown skin had turned a shade of blue.

I stared at the body for a while, then turned to Sue who hadn't budged, and said, "So he's still playing dead, huh? Nice try, but it won't work."

"What the hell're you talking about?" she said. "Have

you totally lost it? You better do something. I can't stand having him in the apartment anymore. I can't look at him."

I continued staring at the body in a daze, the truth setting in. I didn't know how I'd managed to convince myself that it hadn't happened.

"You were supposed to take care of this," I said.

"I couldn't, all right?" Sue said.

"Why not?"

"Because I'm a really shitty liar."

"Then why did you tell me—"

"Because I thought I could pull it off," she said. "I made a mistake, all right? Go ahead—shoot me."

"Call the police now."

"I can't."

"Do it, damn it."

"You do it," she said. "Tell them the truth—say you killed him by accident, self-defense, whatever. That's what you wanted to do anyway, right?"

I considered this, but decided it was too late. The police would run tests, realize the body had been here for about seven hours. They would want to know why there was a delay in reporting the incident. I could tell them that I'd panicked and ran away, which was sort of the truth, but with Ricky's head bashed in they'd never believe my self-defense story—especially not now.

"That won't work," I said.

"Well, you better do something else then. You're the one who killed him."

"I saved your life."

"Bullshit." She sounded ridiculous, getting angry with that high, squeaky voice. "You know how many times Ricky came at me with a blade? He wasn't really gonna hurt me—he just liked to get macho like that. You didn't have to ram his head into the door like some maniac."

Now I knew there was no way I could call the cops. Sue would never back up my story and I'd be arrested for murder.

I couldn't believe I'd let this happen. If I hadn't tried to get my wallet back, I could've been home right now.

"Come on," Sue said, "just call the—"

"We're not calling anybody."

"Then what're we gonna—"

My brain jump started.

"Was Ricky a junkie too?"

Sue stared at me with her glassy, lifeless eyes, then said, "Who're you calling a junkie?"

"Shut up. Was he a junkie too?"

"I'm not a fuckin' junkie."

"Was he a junkie?"

"He shot up once in a while, yeah, but he wasn't a junkie."

"We'll make it look like it was drug-related," I said.

"What're you talking about?"

"The murder, I mean killing—whatever. We'll dump the body somewhere. Tompkins Square Park's right around the corner, right? The cops probably find dead junkies there all the time."

"Ricky wasn't a junkie."

"Shut up," I said, almost shouting. In a much quieter voice I said, "Does he have track marks?"

I leaned over toward the body to get a closer look at the arms. They looked like pincushions.

"Perfect," I said. "So that's what we'll do. The cops'll think some drug dealer killed him. They had an argument over money and started fighting; then the guy rammed Ricky's head into a tree and killed him. They'll come talk to you, but they'd never question you. Why would they?"

"It won't work," Sue said.

"Yes, it will," I said.

"How're we supposed to get him to the park?"

"We'll carry him."

"You crazy? He weighs one-sixty-five."

"So?"

"What if somebody sees us?"

"We'll wait till later—the middle of the night. Four, five in the morning. It's just down the stairs, then a block or two to the park."

"The cops won't believe it was over drugs."

"Why not?"

"Why would a dealer kill him?"

"For money."

"If the dealer killed him he'd never get his money."

"Maybe he didn't mean to kill him."

"If a dealer was after him he wouldn't bust his skull," Sue said. "He'd shoot him, or cut him, or something like that."

"Maybe there was a struggle," I said, "a fight and ... Or maybe it wasn't over drugs, all right? Maybe somebody just tried to mug him—kids. Or maybe he got into a fight—said something to the wrong guy. That happens all the time—two guys fighting over a parking space and one guy flips and starts beating the other guy up."

"Why would they be fighting over a parking space in the park?" Sue asked.

"The fight could've been over anything," I said, losing patience. "The cops'll find his body in the park, they'll think he was killed fighting, and that'll be the end of it."

"I don't care," Sue said. "Say whatever you want. But I'm not helping you carry him anywhere."

"Oh, yes, you are."

"You can't make me."

"You're right, I can't. But you think if I get caught I won't turn you in too? I'll say you were an accessory, or an accessory after the fact, or whatever the hell they call it. They'll put us both away for a long time."

"So let them put me in jail," Sue said. "What the fuck do I care?"

"You can't get any heroin in jail," I said. "They won't give you anything to dry out with either. You think you can handle that? I don't think so."

My last words seemed to have an effect on her. Sick of looking at her face, I turned away; then I realized I was staring at the body, at the blue-gray lips, parted slightly and swelling, and I turned again quickly. I didn't want to look at Sue anymore either, but the apartment was tiny, like a cage, and it was hard to avoid her. I stood with my arms crossed in front of my chest, rocking back and forth nervously, staring at the wall adjacent to the refrigerator.

"So what're we gonna do now?" Sue asked.

"Wait," I said.

Sue remained on her futon, cross-legged, staring at nothing, and I remained facing the wall. I noticed a roach—a good-sized one, about an inch long—moving vertically toward the floor. It was robust, shiny, moving at a good, steady pace, definitely thriving in its environment. I continued to watch it as it reached the floor, went around a plastic Pepsi bottle, around mouse or maybe rat droppings, and disappeared swiftly into a space between the wall and the floorboards.

I realized that my face and neck were sweating.

"You sure that fan doesn't work?" I asked.

"I told you, it broke," Sue said.

"It must be ninety fucking degrees in here," I said, wiping sweat from my forehead with the back of my wrist. "I don't know how the hell you live here."

"Sorry, it's not the fucking Plaza Hotel," she said.

Sue looked away and I noticed another roach coming from near the stove. I stomped on the roach, rubbing the shiny pieces into the floor, and then I sat down on one of the chairs, hoping sitting would make me sweat less. It didn't work. Sweat was dripping off of my forehead like I was a basketball player in the fourth quarter.

"How come this building's such a dump anyway?" I asked.

"What're you talking about?" she said.

"There's garbage piled up downstairs, you got roaches and mice. The rest of the neighborhood's gentrified. How come they didn't gentrify this place yet?"

"You mean how come it's not infested with yuppies yet?"

"Yeah," I said.

"It's a rent-controlled building," she said. "People've been living here for years."

"So lots of buildings are rent controlled," I said, "but they're not hellholes like this place. I mean, the stairwell's disgusting, it's infested with God knows what, it's about a thousand degrees in here—"

"The landlord's trying to get people to move out so he can raise the rents."

"That's against the law."

Sue shrugged and said, "It's not working anyway. People in this building aren't going anywhere no matter what he does."

"Still, you must be paying a decent amount for this place. How do you afford it?"

"What the fuck do you care?"

"I'm just curious. I mean, do you make all your money turning tricks and selling wallets or do you have a day job too?"

"Fuck you."

"I'm serious. Heroin's gotta be an expensive habit, and you must eat, what, once or twice a week, right? After that, there must not be too much leftover for rent money."

"Maybe I don't pay rent," she said smugly.

"What?" I said. "Your psychotic, jealous, knife-wielding boyfriend helped you out?"

"Maybe I just worked out a special deal with my landlord."

"A free-rent deal?"

"Yeah, a free-rent deal."

"And how exactly does that work?"

"Easy," she said. "I meet him in his car a couple times a week and he lets me slide on the rent."

"So you really are screwing your landlord."

"I don't fuck him," she said as if the idea disgusted her. "I just blow him."

"Classy," I said. "You should be really proud of yourself."

"You just wish you had a setup like that."

"That's true," I said. "I wish I was giving my landlord blow jobs. Why didn't I ever think of that?"

"Beats working for a living," she said. "Going to an office every day, having somebody tell you what to do."

"True," I said. "And you can make your own hours too."

"Right." Then, realizing I was being sarcastic, she said, "You can suck my dick, asshole. You think you're all that? Mr. Hotshot Business Writer Man living on West Eighty-first Street."

I gave her a long stare, then said, "You really studied my wallet, didn't you? You know where I live. I bet you know my Social Security number, credit card numbers, place of birth, mother's maiden name ..."

"You think you're so much better than me," she said, "but you're not. Where're you from? Wait, let me guess— you got a New York accent, but you're not from Manhattan. You from Staten Island? Brooklyn? Queens—?"

"I'm from Long Island."

"Ooh, big-shot bridge-and-tunnel man. Probably didn't come from the rich part of the Island either—you're probably from White Trashville, out near Stony Brook. You know where I'm from? Bloomfield Hills, Michigan, buddy. In case you don't know, that's a very ritzy area. My parents had a twelve-room house, filled with classy furniture."

"Sounds like you had a great life," I said.

"I did," she said. "At least, I did till you came along and fucked everything up. I was gonna go on the juice and quit hooking and me and Ricky were gonna open a business together."

"A business, huh?"

"Yeah, a business. An antique store, if you really wanna know. I have a good eye for that stuff. See those chairs? I found them on the street last week and I'm gonna sell them for fifty bucks apiece. Girl's coming to pick them up this weekend. I have a good eye—I always spot bargains. I bought some silverware once—sterling silver—for twenty bucks at a flea market. I sold it the next day to an antique dealer on Lafayette Street for two-fifty."

"And I'm sure the profits went to a really great cause," I said.

Ignoring me, she said, "Yeah, I have a great eye for bargains. If I opened my antique store it would've been a big success. I wasn't just gonna sell antiques; I was gonna sell cheese."

"Cheese?" I said.

"Yeah, cheese," she said. "You know the place uptown that sells cheese and antiques?"

"No."

"Well, it's a really classy place, and my place was gonna be just like it. Ricky was gonna give me the start-up money, but thanks to you, that's all shot to fuckin' hell."

I rolled my eyes and looked away, deciding that I wouldn't say another word to her for the rest of the night.

We were both quiet for a long time—maybe ten or fifteen minutes. Sitting on one of the chairs, I stared at the brick wall mainly, following the paths of a couple of new baby roaches that had appeared, but a few times I couldn't help looking toward the bathroom, at Ricky's body. Sue seemed to be becoming more and more anxious and fidgety—rocking back and forth, making weird clucking noises with her mouth.

I couldn't take sitting anymore, so I started pacing.

"Why don't you just sit down?" Sue said. "You're making me fucking nervous."

I ignored her.

Maybe another five minutes passed, and then Sue said, "Or if you don't want to sit you can lie down here with me."

I did a doubletake, thinking I might've missed

something. Then I looked at Sue and saw her returning my gaze in a way that convinced me that I had been propositioned. I didn't know why I was so surprised.

"Come on," she said, continuing to fidget in a more exaggerated way—wiping her nose every few seconds, her legs shaking. "It'll only cost you fifty bucks."

I imagined climbing on top of her thin, heroin-addicted body; although the idea disgusted me, there was something exciting about it too.

"Come on, lemme relax you," Sue said, rubbing her nose. "I mean you look so nervous, pacing around. I'll make you feel real good, baby. What do you say?"

"The answer's no."

She was quiet for a few seconds, then said, "Okay, I'll give you the Upper West Side business writer's special. I'll suck your cock for twenty-five."

I looked away, shaking my head. When I looked over again she'd taken off her shirt. First I noticed her ribcage—the bones clearly visible—and then my gaze shifted higher, toward where breasts should've been. It looked like a man's chest—or rather a boy's, an emaciated boy's, except for the surprisingly big brown nipples. It was sad because her face wasn't bad-looking, and if she were twenty pounds heavier and hadn't poisoned her body with heroin she would've been very attractive.

"Come on, why won't you fuck me?" she said, stroking her breasts softly. "I could tell you were thinking about it before. Come on, baby, you can have a whole half hour and I'll do whatever you want. I'll make you feel so good."

"Will you just put your top back on?"

"Fuckin' faggot," she muttered as she put her shirt on and continued fidgeting and twitching. I paced from the refrigerator to the stove and back, feeling as pent-up as one of the miserable-looking gorillas they used to have in the Central Park Zoo. My feet were hurting and I was still sweating badly; I wondered if I was starting to get dehydrated. I went to the sink and gulped down water from the faucet, some of it dribbling down my chin and neck. After splashing some water over my face I actually felt slightly refreshed. I glanced at Sue, but she was looking away, pulling on her hair, scratching her arms. I opened the refrigerator, hoping there would be something to eat, but there was nothing except a bag of Wonder bread with only a couple of stale-looking end pieces inside, an empty can of Franco-American ravioli, some blackened banana peels, and a couple of loose slices of American cheese that looked hardened. Then I caught a nauseating whiff of something rotting and I closed the door quickly.

"I eat out a lot," Sue said.

I looked over at her and smiled slightly, then realized she wasn't trying to be funny. I started pacing again. After awhile, I decided I'd better conserve my energy, and I sat in one of the chairs.

Sue was still shifting anxiously from side to side, still making those clucking noises. I was about to tell her to shut the hell up when she said, "So if you don't want to fuck me maybe you'll give me fifty bucks anyway."

I ignored her.

"Come on, it's just fifty," she said. "Fuck, I could've gotten a thousand from you if I met you tomorrow night."

"I guess you blew it then, didn't you?" I said.

A few more minutes passed, and then she said, "You ever shoot dope?"

I didn't want to answer her, so I just shook my head.

"Man, you don't know what you're missing," she said. "The first time I shot up I couldn't believe how good it felt. It feels like you're just floating away, like you're nothing. Hey, I got an idea. You let me go out and get some, we'll shoot up together. Don't worry, I'll get you a clean needle. Come on, I love turning on virgins."

"I have enough problems in my life," I said. "I don't need yours too."

"Trust me," she said, "after you shoot dope all your problems go away."

"Forget about it," I said.

"Faggot-ass fuckin' prick asshole piece of shit," she said, suddenly venomous. "You're just a stupid fucking faggot, that's what you are."

I started pacing again. Sue's tics had gotten even more exaggerated now, and her face was cringing, as if she were in serious pain.

"You okay?" I asked. She didn't answer, and then I said, "Really, are you feeling all right? Is there something I can get you? A glass of water or a piece of that cheese? Or maybe you want a wet towel."

"If you really want to help me you'll give me fifty so I can go out and take a fuckin' walk," she said.

She continued looking pained.

I ignored her for a while, then said, "Not that I really give a shit, but how did your life get so screwed up anyway?"

She didn't answer.

"Come on, I really want to know," I said. "I mean, you seem intelligent, you're not so bad-looking, and you said you were from that nice area in Michigan. You must've had a good family, went to good schools—"

"Fuck you."

"What?"

"Talking down to me like you're a fucking priest or something. You fucking asshole."

"I'm just trying to connect the dots."

"I gotta get the hell outta here," she said, standing up.

"Yeah, right," I said.

"I'll be back in a half hour, tops," she said. "Come on, what do you think I'm gonna do?"

"Oh, I know what you're gonna do. You're gonna go to the first phone booth you see and call the cops. You'll tell them a guy killed your boyfriend and if they don't believe you they can just go up to your apartment and see because he's still there."

"I'm not gonna rat you out, all right? I'll come right back here and we'll do it the way you want—we'll carry Ricky down to the park. I think that's a great idea, so why don't you just—"

"Sit down," I said.

She tried to bolt past me to get to the door, but I grabbed

her skeleton arm and yanked her back toward me. She stumbled over her own feet and I let go of her and she fell down onto the floor onto her side.

"Fucking cocksucking piece of shit," she said.

We glared at each other, the showdown lasting for maybe ten seconds. Finally she settled back down on the futon, fidgeting and rocking back and forth. Although I was looking away, I was watching her in my peripheral vision; if she made a sudden bolt toward the door I was going to block her. I realized that if, later on, she became even more desperate for a fix, it would be harder to restrain her. I started looking around, for rope or something else in the apartment that I could use to tie her up if I had to, but I didn't see anything.

"You know what I don't get?" Sue said. "I don't get why you wanted your stupid wallet back so bad anyway. If you just told me to fuck off right away Ricky'd still be alive."

I was going to remind her that she was the one who called me about the wallet, but I didn't want to get into that again.

"I mean, you paid one-fifty for it," she went on. "That's a lot just to get your license and some canceled credit cards back. I would've taken twenty bucks."

I squatted, facing the wall, noticing a monster-size water bug scamper from under the sink toward the refrigerator. I stared at the bottom of the refrigerator, waiting to see if the bug would appear again.

"You really are a nut job, aren't you?" she said. She sat with her head hanging between her knees for a while;

then she looked up at me again and said, "Say whatever you want about me. Say I'm a junkie, say I'm a whore, say whatever the fuck you want, but look at you. You're the one who's fucked up. Look what you did—look what you fuckin' did. You didn't have to kill him. You could've just got the knife away, held him down, but you didn't. You kept going. I saw the way you looked when you did it. You looked whacked, like you were getting off on it."

I was still staring at the bottom of the refrigerator, waiting for the bug to come out, when the doorbell rang. Sue looked as panicked as I probably did. We stared at each other and the bell rang three more times in quick succession. There was a period of silence, and then a man said, "Come on, I know you're in there. Come on, open up."

"Who the hell is that?" I whispered.

"Shit," Sue whispered harshly, as the ringing started again. "See, I told you we should've called the cops, you stupid fuckin' idiot. I told you.

6

THE BELL MUST have rung twenty times. Sue and I remained still. I was hoping whoever it was would finally give up and go away, but then a harsh voice said, "Hey, Ricky, open up, will ya? Come on, I gotta talk to you, for Christ's sake. Charlotte, I know you're fuckin' there too. Come on, I heard you guys talking. Will you put your fuckin' clothes on and let me in?"

"Who the hell's Charlotte?" I whispered

Sue gave me a *Who do you think, stupid*? look as the bell rang again.

"Come on, what're you gonna do, make me break the fuckin' door down?" the man said. "Come on, Ricky, what're you doing, getting your dick sucked in there? Come on, open up!"

There was more ringing and then the guy started banging on the door. It sounded like he was using his fists.

"I better let him in," Charlotte said, getting up.

I grabbed her arm. It felt like I was gripping a broom handle.

"Sit down," I whispered.

"We gotta let him in," Charlotte said, "or he'll—"

"He'll go away," I said.

The banging was getting louder.

"Come on, Ricky," the voice said. "I know you're fuckin' in there, you little piece of shit."

"You don't know Kenny," Charlotte said. "He won't go away. Ricky owed him money, and he won't leave till he gets it."

The banging continued.

"Take the body in the bathroom," Charlotte said.

"The bathroom?" I said.

"Open up!" Kenny said. "Just open the fucking door."

"I'll be right there!" Charlotte called out.

The banging stopped. I looked at Charlotte, wanting to strangle her.

"Go," she whispered.

Avoiding looking at Ricky's face, I lifted him by the sneakers. The body wasn't as stiff as I expected it to be, but it was stiff enough to remind me that he was dead. I backed into the bathroom, taking little shuffle steps. There was barely enough room for a toilet, a shower stall, and a tiny sink. The body and I didn't fit—at least, not with the body horizontal. The banging on the door continued and the doorbell kept ringing, but I couldn't tell what the guy was saying. I lifted the body up under its shoulders. At first, it was facing me, which was getting me kind of sick, so I turned it around one hundred and eighty degrees. Then I became aware of an odor of shit, probably from a postmortem bowel movement, and I couldn't hold back. Somehow I made it to over the toilet in time, managing to keep the body upright as I vomited. Charlotte poked her head into the bathroom.

"What the hell're you doing?" she whispered.

I upchucked again. It must've been old food, because it felt like battery acid was passing through my throat.

"Come on, just flush," Charlotte said.

Then, from outside the apartment: "Come on, Ricky, Charlotte, just open the fucking door. Jesus."

"I'll be right there!" Charlotte called out, and then she leaned around me and flushed the toilet.

"What're you doing?" I said weakly. Talking hurt, as if I had tonsillitis. "Now he'll know somebody's in the bathroom."

"Just get in there and shut up," Charlotte said.

Gritting my teeth, I lifted the body and carried it in front of me into the shower stall. It was a small, cramped shower, tiled with what had probably once been off-white or light yellow tiles, but they were brown now, covered with soap scum and mildew. I tried to prop the body upright against the back of the wall, but it kept slipping forward.

"Come on," Charlotte whispered urgently.

Grinding my back teeth, I held on to the body as I tried to close the shower door. The door was corroded and kept popping open, so I had to stand there with one hand on the door handle, the other pushing the body back against the wall. The stench of shit was worse now and I was trying not to breathe too deeply.

Charlotte left the bathroom and closed the door. I heard the locks on the front door turning and then the door squeaked open.

"About fuckin' time," Kenny said. "What were you doing, hitting up?"

I heard heavy footsteps entering the apartment.

"So what the fuck took you so long?" Kenny asked.

"I was in the bathroom, puking," Charlotte said.

"What'd you do, suck a rotten cock?" Kenny laughed. "So where's my boy, Ricky?"

"He's not here."

"You're shittin' me. He said he'd be around tonight."

"Well, he's not."

"You sure he's not hiding somewhere? The fuckin' prick owes me money."

Footsteps headed in my direction. My entire body tensed.

"Don't go in there," Charlotte said.

The footsteps stopped.

"Why not?"

"I had the shits too."

"You must've sucked a lot of rotten cocks." Kenny laughed.

The footsteps headed away, but I couldn't relax. It was Kenny's voice. It had sounded vaguely familiar before, but now I knew where I'd heard it—last night, at the bar. Kenny was Eddie Lomack.

My body temperature seemed to go up ten degrees. Fucking Charlotte had lied to me about a lot more than her name.

The conversation continued; I'd missed some of it.

"Gino's?" Kenny asked.

"I don't know, maybe," Charlotte said.

"Why would he go to Gino's?"

"I didn't say he went there. I just heard him saying he might go by there later."

The talking and the footsteps sounded farther away. Maybe they were near the futon now.

"You sure he didn't jump out the window and go down the fire escape?" Kenny said. "I coulda sworn I heard you talking to somebody before I started knocking."

"It was the radio," Charlotte said.

"Son of a bitch," Kenny said. "I lent him a hundred last night, said he needed to buy some food, but I shoulda known he'd just blow it on more junk."

"Look, he's not here. Just check Gino's, all right?" Charlotte said.

"You're really hard up, huh?" Kenny said. "What's the matter, Ricky blew all his money on his own stash last night, didn't share anything with his beautiful whore girlfriend?"

"Look, Ricky's not here, so why don't you just get the

fuck outta here, you fuckin' asshole."

"You don't look too good, sweetheart," Kenny said. "Yeah, you must be hitting it hard these days, huh?" I pictured him smiling, the way he had last night at the bar while he was distracting me with pictures of the centerfolds. "Probably going through, what, ten, fifteen bags a day? Probably hadn't had any in what, a few hours? Yeah, you're real hungry now."

"You got some or not?" Charlotte said.

"Come on, you know I'm on the fuckin' juice," Kenny said. "But look what I do got … It'll buy you a couple bags. Keep you going another few hours … Hey, not so fast. You're gonna have to work for it, baby."

"Come on, Kenny, just gimme it."

"What, Ricky's not around, so what difference does it make? In fifteen minutes you can be scoring, baby. Then you could be back up here, cooking it up nice and sweet— it'll make you feel *so* good, baby. Bet you haven't felt that good in a long time—so long you probably forgot what it feels like. But hey, it's up to you. If you don't want it …"

"You want to fuck me, stop talking and take your little dick out," Charlotte said.

"Little?" Kenny said. "That look little to you?"

The apartment got quiet, and then Kenny said, "Yeah, like that, bitch. Work it just like that." Then, about a minute later, I heard Kenny's moaning. It sounded like a sick animal, or a dying one. He was talking too. At first I couldn't make out the words; then I could hear some of them. It sounded like dialogue from a bad porno movie.

He was saying, "Keep doing it like that ... Yeah, just like that, bitch ... Fuck me harder, yeah ... Keep fucking me that way ... Yeah ... Play with my balls now ... Yeah, play with those balls, you little slut." I didn't know what was making me more nauseous: holding up a dead body or trying to fight off the images of Kenny and Charlotte that kept coming to me. The aftertaste of vomit in my mouth wasn't helping, and I had to concentrate on more pleasant things—sunny weather, the ocean, solid food, a beautiful woman—Rebecca. No, not Rebecca. Shit, anybody but Rebecca. Angie. Yes, Angie. Angie's face—to keep from throwing up again.

As the fucking went on, the only noises came from Kenny until he ordered Charlotte to "Come for me, baby. Come on, come for me," and she let out a series of lame, obviously fake squeals. I imagined her lying there on the futon on her back, just waiting for it to end so she could go shoot up.

Kenny's grunting and bad porno dialogue continued, and then, just when it seemed like the sex might never end, Kenny let out three louder grunts and then there was sudden silence.

There was more talking, but it was low and I couldn't hear what they were saying. Then I heard Kenny, his voice suddenly louder, say, "Wait, I gotta use the John Hancock."

Every muscle in my body tensed.

"Wait, don't go in there," Charlotte said, her voice close now too. They must've both been right outside the door.

"Why not?" Kenny asked.

"I stunk up the bathroom really bad."

"So what the fuck do I care?"

As the door opened, I crouched down, managing to keep one hand on the shower door handle and the other holding the body upright by pressing it against the back of the stall. If it wasn't for the mildew on the shower door, which was denser toward the bottom, Kenny could have easily seen in. As it was, he would've probably been able to see me if he looked in my direction.

Kenny hawked up a wad of spit; it splashed into the bowl, and then he started peeing.

"Liar, it don't stink in here!" he yelled. Then he added, "Hey, some of your chunks missed the bowl!"

He finished peeing. He didn't bother to flush, and then I saw the shadow of his legs pass by the shower door and stop. I thought he was going to look inside the stall, but then I heard the handle on the bathroom door turn and he left. My heart must've been racing at two hundred beats a minute.

"Where's my money?" Charlotte asked.

"Easy," Kenny said. "You'll get your skag, you'll get your skag."

"Come on," Charlotte said urgently. "Let's go."

The front door opened then closed. I waited several seconds, making sure they were really gone. Then I got up, leaving the body propped up diagonally, bent slightly near the neck and shoulders, and left the stall and the bathroom.

I never thought I could feel so relieved to be in the main area of the apartment. I was like a prisoner, released from solitary confinement and put back into his jail cell. But after a few minutes I started feeling pent up again. I had to leave, go outside, or I was going to lose my mind. I considered going downstairs, just for a few minutes, but I decided it was too dangerous. Someone could see me leaving the apartment, or someone could come in the apartment because I'd have to leave the door unlocked. I went to the one window in the room; it was partway open and I opened it further. Child safety bars were screwed into the sill, and it horrified me to think that a child had once lived in this shithole. I leaned over the bars, bringing my nose as close to the screen as I could without touching it, and breathed. The apartment was facing the back of another, taller building, maybe forty feet away, and the air didn't seem to be circulating much better than inside the apartment. Still, I remained there, with my nose near the screen, trying to get a hold of myself. I noticed a young guy in an apartment across from the building. He was lying on a couch in his underwear, watching TV, holding a green bottle—probably a cold beer. I hoped he knew how good he had it.

I started pacing the apartment again, wondering if Charlotte was going to go to the police. I didn't know why she would at this point, but I didn't have any reason to trust her either.

Several minutes went by, and I was becoming increasingly convinced that Charlotte was going to make up a story and turn me in, when my cell phone started ringing. The sudden noise startled me, and I realized how lucky I was that I didn't get a call while I was hiding in the shower. I checked the caller ID—it was my home number—then I shut the phone off.

I knew Rebecca wouldn't give up. She'd keep calling me, on my cell and at work, trying to get through. I didn't care about pissing her off, but I realized that if the police did wind up investigating me I'd have no alibi. If I called Rebecca back and told her I was at my office it wouldn't help, because I still wouldn't be able to prove I was there.

I had to stay positive, pray that Charlotte wasn't dumb enough to go to the cops, and that I'd never even be a suspect in the case.

The heat and the lack of fresh air in the apartment were unbearable, and the entire room was starting to smell like my body odor. Every time I heard a noise outside the apartment I hoped that the next sound I'd hear would be a key turning in the lock.

At midnight, there was still no sign of her. I was exhausted and starving—the turkey sandwich for lunch was all I'd eaten all day—and I didn't know how much longer I could last.

Around one A.M. I heard a noise outside the apartment. Convinced it was Charlotte, I rushed to the foyer, but the noise stopped. Impulsively I opened the door, realizing what a stupid thing I'd done only when I saw that Charlotte wasn't there. Instead, the young black guy who'd knocked into me on the stairwell before was standing by the door to the left. He was fumbling with his key chain, trying to find the key to his apartment. Before I could duck back into Charlotte's apartment he turned around and looked right at me. I mumbled, "Sorry," and he turned away, continuing to jingle his keys.

Back in the apartment, I knelt with my face buried in my open hands. If I hadn't opened the door, if I hadn't let that guy see me, I would've had a chance. But now when the police came to question Charlotte tomorrow they'd probably talk to her neighbors too, asking, "Did you notice anything unusual at Charlotte and Ricky's apartment last night?" The guy next door would mention me, give them a full description and—shit—I'd even *talked*, so now he could ID my voice.

I tried to convince myself that it wasn't as bad as it seemed. The guy had looked out of it, and there was a chance he might not remember me at all tomorrow, or at least he wouldn't remember me well enough to give a description. This gave me some hope, but not much.

The next time I checked my watch it was past two-thirty. I had no idea what was holding Charlotte up. Even if she was planning to bring a cop back with her, it wouldn't take her this long. I wondered if she was dead. She could've OD'd and was lying in an alley somewhere. But if she was dead that wouldn't help me. I couldn't leave because that guy had seen me, and with Charlotte unable to back up my self-defense story, I'd be screwed. I decided I'd give her till about half an hour before dawn. If she wasn't back by then I'd have no choice but to take the body outside by myself.

Another excruciating hour went by, and then I heard the lock in the front door turn. I rushed over as Charlotte entered, and I was surprised by her appearance, by how much better she looked. Her pained expression was gone and she seemed noticeably calmer and more relaxed. Except for her thin, ghostly face, she seemed almost normal.

"Where the hell've you been?" I asked. "It's almost four fucking A.M."

"Thanks for waiting up, Daddy," she said, stepping past me. She tossed her ripped denim jacket off to the side and then plopped down onto the futon. I did a double take, surprised all over again at how thin her arms and shoulders were. She was dangerously emaciated and probably needed medical help.

"You've been gone six hours," I said.

"You gonna ground me, Daddy?"

I hated the way she was suddenly so relaxed, acting like this was no big deal.

"Come on, let's go," I said. "We're doing it right now."

"Doing what?"

"What the hell do you think?"

"We should wait."

"We're not waiting."

"The after hours places are still open," she said. "There're still a lot of people out there. Give it another hour and the streets'll start to clear out."

The idea of spending another hour in the apartment seemed unbearable, but I realized that it probably made sense to wait.

I turned away, but there was no way to get away from her. She had closed her eyes and had her arms flung back over her head. She wasn't fidgeting or twitching anymore, like she had been earlier in the night. She looked like she was spending a relaxing afternoon on the beach. It was easy to imagine how she might've looked fifteen, twenty years ago, when she was a rich girl growing up in Michigan. She could've been lounging next to a pool in her parents' backyard.

"So're you gonna tell me the truth now or what?" I said.

"What do you mean?" she said, not bothering to open her eyes. She sounded like she'd been falling asleep.

"Come on," I said, "I know you've been lying to me since the second I walked in here so just tell me what the hell's going on."

"I didn't lie to you."

"Really, *Sue*."

She opened her eyes, looked at me for a couple of seconds, then closed them again, acting as annoyingly nonchalant as before. Then she said, "Sue's my street name."

"You stole my wallet last night, didn't you?" I said.

"I told you, I found it on the bus—"

"Stop fucking lying to me," I said. "I recognized your friend Kenny's voice—only he told me his name was Eddie. I guess that was his 'street name' too, huh?"

"Kenny's not my friend."

"Sorry," I said, "*Ricky's* friend who you don't mind fucking every once in a while for drug money even if the love of your life happens to be dead in the bathroom at the time."

"You got it all wrong, you stupid asshole," Charlotte said. "Kenny wasn't at the bar you were at last night."

"Yes, he was," I said. "He distracted me while you picked my pocket."

"I told you, I found your wallet on the bus."

I went over and grabbed her arm above her elbow and lifted her up to a sitting position.

"You stole my wallet last night, didn't you?"

"What're you gonna do, kill me? Go ahead—do it. I really don't give a shit."

I continued to squeeze her arm, which felt like a broom handle. She didn't seem to feel any pain.

After maybe ten seconds she said, "If you let go, I'll tell you."

Finally I loosened my grip and she wriggled free. She remained sitting, rubbing her arm, which seemed to have turned slightly purple.

"See, I knew you were a fuckin' basket case," she said.

I moved toward her again when she said, "Kenny and Ricky took your wallet—I had nothing to do with it, and that's the God's honest truth. They stole shit off people all the time. They sometimes worked the subways, but they did midtown mostly. They hung out at bars and looked for drunk tourists—I guess that's what they thought you were. Anyway, they took your wallet last night, and Ricky came home with it. He took all the money out and left the wallet here, so I decided to call you—to give it back to you."

I gave her a *Yeah, right* look.

"It's the truth," she said, "and I don't give a shit if you believe me or not."

"You're lying," I said. "Ricky wasn't at the bar with Kenny last night—you were. If Ricky was there he would've recognized me when he walked into the apartment today."

"Maybe he didn't get a good look at you last night," Charlotte said.

I realized this was possible. Whoever had picked my pocket had been behind me and might not have gotten a good look at my face.

"Maybe," I said, "but I still don't get why he attacked me. I mean, if you bring guys back here all the time—"

"I don't do it all the time," she said defensively. "I usually do it outside—in cars, mostly."

"Still," I said. "That doesn't explain why he'd flip out and pull a knife on me."

"Ricky was in love with me."

I must've rolled my eyes.

"I don't give a shit what you think," she said. "We were gonna get married soon. We were gonna open that antique store too and save up money and move to a bigger apartment someplace. Maybe in Queens or the Bronx. Ricky had family in the Bronx."

"Stop with that bullshit," I said. "If you and Ricky were so in love, why were you fucking other guys for money? Why were you fucking your landlord, for Christ's sake?"

"I wasn't fucking him!" she screamed, starting to cry.

"And why were you so quick to take the rap for his murder?" I said, not letting up. "You mourned for exactly two minutes—then you were out to make a quick thousand bucks off it. That really sounds like true love to me."

"I did love him, you fuckin' prick."

As Charlotte wiped away more tears with the back of her hand, I checked my watch. It wasn't four A.M. yet, but I felt like if I stayed in the apartment another minute I was going to lose my mind.

"We're going," I said.

"It's not late enough," she said.

"You got bed-sheets, a rug, something to wrap the body in?"

"We should wait till—"

"We're not waiting!"

She paused, then said, "All I got is what's on the bed."

"Get up," I said.

She stood up slowly, like an old woman with arthritis. The cotton blanket was too thin to conceal a body. I pulled the sheet off the futon, noticing all the cum and blood stains, but it wasn't nearly big enough or thick enough.

I picked up the rug in front of the bed, but it was too small, maybe two by four.

"You got anything else?" I said. "Another blanket or rug?"

She shook her head.

"Come on," I said. "You must have *something*."

I went to the one closet in the apartment, near the front

door. Hanging from wire hangers were dirty, torn clothes—jackets, coats, shirts, pants—that the Salvation Army wouldn't even accept. On the floor were some boxes of things and a duffel bag, but it was much too small to use.

"Jesus," I said.

"Wait till the stores open in the morning," Charlotte said. She had sat back down on the bare futon mattress. "You can buy a blanket then."

"And wait another day in here?" I said. "Are you out of your fucking mind?" I looked around the apartment again, coming up with no new great ideas, then said, "We'll just carry him between us like he's drunk or he OD'd. It could be better that way anyway. In this neighborhood that'll look less suspicious than carrying a rug or laundry down at four in the morning."

Dropping the sheet on the floor, I went into the bathroom. The body must've slid forward on the soap-scummed wall, because when I opened the door to the shower stall it fell out toward me. Despite my physical and mental exhaustion, my reflexes were quick enough to catch it by its shoulders. It was about as stiff as before, but it seemed to have gotten colder. Ignoring a surge of nausea, I held the body upright outside the shower stall.

"I need something—a rag or shirt or something," I called out.

"What?" Charlotte said.

"I need …" I looked up at the vent above the sink. It was clogged with puffy gray dust, but I knew my voice still might be able to travel to another apartment.

"Just come here," I said in a quieter voice. When Charlotte came into the bathroom I said, "I need a shirt or a rag or something—make it wet."

"What for?"

"Just get it."

Charlotte returned about a minute later with a damp T-shirt. Managing to keep the body upright, I scrubbed the sneakers as best I could, even doing the bottoms, and then I wiped the legs of Ricky's jeans, even though I knew fingerprints couldn't be found there. I wasn't even sure the sneakers needed to be wiped down, but I wanted to be as safe as possible.

When I was confident I'd done the best I could, I said to Charlotte, "Okay, here's what we do. We carry the body down between us as fast as we can, and we don't stop till we get to the park. Tomorrow, when it's discovered, the cops'll come tell you. Just start crying, the way you did before, and there should be no problem. They'll probably ask you—"

"I can't," she said.

"Yes, you can," I said. "Just say you know nothing about it and—"

"No, I mean I can't carry the body down. I can't touch it."

"What do you mean?" I said. "You touched it before."

"I know, but I can't again. I can't even look at him anymore."

She turned away, toward the door. Still supporting the

body with my left hand, I grabbed Charlotte's head with my right hand and forced it back around.

"Look at it," I said. "Get used to it, because you're helping me carry it down."

Her eyes were closed.

"Fuck you," she said. "I'm not going anywhere."

I realized that I couldn't force her to go with me, and arguing with her was just wasting time.

"Fine," I said, "but after I leave, I never want to see your pathetic face again. And when the cops talk to you, you better lie good, because if I go down I'm taking you with me. Got that?"

Charlotte nodded slowly. I tried to lift Ricky's left arm over my shoulder, figuring I'd carry him down that way, but the arm was too stiff and I could barely move it. Instead, I grabbed him from behind in a bear hug and started backing my way out of the bathroom, getting nauseous from the smell of shit. I saw Charlotte, back on the futon, lying on her side, facing away. I'd started walking forward now, shuffle-stepping, holding the body in front of me. When I got to the front door I was already sweating and gasping.

In the hallway I looked in both directions, especially toward the neighbor's door to the left; except for music playing in a lower-floor apartment, it was quiet, and no one was around. I tilted the body horizontally and held it by my side, as if I were transporting a heavy rug. But it didn't feel like a rug; it felt like a stiff, heavy, cold body. Sucking it up, I headed down the stairs as fast as I could.

Halfway down the first flight I was already exhausted, and I didn't see how I could possibly make it. I'd had an off-and-on sacroiliac problem since injuring myself carrying a metal filing cabinet home from a thrift shop a few years ago, and the way I was struggling on the fourth floor landing I didn't see how I could possibly make it all the way to Tompkins Square Park without throwing my back out or having a heart attack.

I considered dragging the body behind me and letting it bounce on the stairs, but I figured it would make too much noise. Then, heading down the next flight, I realized how idiotic the whole plan was. Anyone could leave an apartment at any moment and see me, or someone could come up the stairs, and I'd have nowhere to hide. No one would believe Ricky was drunk or had OD'd, the way I was carrying the body, and even if that was what someone did think, it wouldn't do any good when the cops started asking questions. The person would just give the cops a description of me and eventually I'd be caught.

I considered turning back, but I talked myself out of that quickly. If I had to wait until tomorrow night the medical examiner would figure out that Ricky had been dead for more than thirty-six hours, and the cops would never believe that he'd been in the park for so long without being discovered. It was now or never, and I just had to pray that I could make it without being seen.

As I approached the third-floor landing my arms were killing me and I was breathing so hard my lungs hurt, but I didn't let myself rest. Jazz music with a strong sax sound was playing in the apartment adjacent to the bottom of the landing. Hopefully, someone had gone to sleep with the stereo on and there was no one awake in the apartment. I'd barely finished having this thought when I arrived on the landing and the music suddenly stopped. I froze a few feet in front of the door to the apartment where the music had been playing, holding Ricky's body by my side, his head jutting toward the doorknob. I heard heavy footsteps in the apartment, and if the person had heard me or opened the door for any other reason I could get ready to spend the rest of my life in jail.

The footsteps were closer now, and I imagined a surly, muscular guy with a goatee—like my future cell mate was going to look—opening the door at any moment. He'd scream for help, tackle me to the floor, and hold me down until the cops came. Aunt Helen and some of my other relatives would be shocked when they heard the news, telling reporters, "He was such a nice, easy-going guy—he could never have done something like that." I'd plead innocent, say the whole thing had been an accident, but everyone watching the news would think, *Sure, that's what they all say*. People at my office would have the same reaction, but Rebecca wouldn't give a shit. She'd just move on and start mooching off some other guy.

The two locks on the door turned and I knew this was it. The door would swing open and—

The footsteps started again, dissipating into the apartment. It took me several more seconds to realize that the person was *locking* the door, not unlocking it, and I wasn't going to get busted—not yet anyway. I waited until there was total silence, and then I continued around toward the stairs leading down to the next floor.

The short rest had given me a surge of energy, and I was able to move faster than before. Fatigue set in again as I neared the second floor, but I was able to push myself to keep going. I kept telling myself that once I got outside I could find a dark area and rest for a while, and then it would be only a block and a half to the park.

When I reached the ground floor and saw the double doors leading to the outside several yards in front of me, I didn't think I could make it. I was going to pass out and collapse—what a pathetic way of getting caught. Then I was opening the first door, which seemed like it weighed a thousand pounds, and I made it into the vestibule, and I opened the second door, which seemed to weigh even more. I made it outside, but I couldn't go any farther. I squatted, resting the body against an overflowing garbage can. It was okay—the street was dark, empty, and quiet; the only noises I heard were distant traffic on Avenue B and, somewhere, a dog barking. I could rest for a few minutes and go on, but then I thought, *Why not just leave the body here?* It was going to be discovered anyway, so what difference did it make when or where it was found? Somebody could've fought with Ricky and bashed his head into the concrete right here as easily as in the park.

I thought it through a few more times, making sure I wasn't making a stupid, rash decision. When I was convinced I wasn't, I started walking up Sixth Street, as fast as I could without running. Crossing Avenue A, continuing west, I couldn't hold back any longer. I broke into a full sprint.

7

APPROACHING FIRST, I started walking again toward the West Side. I figured it would be a good idea to hail a cab in the West Village or Chelsea, far away from Charlotte's. Desperate voices in the dark asked me for change—"Yo, you got twenty cent?"—or offered me drugs—"Smoke, man, smoke"—but I kept going, not making eye contact with anybody. I was sick of all the zombies who just existed to make other people miserable. Everyone who thought the scum was gone from the city didn't leave their apartments at night.

Around Broadway my fatigue started to set in again, but it was nothing compared to how I'd felt lugging the body. I continued along Eighth Street, past all the closed stores, the streets emptier. On Sixth Avenue I finally hailed a cab, and I sat in the car, staring blankly straight ahead as Aziz Amir sped uptown, making almost every light. A wave of euphoria had set in—I was really out of that apartment, on my way home. The situation had seemed so hopeless, especially when I'd heard those locks turning, but now I was free. My arms, shoulders, and lower back ached badly, and I knew my muscles would hurt even more tomorrow, but the pain would be worth it. I'd lie on a bed of nails for months if it meant getting through this.

In the back of the cab I felt filthy, like the whole day was sticking to me, and I couldn't wait to wash it away. It was going to be so great to take off all my clothes, stand on the soft, shaggy bath rug, then get under a hot blast of water. I'd just stand there and let the water pound on my head and run down my neck, and I'd feel my muscles relax and peace overtake me, and I'd know I was away from Charlotte and that whole nightmare.

I paid Aziz, giving him a two buck tip, and I went into my building. Opening the door to my apartment I was thinking about the warm water, my tension releasing, the filth swirling down the drain. Then I saw Rebecca standing in front of me, wearing the same black dress she'd been wearing when I'd left, but she was obviously drunk and wasted. Her eye makeup had run, giving her dark "raccoon eyes," and she was swaying as she tried to stand still. The apartment had a faint odor of pot.

"Where the hell've you been?"

I'd almost forgotten about Rebecca and all our problems.

148

"Where do you think I was?" I said. "I was at work."

"Work, my ass."

I noticed the empty bottle of wine, on its side on the dining room table, next to a few empty beer bottles. She was acting like she was coked-up too.

"I'm not gonna deal with this shit again," I said.

I headed along the hallway toward the bedroom, watching over my shoulder for flying bottles, but Rebecca was following me.

"What's her name?"

"I don't know what you're talking about."

"Come on, why can't you be a man and tell me? What's the bitch's name?"

"Leave me the hell alone."

We were in the bedroom.

"Who is she?" she asked. "How long has it been going on? Have you been cheating on me since we met? Is that why you never want to go out with me anymore, why you want to break up with me, because you started screwing some ho? Come on, tell me who the bitch is. I have a right to know the slut's name."

In the middle of taking off my sweatshirt, my face covered, I said, "I know you're dying to fight with me again, but it's"—I finished taking off my sweatshirt and glanced at my watch—"shit, four-thirty, and I'm going to sleep."

I took off my jeans and plopped onto the mattress. The pillow against my head would've felt so good if Rebecca weren't still standing there, shouting.

"I should've known you've been getting some on the side. Making it out like you have all these *problems* with me—I go out too much, I spend too much, I do this, I do that. Meanwhile, it's you—you're the bad one, not me."

I ignored her, hoping she'd leave me alone.

"So who is she?"

I was starting to conk out, but I knew she wouldn't shut up if I didn't answer her.

"There's nobody," I mumbled.

"You're lying," she said.

"I'm not lie … li … lying," I said, my voice fading.

"Do you work with her? You screwing some cunt at your office?"

Her voice jarred me awake.

"No," I said crankily. "Will you just stop with this already?"

"So where were you tonight? Her place?"

"What the hell're you talking about?" I said, burying my head under the pillow. "You know where I was."

"No, I don't know."

"I was at work."

"What?"

She couldn't hear me through the pillow. I pushed the pillow up slightly, revealing my mouth, and said, "Work. Work, all right?"

"I called work. Your voice mail kept picking up."

"That's because I was working. That's what people do when they're at work—they work, but I guess you wouldn't know about that."

"What's that supposed to mean?"

I didn't want to get into another senseless argument, so I didn't say anything. The room got quiet. I was hoping I'd hear footsteps and the door slamming but instead she said, "I called your cell too, but you didn't pick up. Why didn't you pick up?"

I waited, then said, "I didn't have my phone on."

"Bullshit. It was on because it rang—the first time I called anyway. You didn't answer, then you turned it off. You didn't bother checking your messages either—I left, like, five of them."

"I didn't know it was you calling."

"You have caller ID."

"My battery was running out."

"Bullshit!"

I burrowed my face deeper into the mattress, the pillow still atop my head. But Rebecca wouldn't let up.

"What were you doing at work?"

"Working," I said, "what do you think? Now can you leave me the hell alone?"

"I thought you just had to give them a file or something?"

"The whole system crashed, and I didn't back it up after all. I had to rewrite it from scratch."

"Why didn't you check your messages?"

"Because I didn't," I said, angry that I'd been explaining my whereabouts to some crazy girl I didn't even want to be with.

Rebecca grabbed the pillow.

"Give it back," I said.

"Not till you tell me her name."

"You're so pissed off, what're you waiting for? Why don't you just leave me? Get out of my life!"

"I want to know her name!"

She stopped, staring at something to her left. I realized what it was right away. Before I'd taken off my jeans I'd put my wallet on the dresser.

"What's that?" she asked.

"What's what?"

"That ... Your wallet."

"Oh, yeah," I said. "It was returned to me."

"By who?"

"I have no idea."

"What do you—"

"Somebody dropped it at the office—I don't know who."

I reached for the pillow, but Rebecca yanked it back away.

"Can you please give me my pillow back?"

"You're such a liar," she said. "Your wallet wasn't stolen—you just made that up because you thought I wouldn't be able to use my credit cards. You thought if I didn't have any credit cards I'd leave you, because that's why I'm with you, right? Because you're like my sugar daddy or something."

"A woman found it on the First Avenue bus."

She swung the pillow hard against my head. The force jerked my head back, stunning me.

"Are you cheating on me?" she said.

"Yes," I said, dazed. "I'm cheating on you, all right?"

She glared at me with the pillow cocked, ready to belt me again. Then she said, "With who?"

"I don't see what difference that makes."

"I want to know her name."

"I'm not telling you her name."

I was ready to raise my arms to block the blow.

"Do you love her?" she asked.

"Yes," I said. "I love her."

She would belt me with the pillow again at any moment, or maybe she would forget the pillow—go for the picture frames on the dresser. She would fling them at me one after the other and there would be more broken glass, and this time there wouldn't be anything I could do to stop her. She would keep coming after me, or maybe she'd pick up pieces of broken glass and try to cut me. I'd try to fight her off, and maybe I'd get her in a headlock. I'd just be trying to defend myself, but I'd lose control and start ramming her head against the wall.

But Rebecca wasn't coming after me. She was staring at me, looking wounded, and then she shook her head slowly and turned and left the room without saying a word, closing the door quietly behind her.

I felt like I'd finally gotten through to her. Later, or even right now, she'd start packing her things, and by the end of the day she'd be gone. I wished I'd thought of the "other woman" breakup technique sooner.

I fell asleep quickly, but it felt like I'd been out for only a few minutes when I was jarred awake by a nightmare. I was carrying Ricky's body down the stairs in Charlotte's building, but the body in the dream weighed much more than the actual body, and the stairs were at least twice as steep. I wasn't making any progress; it felt like I was trying to go down an up escalator. As I became more frustrated, I realized that Ricky was alive, squirming in my arms. He kept saying, "You fucking my lady?" Then he was behind me—chasing me, his head hanging to the side, as if it were attached to the rest of his body by a piece of string.

I waited for my heart to stop throbbing and for my breathing to return to normal, and then I glanced at the clock on the night table. It was 4:58, meaning I'd been asleep for only about twenty minutes. The light in the bedroom was still on, and the door was still closed. Rebecca was probably in the living room, sleeping on the couch, or maybe she'd gone to a friend's apartment or, better yet, a boyfriend's. Hopefully she'd move out by later today and I'd never see her again.

I turned out the light and tried to go back to sleep, but I was too wound up. I kept thinking about Ricky's body, lying there against the garbage can. Anybody who'd passed by until now had probably assumed it was just another strung-out junkie, but as the morning went on there would be more people on the streets, and eventually someone would realize that Ricky was dead and call the cops. Then the cops would go talk to Charlotte, and I had to count on her to keep her mouth shut. I didn't think she'd turn me in on purpose, but if the cops started putting pressure on her, she could blurt out my name. Or what if Charlotte's next-door neighbor told the cops he saw a guy in Charlotte's apartment? Charlotte would have to think fast and make up some story, and I knew I couldn't count on that.

I lay on my back, my mind spinning. I wished I could call Barbara, or go over to her place. She would've told me exactly what to do.

"I have a surprise for you," I said.

It was late one Saturday night. Barbara had been working long hours at her job, promoting a new IPO, and I'd been working hard too, having returned that afternoon from a business trip to San Francisco. I went to a video store on Columbus and rented the DVD of Barbara's favorite movie, Pretty Woman, *and bought a container of her favorite Ben & Jerry's flavor, Chunky Monkey, then went to her place on Eighty-fourth Street.*

"It's not a good time," she said into the intercom.

"Come on, buzz me up," I said. "I've got Chunky Monkey and Pretty Woman. *It doesn't get any better than that."*

"I'll call you tomorrow," she said.

I remained in the vestibule, suddenly getting a bad feeling, making up stories to myself. Maybe someone was robbing her apartment, tying her up, about to rape her.

I rang the buzzer again.

"Buzz me up, Barb."

"Go away."

"Buzz me up," I insisted.

A few seconds passed, and then the buzzer sounded. I went up to her apartment, and she talked to me with the door open a crack, with the chain on.

"Is everything okay?" I said.

"I have someone here."

"Who?"

"Just someone."

"Let me in."

Then the door closed. I heard Barbara saying, "No, don't, come on," and then the door opened all the way and Jay was standing there with that slicked back hair and that fake tan.

"Your sister said she didn't want to see you," Jay said. "Can't you get the message?"

"Stop it," Barbara said to him.

"I thought you two broke up," I said to Barbara.

"We got back together," Barbara said.

"When?" I said.

"It's none of your business," Jay said. "Why don't you just get the hell out of here?

"Don't talk to him like that —"

"Shut up," Jay said to Barbara; then he said to me, "Your sister's sick of you. She doesn't want you coming by here anymore."

"I never said that," Barbara said.

"Shut up," Jay said to Barbara. Then he said to me, "Why don't you get the hell out of here before you get hurt?"

"You okay?" I asked Barbara.

"I told you to go," Jay said.

"I'm talking to my sister," I said.

Jay pushed me.

"Stop it," Barbara said.

"Your sister wants you to leave," Jay said.

"Jay!" Barbara shouted.

"You deaf?" Jay pushed me again, almost knocking me down, and then I went after him. He was taller than me and stronger, but I didn't let up. I tackled him, punching him in the face till his nose was gushing blood and there was blood all over my fists and he was squirming on the floor, trying to get up.

"Get out of here!" Barbara screamed at me. "Go!"

I turned over onto my side and punched the bed as hard as I could.

I lay awake for a long time, sweating and agitated, until grayish-blue light started filtering into the room through the blinds. Then I watched the ceiling brighten—it was after six already—and I was expecting the phone to ring at any moment, or the police to show up, banging on the door. I'd given up on trying to sleep, but I stayed in bed until eight o'clock anyway. I'd been planning to take the day off to get some rest, but I wasn't getting any, and I decided it might be a good idea to go into work. When the police investigated, it would be better to show that I was going about my normal, everyday life.

I left the bedroom, on my way to shower, when I decided to check the living room to see if Rebecca was there. Sure enough, she had crashed on the couch, still in the clothes she'd been wearing last night. I hoped she was planning to move out today, although I realized it didn't matter what she did if I wound up in jail.

Showering didn't relax me at all. Afterward I shaved sloppily, cutting myself in several places. Looking in the mirror, I appeared, appropriately, as if I'd been through hell. My lower lip was still swollen—although not as badly as yesterday—and my eyes were bloodshot with dark circles underneath.

Riding downtown on the crowded 1 train, I felt like it could have been any morning. People's pissed-off faces were inches apart, everyone trying to avoid eye contact, and when the one-legged, homeless ex-vet with AIDS came through the car, pushing through on his crutches, rattling his cupful of change, everyone groaned and muttered curses. But instead of getting annoyed or depressed about my commute, I enjoyed every second of it. I knew if I wound up in jail I'd spend years missing shitty mornings just like this one.

When I got to my building I had a scare when I saw two cops waiting in front. My first instinct was to turn around and run, but then I realized I'd seen the cops in the area before, and they were just on their normal beat. I walked by them and headed into the building through the revolving door, moving quickly because a guy was turning the door fast behind me. In the elevator, I imagined some guy in Alphabet City saying to his friend right now, "Hey, I think that guy over there's dead," and his friend saying, "No, he's not." But the first guy would insist, and they'd take a closer look, and the friend would say, "Holy shit, you're right," and that would get the ball rolling. The police would question Charlotte and her next-door neighbor, and it wouldn't be long before they questioned me. They could already be on their way over.

In the *Manhattan Business* office, I went right to my desk and booted up my computer. Peter Lyons had sent me a revised version of my story. I started proofreading it on the screen, but I couldn't concentrate. I kept thinking about all the ways I could be caught, even if Charlotte or her neighbor didn't tell the police about me. I could've left physical evidence on the body—hair or fibers from my clothing. There was a chance I'd stepped in something in the hallway or outside the building—I vaguely remembered my sneakers sticking slightly against the stairs—and for all I knew I'd left a footprint somewhere. Or someone could've seen me—a neighbor who'd heard a noise and looked through a peephole out to the hallway. And then there was my bruised lip and the cut on my arm. If the cops questioned me for any reason it was doubtful they'd believe my falling-in-front-of-the-bank story, and the more explaining I did the more convoluted my story would become.

A noise behind me startled me. It was only a creak in the floor, but I wheeled around in my chair as if a bomb had gone off. Angie was standing there.

"Sorry," she said, "didn't mean to scare you."

"You didn't," I said, catching my breath.

"Is everything okay?"

"Yeah. Why?"

"No reason."

She came into my cubicle and sat down in the chair, mindlessly sifting through a stack of magazines. She was wearing her red-blouse-with-a-short-black-skirt-and-shiny-black-boots outfit that I'd always thought she looked really cute in.

"So what're you doing?" she asked.

"Oh, nothing much," I said. "Just looking over Peter's idiotic edits."

"How's the damage?"

"Listen to this," I said, looking at the computer monitor. "My original sentence was 'Byron took a major risk last year, expanding abroad in the face of fierce competition at home.' The schmuck changed it to, 'Byron took a terribly odd gamble last year, spreading its operations too thinly abroad, while competition from industry leviathans swelled in the States.'"

"You know what he did to my last story?" Angie said. "He said the company I was writing about had 'indefatigably gained market share.'"

I laughed. It felt good to have something to laugh about.

"I wish we could do something to get even with him," Angie said, "like expose him somehow. Like maybe we could start a web site—Peter-Lyons-is-a-fucking-asshole-dot-com, or something like that. We could post all this trash about him and everybody in the world would know what a prick he is ... What's wrong?"

Laughing with Angie had managed to distract me from my real problems for a while, but it had all set in again.

"Nothing," I said.

"God, you scared me," Angie said. "For a second I thought you couldn't breathe or something."

"I'm fine."

"You sure?"

"Maybe it's allergies—pollen. I'll have to stop by the drugstore later."

Angie still seemed very concerned, and I wished I could've opened up to her about everything that was going on in my life. It would've been great to have someone to talk to.

Wanting to change the subject, I said, "So how're you and the frat boy doing?"

"*Please*," Angie said, blushing.

"What? You and Mike are dating, right?"

"*No*," she said, overly defensive. She got up and peered over the tops of the cubicles to make sure Mike wasn't around, and then she sat back down. "We went out last night to dinner at City Crab on Park. I had the shittiest time. He kept going on and on, talking about some hockey game he went to with his friends, even though he knows I couldn't give a shit about hockey. Then he starts taking all these cell phone calls. Just stupid calls from friends of his—'Hey, man, what's goin' on?' 'Not much, dude—just sittin' here chillin', havin' dinner with this hot chick from my office.'"

I laughed.

"So finally he gets off the phone and the rest of the meal we barely talk at all. I'm just checking my watch, hoping

I'm home in time to do my laundry; then the check comes and he's like, 'So do you want to go back to my place and fool around?' I look at him like, Are you out of your fucking mind? I mean, what was he expecting me to say? 'Yeah, let's go fool around—that sounds like a great idea. Why don't you invite some of your hockey goons over too?' So we get outside and I just get in a cab and tell the driver to drive away as fast as he can. I don't know what I'm gonna say when he sees me today. Hopefully he'll just blow me off."

"If you want to go on another date we'll pay for it," I said.

"No, thanks, Chuck," Angie said, and then she glanced at her watch. "Well, I better get to work. I have to talk to this analyst, then write this story about some company I know nothing about."

"What company?"

"Cornwell and Wallace. They're a search firm specializing in accountants."

"Fun."

"I know, right? It sounds like some bad joke. What's more boring than headhunting? Headhunting for accountants."

Angie got up to leave.

"Stay," I said.

She looked at me, noticing the strange desperation in my voice. I liked the distraction of having Angie to talk to. It made me feel safe, as though as long as I was with her nothing could possibly go wrong.

"I can't," she said. "My story's due this afternoon and I haven't even started it yet. But if you want to do lunch later, maybe around twelve-thirty ..."

"Lunch sounds great," I said.

"Cool," she said, looking at me—I thought—flirtatiously. "See ya later."

I continued reading through the edited version of my story, but I couldn't concentrate, reading the same lines again and again. Every time I heard a noise behind me I felt a pang in my chest and I looked over my shoulder expecting to see police officers. I hoped it wouldn't be a big production—six or seven officers, guns, handcuffs.

The tiny clock in the lower right hand corner of my computer monitor seemed to take up the entire screen. When ten o'clock came I knew it wouldn't be much longer. The body had to have been discovered by now. Charlotte had told the cops my name and where I worked, and they were probably in the building, getting on the elevator right now. Maybe they considered me a dangerous felon and had cordoned off the building. Dozens of cops—no, a whole SWAT team—could be on their way up to get me.

I was sweating through my shirt. I went to the bathroom to wash up, and then I used the urinal, wondering if it was the last leak I'd take as a free man.

Back at my desk, I skimmed the story on the screen, noticing more Britishisms and awkward sentences. I started to write an angry e-mail to Jeff; then I had a better idea. I forwarded my original version of the article to Jeff, without Peter's edits. It was against the magazine's protocol to bypass the associate editor, but at this point what did I have to lose?

At 10:42, the police still hadn't arrived, and I decided that something must be holding them up. Maybe Charlotte wasn't home when they went to question her and they were waiting outside her apartment. So I'd gotten a couple extra hours of freedom, but maybe it would've been better to have been put out of my misery.

Another excruciating few minutes went by, and then Jeff IM'd me, telling me he wanted to see me in his office.

"Take a seat," he said when I arrived.

Jeff had turned forty last year, but he looked at least fifty. His hair had been totally gray since I'd known him, and he had a wrinkled, prematurely aged face, probably from years of alcohol abuse. Everyone at the magazine knew to stay away from him after two in the afternoon, when he was known to be irritable after his long martini lunches. Once, during my first year at the magazine, I'd made the mistake of asking him for some advice about a story while he was lit, and he blew up at me, screaming, "Get out of my motherfucking office!"

I sat down in the chair across from his desk when he said, "Are you okay?"

"Fine," I said. "Why?"

"You look exhausted."

"Oh, I'm just trying to fight something off."

"You mean you came into work *sick*? What's wrong with you? I have kids at home, for Christ's sake."

164

"I don't think I'm actually sick," I said, wondering if he'd started drinking earlier than usual today. "I just have a scratchy throat."

"Still," Jeff said, shaking his head, and then he became distracted by his computer monitor and he swiveled in his chair to face it head on. "So I was looking over your story on this, er … Byron Technologies …"

"I was going to write you about that," I said. "I sent you my original version because I don't think it's fair what Peter's been doing. He doesn't edit; he rewrites."

"So this writing is entirely yours?" Jeff asked.

"Yes," I said.

"Well, I think it's one of the best stories you've done since you've been here."

"Really?"

"Love it," Jeff said. "It's angry, it's biting, it takes a strong point of view—you know that's what I always look for. I love this line when you say Wall Street needs to reserve a plot in the high tech graveyard for Byron, and how the company has had more fumbles than a high school football team. That's perfect."

"I'm glad you enjoyed it," I said.

"The writing's very straightforward," Jeff said. "It has none of those awkward words and overly complicated sentences that your other articles have had."

"Peter always adds that crap," I said. "I mean, if you check out some of the articles I wrote for the *Journal*—"

"Look," Jeff said, ignoring me. "I know we've had our differences in the past, David, but the past is just that—the past. What I'm trying to say is, how about we put our differences behind us and move on with a clean slate?"

"Okay," I said with no idea what he was getting at.

"Great," he said. "So how'd you like to be my new associate editor?"

I thought he was joking. He'd never even hinted about a promotion before, and besides, associate editor was Peter's position.

"You're kidding," I said.

"Why would I kid about that?"

"What about Peter?"

"We've been getting too many complaints about him lately. We were all discussing it at the management meeting this morning, and we think it's time to make a switch—at the very least to boost the morale at the magazine, which, if you haven't noticed, has been pretty dismal lately. Peter doesn't know about this yet, so this is between you and me. Gossip gets around this office faster than the flu, and I don't want Peter to find out about it third hand. I just wanted to get a feel for whether you're up for the job before I take the next step. So? Are you?"

I heard a siren on Broadway outside Jeff's window—I wondered if it was the cops coming to get me.

"Sure," I said.

"You sound noncommittal."

"No, I'm very committal," I said. "The job sounds great."

"You sure you're just feeling under the weather? Because I get the feeling you don't want this job."

"I want it," I said.

"Great, then it's yours."

Jeff reached across to shake my hand, then yanked his back before it touched mine.

"Germs," he said.

I stayed in Jeff's office for the next half an hour or so, discussing the new job and my new responsibilities. My new salary would be fifty-two a year—a far cry from what I used to make at the *Journal*, but it was still a ten-grand-a-year raise. At another time in my life, even a couple of days ago, I would've been excited about the promotion, and would've started plotting using it as a stepping-stone toward getting a job at *Forbes* or *BusinessWeek*. Now, with my arrest looming, it was hard to really give a shit.

Surprisingly, twelve-thirty came and the police still hadn't shown. Angie came by my cubicle, smiling—she'd reapplied her lipstick—and asked if I was ready for lunch.

"You betcha," I said, in a better mood than I should've been in.

We went around the corner to the deli with the good salad bar on Fiftieth Street. Eating our combinations of California rolls and oily salads, I told Angie about my promotion.

"That's unbelievable," she said.

"It's a secret," I said, "so don't tell anybody."

"My lips are sealed." She mimed locking her lips and throwing away the key. "It's so funny—we were just talking about Peter."

167

"I know."

"It's gonna be so great not having that loser editing my stories anymore."

"You never know," I said. "I might start inserting some indefatigablys myself."

"As long you don't put in any terriblys."

We laughed and I impulsively reached over and held her hand, caressing it with my thumb. She looked at me intensely for a few seconds, then pulled her hand away.

"What about your girlfriend?"

"She's not really my girlfriend."

"But I thought you live together?" She looked confused.

"Yeah, but it's ending," I said. "Besides, it was never very serious to begin with. I know you've never met her, but she's this young club girl. I mean, you should hear the way she talks. She has this upspeak, you know, making everything sound like a question, and she has this weird Southern accent. It's hard to describe, but it's really funny to listen to—trust me."

I was smiling, trying to get Angie on my side, the way she was always on my side when we made fun of Peter or Jeff, but she remained very serious.

"I don't get it," she said. "If you don't like her, why did you start dating her to begin with?"

I wished I'd kept my mouth shut.

"There are some good things about her, of course," I said, trying to do damage control. "I mean, she's fun to be with and I like a lot of other things about her, but we're not really compatible."

"So if you're not compatible, why are you still living together?"

"Good question." I was smiling, trying to make light of the situation. "Like I said, we're in the process of breaking up. I mean, we're going to be broken up very soon."

"But you're still together."

"Kind of."

She was squinting, looking confused, and I didn't know why I'd opened my big mouth about any of this.

"I've been trying to get her to move out," I said, "but it's been kind of difficult."

"Difficult how?"

"Well, I've asked her to move out, but she kind of has attachment issues, I guess. She had a difficult childhood, so maybe that has something to do with it, or maybe … Anyway, she just doesn't get that it's over. I mean, the other night, when we talked about it, she started throwing vases at me."

"What do you mean she threw vases at you?"

"She was drunk," I said. "I mean, she was just out of it, that's all, and she kind of lost her temper for a second and picked up some things from the mantle and threw them. It was nothing, really … So how's your salad?"

"Did she hit you with the vases?" Angie asked.

"No, of course not," I said. "The hitting came later."

I smiled, but she didn't.

"Is that how you hurt your lip?"

"What? No."

"It sounds like you're in an abusive relationship."

"Whoa, come on," I said, "don't you think you're exaggerating just a little bit?"

"What if I told you my boyfriend was hitting me and throwing vases at me? Wouldn't you say that was abusive?"

"It's not the same thing."

"Why not?"

"Because it just isn't," I said, getting frustrated.

"Sorry, I guess it's really none of my business," Angie said as she speared a cherry tomato with her fork. "I just want you to know that, as an outsider looking in, it sounds like your girlfriend has some serious problems."

"Look, I know she has problems," I said. "Why do you think I'm breaking up with her?"

We continued eating in silence. After a few minutes I broke the ice and said, "So how's your new article going?"

Our conversation was uncomfortable for a while, but then we settled down and things seemed more normal again.

At around one o'clock we headed back toward our office building. As we turned the corner onto Broadway, reality set in as I realized that Rebecca wasn't my real problem. My real problem was lying against that garbage can in Alphabet City.

"What's wrong?" Angie asked, concerned.

"Nothing," I said. "Why?"

Back at the office I walked Angie to her cubicle. The way she said, "See ya later," I could tell she was still upset about our conversation over lunch, and I felt frustrated too that there was suddenly so much awkwardness between us.

At my desk, I was more anxious than I had been in the morning. Time seemed to go by even slower as I waited to hear the commotion of the police arriving. But the hours crept by, and at five o'clock the police still hadn't come. I had no idea what was going on. The body had to have been discovered by now. Maybe the police hadn't had a chance to talk to Charlotte yet, or maybe she'd handled herself better than I'd expected. Maybe the plan was going to work out after all.

As I was getting ready to leave, Angie came by and asked if I wanted to walk out of the building with her. I told her to go ahead without me, that I had some last-minute stuff to take care of, and that I'd see her tomorrow. I wanted to leave with her—hell, I wanted to do more than that with her—but I realized that holding her hand had been a big mistake, and I didn't want to lead her on more than I already had. If I lucked out and the police never bothered investigating Ricky's death, and I finally got Rebecca to move out of my apartment, then I'd attempt to start a normal relationship with Angie. Until then, I'd try to keep some distance between us.

I walked home from work. Every time I saw a cop I crossed the street to avoid being seen, afraid that a description of me had been radioed around the city. I made it to my block, relieved that no cop cars were in front of my building.

In the hallway outside my apartment, I stopped when I

heard the Police's "Hole in My Life" playing inside. I was upset that Rebecca was home, that she hadn't moved out today, but I was also confused. She never listened to my CDs and always made a big fuss whenever I played them.

I opened the door and went to the living room and saw Rebecca lounging on the couch, reading a copy of *Vibe*.

"Hi, honey," she said in a domesticated, 1950s way. "How was your day?"

I stood there near the door, taking in the scene. Then Rebecca looked up at me again, smiling.

"What's going on here?" I asked.

"Not much," she said. "Just chillin', listening to some Police. I decided you were right—I should start listening to other types of music—widen my horizons? That song 'Roxanne' is dope, yo."

"Is this supposed to be funny?"

"Is what supposed to be funny?"

"Don't you remember our conversation last night?"

"Yeah, I remember it. You told me that you're in love with somebody else."

"So if you know that, what're you still doing here? Why don't you move out? Go stay with a friend."

"Because I don't believe you."

"You don't believe I met someone else?"

"No, *that* I believe. I just don't believe you're in love with her. Maybe you had a fling with someone at your office, because you were mad at me, but I forgive you." She resumed flipping pages of the magazine. "Oh, sorry I didn't cook tonight—I didn't have any money. I have an

172

idea—let's go out to dinner. We can go downtown to this cool Spanish place in Soho Ray told me about, then we can swing by Key Club or Exit? Unless you wanna listen to some rock—I'm down for that too. Or maybe you just wanna go barhopping. When was the last time we got wasted?"

I was staring at her. Finally I said, "It's not a fling. I met somebody else, I love her, and I want to be with her."

I was just saying this to hammer a point home, to convince Rebecca to leave, but I wondered if I was talking about Angie.

"Pul-leeze," Rebecca said, shaking her head and smiling. "Do you really expect me to believe that?"

"Why would I make it up?"

"Because you're still mad at me and you're trying to hurt me. Just stop it already."

"You're wrong," I said. "I really did meet someone else—someone I'm very serious about. Her name's Angie."

Rebecca tossed away the magazine and got up from the couch. She came over to me, wrapped her arms around my back, and moved her mouth up toward mine, her lips parting slowly.

"You look so hot tonight," she said. "How about we pop some E and go into the bedroom and get busy?"

She started kissing me. I pushed her away and said, "What the hell're you doing?"

"Come on," she said, reaching around and squeezing my ass.

173

As she leaned in again to kiss me, I pushed her away and said, "I'm serious. I'll give you two days to pack up and move out. I think once you're gone you'll see how good this is for both of us."

She looked at me as if she didn't recognize me, and then started to smile.

"That was really good," she said. "How long did it take you to think that one up? Seriously, I bet you were thinking about that all day. You were thinking, 'I'll tell Rebecca "Once you're gone you'll see how good this is for both of us."' You thought that would really get me back."

"I'm not trying to get you—"

"You probably made up that whole Angie story too."

"I'm not making up anything," I said very seriously.

I could tell she was starting to believe me.

"So how is she?" she asked.

"How is she what?"

"You know …"

She tried to grab my ass, but I moved away in time.

"… in bed," she continued. "Is she in shape? I bet she isn't. I bet she has flabby thighs and a blubbery stomach, and I bet she has zits." She made a disgusted face.

"You have two days to get out," I said. "I think that's a reasonable amount of time to find someplace to crash. Maybe you can move in with Ray."

I went into the kitchen and Rebecca remained in the living room. I opened the refrigerator and took out the Brita water pitcher.

"Two days," I said as I turned on the faucet and filled

the pitcher. "I'm giving you two days."

With the water running I couldn't hear what Rebecca was saying—not that I cared. I turned off the faucet and said, "Two days," again.

Rebecca entered the kitchen. She watched me pour a glass of water and drink it, and then she said, "So you expect me to just leave? Just walk out the door and that's it?"

"It doesn't have to be like that," I said. "We could still stay in touch—be friends, do lunch every once in a while."

"And what about me? What do I get out of all this?"

"What're you talking about?"

"I didn't invest all this time with you for nothing."

"I wasted time too."

"I didn't say *wasted*!" she screamed in a shrill voice. *Great*, I thought. Now Carmen or the other neighbors would complain about the noise to the landlord—I'd be lucky if I could keep my lease.

"Brilliant," I said.

Rebecca picked up the glass from the counter and flung it behind her. It smashed against the wall above the stove, shards going everywhere.

"That's it—we're over!" I screamed.

"Nothing's over," she said, "until *I* say it's over or until one of us dies."

"Really?" I said. "And what's that supposed to mean?"

"Whatever you want it to mean." She smiled ambiguously.

"So what're you saying?" I said. "You're saying if I try

175

to force you to leave you're going to kill me?"

"You never know," she said. "I could strangle you while you're asleep one night. Or maybe I'll get a gun." She held her index finger and thumb up to my forehead, then bent her thumb down and said, "Pow."

"You're really scaring the shit out of me," I said sarcastically, but I kind of meant it.

She was staring at me, doing her best to look like a maniac.

"You're right, I could never hurt you," she said. "Besides, what reason would I have? I know you'd never really try to leave me."

"What're you talking about? I'm telling you to leave."

"You don't *tell* me to do anything."

She came over to me and put her hands around my waist and rubbed up against me. I wanted to move away but I didn't, or couldn't.

"When I found you that day in the park you were like a stray dog," she said. "I rescued you and now you're mine."

"I think you need help."

She kissed my neck a few times; then she kissed my lips.

"You belong to Rebecca now," she said. "You only do what I tell you to do, but you don't have to worry—you can sleep tight tonight, cutie. Rebecca would never, ever hurt you."

She kissed me again, longer this time, then strutted out of the kitchen and headed along the hallway. Moments later I heard the bathroom door shut.

I stayed in the kitchen, wondering who was crazier—Rebecca, or me for staying with her all these months.

After ruminating for a couple more minutes, I tiptoed over the broken glass, figuring I'd clean up the mess later, and went into the living room. "Can't Stand Losing You" was playing and I remembered how Barbara and I used to listen to Bowie and the Police all the time in high school and college, and how I was listening to a Bowie CD that night Barbara came over to my apartment.

"I'm sorry," she said. "You were so right. You were so right about everything."

She looked awful, like she'd been crying for hours. I hadn't spoken to her at all in over two weeks, since the night I beat Jay up. I'd tried to call her at home and at work, but she kept screening my calls and hanging up on me.

"Jay's a fucking scumbag," she said. "He was seeing his old girlfriend the whole time, right behind my back. I'm such a stupid idiot."

I held her for a long time as she cried.

I read part of some boring, poorly written story about the divas of hip-hop in Rebecca's copy of *Vibe*, and then, with the Police still playing, I started thinking about the police. I looked at my watch—it was 6:25. I'd once read somewhere that most crimes are solved within twenty-four hours after they're committed and I hoped that every hour that passed without the police showing up made it more likely that they'd never come.

The CD ended and the apartment was suddenly silent. Having an apartment in the back of the building with no street noise was great most of the time, but when you didn't want to listen to yourself think, the quiet was unbearable. I considered playing another CD, but somehow the idea of listening to more music depressed me. I turned on the TV to some dumb reality dating show just for the comfort of noise.

Not that I really cared, but I looked down the hallway every once in a while, noticing that Rebecca was still in the bathroom. I figured that she was taking one of her annoyingly long baths. She'd done a lot of damage on my credit cards, buying exotic bath soaps and massage oils and she often hogged the bathroom, taking baths that lasted an hour or longer.

Eventually I heard Rebecca leave the bathroom and go into the bedroom, the odors of whatever shampoos or soaps she'd used seeping into the living room. It was past eight o'clock now, and there was still no sign of the police. As I expected, there was nothing about Ricky's body being found on the TV news. Even if the police were investigating, the death of a scumbag drug addict wasn't exactly newsworthy.

I heard a noise to my right and looked over and saw that Rebecca was sauntering into the living room in a black satin nightie.

"I'm sorry," she said, in a soft, vulnerable voice. "You know I'd never really hurt you, right? I just get upset because I love you so much and I don't want to lose you.

You can understand that, can't you, baby?"

"Move out in two days," I said calmly. "Please understand that it's the best thing for both of us."

"I'll be waiting for you in the bedroom," she said, as if she hadn't heard me. She popped an Ecstasy tablet into her mouth and swallowed. Then she headed back down the hallway, swinging her hips from side to side in a slow, exaggerated way.

I shut off the TV and lay on the couch, squeezing my thighs together against my hard-on. Then I remembered having lunch with Angie—how normal and right it had felt to be with her. I imagined that we'd gone out for a drink after work and then she'd invited me back to her place. We'd sat on her couch and started making out. Things had progressed and we'd moved to the bedroom, where we'd undressed each other and started making love.

Unconsciously, I had started to masturbate. I continued, pulling down my underwear for easier access, imagining that I was lying on my back and Angie was next to me, taking off her panties. Then she climbed on top of me and I slid into her. She started bouncing up and down as my hands squeezed her heavy breasts. My hand action quickened as I saw Angie's face, and then Angie turned into Rebecca. I was getting closer and I wanted to get rid of Rebecca and see Angie again, but then Rebecca became Charlotte. I tried to think about Angie again, but Charlotte was sticking. I could see Charlotte clearly, her tiny breasts in my face. It was too late to stop, and I concentrated on

Angie, seeing her again for an instant, and then there was a rapid flux. I was thinking about Angie, Charlotte, Angie, Charlotte, Rebecca, Charlotte—shit—Angie, Charlotte, Angie, Angie, Angie, Angie, then—right as I started to ejaculate—Charlotte.

Miserably, I rubbed the semen onto my leg until it had mostly absorbed. A few minutes later, I was asleep.

8

THE RINGING PHONE jolted me awake. I sat up, disoriented. The lights in the kitchen and in the hallway were still on. The phone rang again as I glanced at my watch: 1:03.

I picked up the phone during the third ring, thinking, *Shit, it's the fucking police. Why did I pick up?*

"Hello," I said wearily.

"David, you gotta come meet me. Right now!"

Charlotte's annoying, squeaky voice made me wonder if I was having a nightmare. I didn't say anything, still trying to process what was going on.

"Hello, you there?" Charlotte said.

"I'm here." Then I thought about Rebecca. "Hold on."

I left the phone on the couch, hearing Charlotte

protesting, "Hey, where're you going? Get back here!" and then her voice fading to nothing as I headed down the hallway. I opened the door to the bedroom carefully. The room was dark but I could see the shape of Rebecca's body asleep in bed. I closed the door and returned to the living room, where I could hear Charlotte's screaming voice still coming through the receiver.

She was saying, "You there? … Hello? Hello?"

"Are you crazy?" I said. "Why are you calling me?"

"We gotta talk," she said. There was background noise—a car honking, Spanish-accented voices.

"Talk about what?" I said.

"Meet me at the Holiday Cocktail Lounge on St. Marks—"

"Tell me—"

"Just meet me at the cocktail lounge—St. Marks and First—"

"Are you out of your mind?" I said. "It's one in the morning."

She breathed deeply, then said, "Be there."

"Charlotte," I said, but she'd already hung up. I called her back, using the star-69 method, and a guy answered.

"Is Charlotte there?" I asked.

"What?" the guy said.

"Charlotte," I said. "She has brown hair. She's very thin."

"You got a fuckin' phone booth, man."

"I know it's a phone booth. Can you just look around and—"

The guy hung up.

"Fuck," I said, and slammed the phone down.

I wanted to pull the phone out of the wall and go back to sleep, but I knew that would be a mistake. Charlotte could be trying to scam me again, or something could have gone wrong with the police. Either way, I had to find out what was going on.

I'd fallen asleep in my clothes, so I didn't have to get dressed. I put on my shoes and jacket and headed out.

On Columbus I hailed a cab downtown. The thought of seeing Charlotte's face again was making me sick. I wondered if she'd told the police about me and they'd talked her into wearing a wire. I could be walking right into a trap.

The cab sped past Lincoln Center, looped around Columbus Circle, and continued downtown.

* * *

I got out at Second and St. Marks and walked down the block to the Holiday Cocktail Lounge, a dive bar with a metal facade and a black, graffiti-covered awning. Inside, a mix of derelicts and college students trying to look like derelicts were seated at or standing around the horseshoe-shaped bar. The juke box was cranking "Tangled Up in Blue."

I didn't see Charlotte anywhere in the front of the bar;

then I went farther inside and saw her seated at one of the booths in the back. I looked around at the only other people nearby—four guys drinking a pitcher of beer at another booth—but they didn't seem to be paying attention.

I sat across from Charlotte on the red, cracked vinyl cushion. She was visibly agitated—wiping her nose obsessively with the back of her hand, rocking from side to side. She was wearing her old, ripped denim jacket.

"I didn't think you were gonna show," she said.

"What happened?" I asked.

"Buy me a drink."

"What the hell happened?"

"Come on, I need something to calm down with. Just one fuckin' drink."

The guys at the other booth started laughing. I looked over at them, then turned back to Charlotte and said, "Are you gonna tell me what's going on now, or am I gonna go home and get back into bed?"

"We're in trouble," she said. "Big trouble."

"Why's that?" I wondered where the wire was. On her leg? Her arm?

She reached into the pocket of her jacket and took out three photographs and put them facedown on the table. I didn't move, getting the sense that I didn't want to see them.

"Go ahead and look," she said.

I waited several more seconds, then picked up the photos and stared at the first one. It was difficult to make out, but maybe that was because I was so shocked and wasn't focusing well. It was actually a very clear picture, considering it was taken at night, showing me leaving Charlotte's apartment building, carrying Ricky's body. It took a while to get a hold of myself, and then I looked at the next photo—a head-on shot of the body and me. The third picture was of me leaning the body against the garbage can. Although the pictures were taken from a distance, maybe from across the street, the general features of my face were unmistakable.

I stared at the third picture for a while longer, trying to think of something to say that made sense. The best I could come up with was, "What are these?"

"What do they look like, you idiot?" Charlotte said.

The guys at the other booth were getting up, putting on their jackets.

In a softer voice, almost whispering, I said unsteadily, "I mean, where did they come from? How did you ... Who took them?"

"Kenny," she said. "And he said he's gonna show them to the cops if we don't pay him off."

"What?"

"He's gonna show them to the cops if we don't give him the money. You deaf or something?"

"Money?" I said, because that was all I'd really heard. "How much money?"

"Twenty thousand bucks."

I looked at the last picture again, remembering how I'd been so determined to get away that I hadn't really looked around carefully. Kenny must have been hiding behind a car or a lamppost, or maybe he'd taken the pictures from inside a car.

"What'd you do," I said, "set this all up when you went out for your fix?"

"Fuck you," she said.

"What'd you think, I'd fall for this bullshit?"

"I had nothing to do with any of this."

"And why should I believe a word you say?"

"Because it's true," Charlotte said. "I don't know why Kenny was out there. He must've figured it out on his own."

"He figured out that I'd just happen to be dumping—" I cut myself off and looked around. The guys at the other table were gone, and the nearest people were at the bar, about thirty feet away. "Wild Horses" was much louder than our voices, but I continued whispering anyway. "He figured out that I'd just happen to be out there at four in the morning? Give me a fucking break."

"Look, I'm telling you the truth—I swear on my grandmother's grave." Charlotte crossed herself. "I don't know how he figured it out, all right? Maybe he saw you and Ricky in the shower."

"And why did he decide to get his camera?"

"Kenny's crazy," she said. "He's always looking to make a buck."

"And you're not?"

She gave me a piercing, narrow-eyed stare, then said, "At least I don't go around killing people."

She was speaking at a normal level, and "Wild Horses" had ended and someone could have easily heard her. I looked around, trying to be nonchalant, but no one seemed to be eavesdropping. Some grunge song came on—maybe Pearl Jam. An old drunk guy was stumbling toward the bathroom, almost tripping a couple of times, but he didn't look over.

"You'd better keep your fucking voice down," I said.

"We have to give him the money," Charlotte whispered harshly, "or we're both fucked."

I still knew Charlotte and Kenny were working together, but I decided it didn't matter. The pictures existed and I was being blackmailed—it didn't really matter who was blackmailing me.

"Why do you care if he goes to the cops?" I said. "You're not in the pictures."

"That's what I told Kenny," Charlotte said. "But he said if he goes to the cops he's gonna tell them that he saw Ricky's body in my apartment. I don't know, maybe he's just using me to get to you. How the hell do I know what he's thinking?"

I picked up the pictures again, looked at each of them for a good five seconds, then ripped them up disgustedly.

"You're wasting your time," Charlotte said. "Kenny said he's got negatives."

Looking at her face was making me sick. I leaned over the table and rested my head in my hands, kneading my scalp with my fingers. Then I looked up and said, "What happened with the cops?"

"Nothing," Charlotte said.

"What does nothing mean?" I said. "Did they talk to you or not?"

"Yeah, they talked to me," she said. "Two cops came to my door and told me Ricky was dead. I pretended I was shocked; then I went down and ID'd him. They asked me if I knew how it happened, some other bullshit, and that was it."

"Did the cops follow you here?"

"No."

"You sure?"

"I just told you, no."

I glanced toward the bar, where mostly drunk-looking guys sitting alone were nursing drinks. No one was looking at us, but that didn't mean one of them couldn't be a cop.

"So you gonna get the money or not?" Charlotte asked.

"Where am I gonna get twenty thousand dollars?" I said.

"You got a bank account."

"I'm a reporter. You know how much I make?"

"So you must got a few thousand bucks in the bank. That'll keep Kenny quiet till—"

"Do you have wax in your ears?" I said. "I'm broke. My credit cards are maxed out, I have nothing in savings. You'd be better off going out on the street and trying to blackmail a homeless guy."

"I'm not blackmailing you," she said.

"Wait, I have an idea," I said with fake enthusiasm.

"Why didn't I think of this right away? What was your bottom price for sex—twenty-five bucks? That means you'd only have to fuck eight hundred guys to make twenty grand. Better get started."

Charlotte managed to maintain her serious, slightly frightened expression, but I knew she was in on this. Kenny was probably at her apartment right now, waiting for her.

I looked away again. There were still about a dozen drunks at the front of the bar, but Charlotte and I had the back to ourselves. The grunge song ended and the bar was much quieter again; it was possible to make out people's voices.

"Let's say I come up with the money," I said, nearly whispering. "How do I know you'll stop?"

"*I'll* stop?"

"You and Kenny."

"I don't know why you keep—"

"Okay," I said, placating her. "How do I know Kenny'll stop? I could give him the twenty grand tonight and tomorrow he'll ask for another twenty."

"He won't."

"Really? And what makes you so sure?"

"Because he said he wants twenty grand—that's it."

"Oh, so now I'm supposed to trust a guy who makes his living picking pockets and running blackmailing scams? You think I'm gonna give him twenty grand, shake his hand, walk away, and think it's all over?"

"You got a better idea?"

She was looking right at me, and there was a different, more sincere tone in her voice. I was starting to believe her, at least about not planning all of this with Kenny.

"There might be another problem," I said. "I saw one of your neighbors last night, while you were out with Kenny. I mean, one of your neighbors saw me."

"What neighbor?"

"Light-skinned black guy."

"Andre?"

"We didn't introduce ourselves."

"What about him?"

"He looked out of it," I said, "but he saw me—in the hallway."

"Why were you in the hallway?"

"I was just … It's not important."

"Forget about Andre," Charlotte said. "He's an ex-con and a dealer—he'll never talk to the cops. What about Kenny's money?"

"Tell him I need time."

"He won't give us—"

"One day," I said. "Tell him we'll give him a payment tomorrow night."

"Why can't you get the money tonight?"

"Because I don't have any fucking money," I said, raising my voice.

A couple of guys at the bar looked over. I ignored them and they turned away.

"Can't you get anything tonight?" Charlotte asked.

There was a different kind of desperation in her voice,

and I realized she was more concerned about getting her next fix than getting Kenny his money.

"Just get the hell out of here," I said. "I can't deal with any more of this bullshit right now."

"What about the—"

"Just go."

Charlotte sat there, rubbing her nose with the back of her hand, then said, "You better get some money tomorrow—at least a thousand bucks. I'll meet you tomorrow morning at Starbucks on Astor."

"I won't have the money in the morning."

"Then I'll meet you at noon."

"I have to work tomorrow—"

"Six o'clock," she said. "You better fucking be there."

Charlotte got up and wobbled toward the door. As she passed a few drunk guys at the bar, she stopped and said something to each of them, obviously trying to pick them up. Two guys ignored her, and then one old guy grabbed her arm, trying to pull her toward him. The bartender said something, and the guy, laughing now, let go. Rubbing her arm where the guy had grabbed her, Charlotte left the bar.

I remained seated, figuring I should allow some time for Charlotte to leave the block before I left.

After listening to the end of "Wish You Were Here" and a live version of "Sweet Jane," I put the scraps of the ripped-up photos into my jacket pocket and went outside. It was raining lightly. I didn't see Kenny or anyone else who looked suspicious, so I headed toward

First Avenue. No cabs were coming, so I put my hood on and started walking uptown with my head down against the wind.

9

ICONTINUED WALKING in the rain. Somewhere around Fourteenth Street I dropped the ripped-up photo pieces into a sewer grating. At Twenty-third Street, the rain started coming down harder and my jacket was getting soaked and my face was wet, so I gave in and took a cab the rest of the way home.

At my apartment, Rebecca was still asleep in the bedroom. I changed out of my wet clothes into sweats, and then took a spare blanket and pillow out of the closet.

"You can join me anytime you want to, baby," Rebecca said seductively, sounding wide-awake.

Without answering, I went out into the living room and plopped down on the couch. Eventually, I fell asleep.

*

At eight A.M., out of the shower and getting dressed for work, I decided I'd have to bring Charlotte the thousand bucks. I'd been going back and forth on it since leaving the bar last night, but I realized I had no choice. Paying off a blackmailer for something I hadn't even done still seemed crazy, but the pictures were just too incriminating. Maybe if I made it clear to Charlotte that the thousand was all I had, Kenny would leave me alone. My only problem was that I didn't have a thousand bucks, although I had an idea where I could get it.

I'd managed to get my work clothes out of the bedroom without waking Rebecca up and I made it out of the apartment without another confrontation.

It felt strange arriving for another day of work when, after I'd left yesterday, I was convinced that I would never be back.

I was hanging up my coat on the hook in my office when Peter Lyons came by. He craned his head down to glare at me, and then, in the voice of a wanna-be Shakespearean actor, he said, "*E tu, Brute?*"

I looked at him, confused. "Excuse me?"

"You'll get your just desserts," he said. "All backstabbers ultimately do."

Suddenly I remembered my conversation with Jeff yesterday and realized Peter must've been fired.

"I swear, Peter—I had nothing to do with this."

"I'm sure you didn't," he said sarcastically. "I'm sure you haven't been campaigning for this behind my back for months. I'm sure you didn't spread nasty rumors about me throughout the office and create a general feeling of malcontent about my editing style."

Peter sounded like a parody of himself, and if I hadn't been in such a bad mood to begin with, I probably wouldn't have been able to restrain myself from laughing.

"Look, I really didn't want to see you lose your job," I said. "If you want me to talk to Jeff—"

"Don't bother," Peter said. "To be quite honest, I've been contemplating jumping ship for some time. The quality of this magazine has been deteriorating rapidly over the past few years, and with you as associate editor I am quite certain that the pattern is not likely to correct itself."

Peter stormed away melodramatically. I felt bad that he'd been fired on account of me, and then it sank in that I was the new associate editor. It wasn't exactly like getting an editor's position at the *Journal*, but *Manhattan Business* had a lot of subscribers in the New York area, and the job title would certainly help my résumé stand out. If I weren't being blackmailed for murder I might've been excited about it.

I sat at my desk and called my aunt Helen at her work number. Helen had had the same job for years, as an office manager for an outerwear distributor in the Garment District. When I was a kid it was great, because I always got a new parka or down jacket every winter. Over the years, she continued to offer me free coats, but they were all so dorky-looking I always had to think of inventive ways to decline. I spoke with my aunt on the phone every once in a while, but I hadn't seen in her in over a year. She still lived alone, in the house I'd been raised in, in Dix Hills, Long Island. Her husband, my uncle Howard, had died of a heart attack a few years after my parents were killed, and Helen had never remarried.

Helen's voice mail answered. I left a message for her to call me back as soon as she could, and then I booted up my computer. A memo had been added to my calendar about a two o'clock staff meeting that Jeff was conducting in the conference room. I wondered if the meeting was to announce my promotion.

My phone rang and I answered it. It was Helen.

"Thanks for calling me back so soon," I said.

"No problem, David. I was just on the other line—it was so good to hear your voice. How are you?"

"Okay," I said.

She must have detected my uncertainty. "Is something wrong?"

"No, everything's fine—totally fine," I said. "I just need to see you. Can we meet for lunch today?"

"You sure everything's okay?"

"Yes, everything's fine. Can you do lunch?"

"Of course."

"How's noon?"

"Noon's okay," she said, sounding concerned.

"Great, I'll come by your office," I said, and hung up.

I called my voice mail and listened to an angry message from Robert Lipton, the CEO of Byron Technologies. He said that a fact-checker had faxed him a copy of the story I'd written, and that if the magazine published "this bullshit" he would take legal action. He was still screaming at me when I deleted the message.

I went down the corridor to where Theresa, Jeff's assistant, sat and said, "Who fact-checked my Byron Technologies story?"

"Sujen," Theresa said. "Why? Is there some problem?"

Sujen was the new intern, a young Korean-American student from Columbia University.

"She faxed the CEO the entire story," I said.

"She wasn't supposed to do that," Theresa said.

"Really?" I said sarcastically.

I went to Sujen's cubicle, ready to give her hell, but when I got there and saw this pretty, innocent girl sitting in front of her computer monitor I lost my edge. She'd been working at the magazine for only a few weeks, so it was understandable that she'd had a slipup. We'd had one conversation, in the elevator one morning. She'd told me she was a journalism major and hoped to write for the *Times* someday.

"Hi, Sujen," I said.

"Oh, hi, David."

I was surprised she remembered my name.

"Did you fax Robert Lipton my article?"

I could tell she was nervous.

"Yes," she said, "but only because he said I should."

"Weren't you told not to do that?"

"Yes," she said, "but he said he spoke with you and—"

"In the future could you try not to do that?" I said. "I mean, it's no big deal, but in the future just check the quotes, okay?"

"I'm so sorry, David. He swore to me he spoke to you and you okayed it. You weren't around, so I just faxed it to him. I'm really sorry."

"It's okay," I said. "Just don't do it again, please."

I headed back toward my cubicle, feeling like a wimp. Sujen was a bright girl and she should've known better than to fax that article. Anyone else would've given her hell for it.

Sitting at my desk, I was checking my e-mail messages when Angie entered.

"Did you hear?" she said in a gossipy tone. Then she whispered, "Peter was fired."

"I heard," I said. I didn't feel like having this conversation.

"So it's official—you're the new associate editor."

"I guess so."

"That's so unbelievable."

"I know."

"How come you're not more excited?"

"I am."

"This is *so* great. I'll have a normal person editing my stories now—not some pseudo-British freak. Do you want to go to lunch to celebrate?"

"I can't," I said. "I'm meeting my aunt."

Angie looked at me as if she thought I might be lying, and then she said, "That's cool—I guess we'll do lunch some other time. Maybe Monday."

"Sounds like a plan."

Angie started to leave; then she turned back and said, "I just wanted to say sorry for yesterday."

"Sorry for what?" I said.

"I shouldn't've butted in."

"Come on," I said, "you didn't—"

"No, it was wrong," she said. "I just got a little concerned, that's all, but I should've kept my mouth shut. I just hope you're not mad at me."

"Why would I be mad?"

"I felt bad about it all night."

"Stop it," I said.

Angie smiled, looking especially cute, then said, "Stop by later and say hi?"

"I will," I said, and then I watched her leave.

I was glad that things seemed smoothed over between Angie and me, but now I was even more frustrated that I couldn't ask her out.

To distract myself, I made some calls about the story I was doing on PrimeNet Solutions, a Silicon Alley DSL company. The company had recently downsized its operations and had a questionable financial position, but their subscriptions were soaring, thanks to outstanding customer service and competitive price points along its entire product line. Deciding that the article would definitely have a positive spin, I conducted a phone interview with the company's

CFO and scheduled calls with several analysts who I knew were familiar with the DSL industry.

At twenty to twelve, I left the office and took the subway downtown to Thirty-fourth, then walked back up a few blocks to the Garment District. My aunt Helen worked in one of the bleak, prewar, industrial-looking buildings on Thirty-seventh Street between Seventh and Eighth Avenue. I took the rickety elevator up to the sixth floor and rang the doorbell to her office.

A young gay guy greeted me, and then Helen came over and hugged me. She was sixty-three, but except for some deepened wrinkles she looked the same to me as she always had. Her short, curly hair had been dyed the same shade of maroon for years, and she was still about twenty pounds overweight. She always seemed to be cheerful and optimistic no matter what was going on in her life. I wished I had some of that quality.

"It's so good to see you, David," she said.

Her raspy, Joan Rivers-like voice reminded me of the way Barbara could impersonate her so perfectly.

"What's so funny?" Helen asked.

"Nothing," I said. "It's good to see you too."

Helen introduced me to several people in her office, and then she reached into a big box of ugly brown winter jackets and asked me if I needed a medium or a large.

"It's all right," I said. "I just bought a new jacket last winter."

"So?" she said. "You'll need a new one next winter. Just take one."

"It's okay," I said. "My closet's so crowded—I really have to start throwing things out."

"I'm gonna get you to take a free jacket one of these years," she said, smiling.

We rode back down in the elevator and left the building.

"What do you want for lunch?" she asked. "Chinese, Italian, Japanese—it's on me."

"No, I'm taking you out."

"Don't be ridiculous," she said. "I haven't seen you in ages. This is my treat."

I suggested that we go to wherever was closest, so we went to a Chinese place near Eighth Avenue. As we were looking at our menus we caught up on each other's lives. She was considering selling her house and moving into a condo closer to the city, and she and a few friends had recently had a great time on a Carnival cruise to Nova Scotia. She asked me about Rebecca—she'd never met her, but they'd spoken on the phone a couple of times—and I told her that Rebecca was fine and everything was great. Then I told her that I needed a favor.

"Anything for you, David."

"Something's come up and I need to borrow some money," I said. "It's not much, and I promise I'll pay you back."

"Of course," she said tentatively. "How much do you need?"

"A thousand dollars."

She hesitated then said, "Okay, I can lend you a thousand dollars."

"Thank you," I said. "I'll give you the money back in a few weeks. I promise."

"How's your job going?"

"My job's fine. I'm getting a promotion, actually."

"That's great. Congratulations."

She was looking at me, confused, waiting for me to tell her why I needed the money.

"I just got into a little situation," I said. "I got in over my head with something, but it's going to be fine."

"Is it drugs?"

I laughed. "No, of course not."

"Because I remember in high school you had that pot problem—"

"I didn't have a pot problem," I said. "I smoked less pot than half the kids in my class, but, to answer your question, no, the money isn't for drugs—I swear to God."

"I trust you, David, but if you're in some kind of trouble—"

"It's nothing like that," I said. "It's just for something … personal."

"Is Rebecca pregnant?"

"No, of course not—"

"Because if she is, I'd understand—"

"She isn't pregnant," I said. "Someday I'll tell you all about what's going on—I promise. I just can't tell you about it now. I hope you can understand that."

Of course, I had no intention of ever telling her anything about what was going on, but I couldn't think of any better way to stop her probing.

"Fine," she said, "we can go to a cash machine after lunch."

"A thousand may be over the ATM's limit. Can we withdraw the money instead?"

Sensing the desperation in my voice, Helen gave me a long stare.

"Yes, we can do that if you want," she said.

The waiter came over and took our orders. I welcomed the distraction, and when he left I changed the subject, asking Helen if she was planning to retire.

"Me, retire?" she said. "What would I do without work?"

"You could move to Florida with your sister, I guess."

"And play bingo until I drop dead? No, thank you. I love my job and I'm gonna stay till they get sick of seeing my face. So what's with this promotion?"

"I'm the associate editor now."

"That's wonderful," she said. "I read your articles all the time, and I tell all my friends to read them too. I liked the one you did about how the price of office space is starting to go up downtown."

"Yeah, that was an exciting one."

"I enjoyed it," she said. "It was a very interesting article, and very well-written too. You shouldn't put yourself down that way."

I couldn't think of anything to say, so I dipped a couple of fried noodles into duck sauce and chewed. Our wonton soups arrived and I started eating mine quickly, bringing the bowl up to my face the way the Chinese do.

"Don't take this the wrong way," Helen said, "but have you gone to see someone?"

"What do you mean?" I asked without looking up.

"I remember how devastated you were at Barbara's funeral and how depressed you were afterward. I was very worried about you."

"I got through it," I said, trying not to get upset.

"Are you sure?" she said. "I know after Howard died my depression lasted for years. I wasn't aware of it at the time either—I probably did a good job of hiding it from you kids. You and Barbara were so close, it's natural that it would be harder than you think to get over her passing."

"We weren't that close."

"Come on, you two were practically inseparable," Helen said. "I remember the way Barbara used to light up whenever you came into the room. It was like there was a spark between you. And you used to spend so much time together."

"I'm over it—really," I said, and I started eating my soup even faster.

"My friend Alice's son Benjamin is a grief counselor," Helen said. "He's a nice guy too. I met him a few times— your age, from West Orange. There was a write-up about him in *New York* magazine last year. Call him—maybe your insurance'll cover it."

"I'm not calling anybody," I snapped.

I hadn't raised my voice to Helen in years, maybe since I was a teenager, and she was visibly taken aback.

"I'm sorry," I said.

"No, I'm sorry," she said, starting to eat her soup. "I shouldn't've pried."

Our dishes arrived. We ate for a while without speaking, and then Helen said, "Good, huh?" and I said, "Yeah." We had some more awkward conversation about minutiae. I was suddenly full and couldn't finish my chow fun. Helen left over most of her chicken with cashews.

When the waiter asked us if we wanted any dessert I said to Helen, "I think we should get to the bank now."

We went to the Citibank on Thirty-fourth and Seventh. I waited near the front while she went up to one of the tellers and withdrew the money. Then she came over to me and handed me ten crisp hundreds.

"I really appreciate this," I said. "And I'll pay you back in two weeks, tops."

"You pay me back whenever you can, dear."

We went outside. The sun had been out, but now it was cloudy. We hugged good-bye; she squeezed a lot harder than I did.

"Take care of yourself, David."

I smiled, as if she were being frivolous. Then I realized she meant it.

"I will."

* * *

At a few minutes past two, I arrived back at my office. No one seemed to be around—even the secretaries' desks were unattended—then I noticed people crowded inside the conference room and I remembered Jeff's meeting.

When I entered the conference room everyone seemed to say at once, "Ah, here he is." Someone made a crack about having to send out a search party, and then there was so much talking and laughing I couldn't make out what anyone was saying.

Jeff was at the head of the conference table. Raising his voice above the din he said, "We were getting worried about you."

"Sorry," I said.

"Come up here," Jeff said. "Let's get this started."

I went and stood next to Jeff, feeling suddenly hot, the way I always did when I was the center of attention. I noticed Angie, standing in the back next to Roger Gibson, another reporter, and Debbie D'Mato, who worked in Sales. Angie was smiling, giving me the thumbs-up sign.

"I'm sure most of you have already heard the news by now," Jeff said, "but this morning Peter was let go."

A few people yelled out, "Yeah!" and "Hurrah!" and then everybody laughed, the way people at office meetings always laugh—a little too boisterously—at things that aren't really funny.

"I know Peter wasn't the most popular member of our staff," Jeff continued, "but we have a great man to replace him. I'm proud to announce that David Miller will be *Manhattan Business*'s new associate editor."

People cheered and shouted their congratulations. I smiled modestly.

"David, of course, has an impressive background," Jeff said. "He worked for years at *Barron's*."

"The *Wall Street Journal*," I said.

There was more overly enthusiastic laughter.

"Right, the *Journal*, the *Journal*, right," Jeff said, obviously not giving a shit. "Anyway, he's been with us for just three months now and—"

"Nine months," I said.

More fake laughter.

"Sorry, nine months, nine months," Jeff said. "Nine short months and he's already the associate editor. The way this guy's going I better look out or soon he'll have my job."

Everyone laughed again, harder than before, as if my running the magazine someday were absurd. Kevin from Payroll, a big, burly guy with a booming voice, shouted, "Yeah, better watch out, Jeff!" and James, who worked with Kevin, yelled, "Go get 'em, Dave!"

Jeff said, "But seriously. David certainly deserves this opportunity and I expect him to do an outstanding job. Congratulations, David."

Jeff and I shook hands.

"Thank you," I said, trying to sound upbeat. "I'm really excited about this opportunity, and I look forward to working with all of you."

Everyone applauded as I backed away, smiling. Jeff had ordered a few boxes of Krispy Kremes, and people hung around the conference room for a while, eating and talking. Just about everyone came over to congratulate me personally. Angie was one of the last to come by, and she said, "Better watch it with those adverbs, buddy," then slapped me on the back of the shoulder, the way a guy would.

When the meeting broke up Jeff took me aside and told me that I could start moving my stuff into Peter's old office immediately. I spent most of the rest of the day moving my things over. Like my old office, the new one was really a cubicle, constructed with portable carpeted walls. But the new office was at least twice as big as the old one, and it had a door, and there was an L-shaped desk and much more shelf and file space.

By four o'clock I'd almost completely moved into my new office. Charlie, the office manager, said he would move my computer and have it installed onto the network by tomorrow morning.

I was in my old office, filling a last box with disks, pens, and other crap from my desk, when the phone rang. I had a feeling it was Charlotte, or maybe even Kenny, and I hesitated, preparing myself, before I answered, "David Miller."

"David, Robert Lipton," the man said.

Fuck.

"You didn't return my call," Lipton said.

"I'm on the other line," I said, knowing this excuse sounded lame.

"You're not printing that article."

"I'm really sorry," I said, "but it's out of my control—"

"I swear, I'll sue your ass off if you run that article."

"I have to go," I said. "My other line's—"

"That article's full of lies—it's libel. Our company's in the midst of a major recovery, and you made it seem like we're going bankrupt, for Chrissake. Our gross revenue quadrupled last quarter compared to the same quarter last year, our balance sheet's improving—"

"I'm sorry if you're disappointed with the article," I said.

"You also misquoted me in several places, and you misquoted that analyst, Kevin DuBois. I faxed him what you wrote, and he's considering legal action too if you print this shit."

"I really have to go now."

"You better not print this garbage. I'm warning you, if you print this—"

I hung up and turned on my voice mail.

I continued setting up my new office, and then I checked my watch and saw that it was already ten to five. I put on my coat, making sure the ten hundred-dollar bills Aunt Helen had given me were secure in my wallet, and then headed between the cubicles toward the office's exit. Although I didn't have to meet Charlotte until six o'clock and it would take me only a half hour to get downtown, I wanted to avoid the rush hour crowds.

I was about ten yards from the door when Jeff appeared from one of the aisles in front of me and said, "Ah, there you are."

I thought he was going to make a comment about my leaving early my first day on the job, but he said, "That CEO you wrote about called me before. He was screaming mad, talking about a libel suit."

Jeff's eyes were bloodshot, and I knew he'd probably had at least a few drinks.

"I know, he called me, too," I said.

"I told him I stick by my reporters," Jeff said. "I know you wouldn't write a story that was inaccurate."

"I only wrote it because you—"

"You don't need to defend yourself," Jeff said. "He's probably just desperate. It reminds me of how it was when all those Silicon Alley companies went under. He knows his company's sinking and he's clinging to a life jacket."

"That's probably true," I said, "but—"

"Don't sweat it, big guy," Jeff said, slapping me on the back. "By the way, I just fired that Chinese girl, what's her name?"

"You fired Sujen?"

"That's it. She didn't cry when I told her to get the fuck out of my office—I'll give her that much."

"You didn't have to fire her."

"Why not?" Jeff said. "Theresa told me the whole story, how she faxed your article to that CEO. That girl's just an idiot."

"She's a journalism major at Columbia."

"She's a fucking intern. I'll make a phone call right now and there'll be ten more Japanese girls begging for that job."

I was going to tell him that Sujen was Korean, but I didn't see the point.

"I've got an idea," Jeff said, resting a hand on my shoulder. "I'll take you out to lunch on Monday. We'll have a drink or two to celebrate and we'll talk about your new job."

"Sounds like a plan," I said.

I left the office, thinking about Monday. I hoped I wouldn't be spending it in jail.

* * *

I made it to the Forty-ninth Street subway station by a little after five. A train came right away, and at 5:22 I was heading along Astor Place toward Starbucks. I bought a tall decaf and sat on a stool by the window, waiting for Charlotte to arrive.

All day I'd been rehearsing in my head what I was going to say and I prepared one last time. After I gave her the thousand dollars I'd look her right in the eyes and say, *Look. Kenny can try to threaten me and blackmail me all he wants, but it won't do him any good, because this thousand's the only money I have. I was fired from my job today and I'm broke. If he wants to go to the cops right now he can be my guest, because he's not getting another penny from me.* I figured if I spoke forcefully enough, she'd get the point, and I doubted Kenny or Charlotte was swift enough to check out whether or not I'd been fired. Then, hopefully, they'd forget about me and go on to scamming somebody else.

I finished the coffee in several minutes, without realizing I'd taken more than a couple of sips. I bought a refill, then returned to my stool and stared outside. It was a mild evening and the sidewalks were crowded with college kids and people returning from work. A butch, militant-looking woman stood by the subway entrance shouting about the evils of pornography, trying to get people to sign a petition, but everyone passed by, ignoring her. On the island between Lafayette and Astor, near the giant cube sculpture, kids in baggy pants with cigarettes dangling from their mouths did tricks on skateboards, jumping off the curb, sometimes into traffic, coming dangerously close to killing themselves.

For the next half hour or so, I watched the activity outside and the nearly constant flow of pedestrians, waiting for Charlotte to appear. By six-fifteen, there was still no sign of her. Uncomfortable sitting, I went outside and paced from the entrance to the subway to the corner of Astor and Lafayette. At six-thirty, I started getting the feeling that something wasn't right. I wasn't sure why I expected promptness from a slimy heroin addict, but I didn't understand why Charlotte would be late for a meeting where collecting money was involved.

I waited another five or so minutes, then remembered that there was another Starbucks a block away, on the corner of Third near St. Marks. She'd told me to meet her at the Starbucks on Astor, but maybe she'd gotten confused.

I went to the other Starbucks, but Charlotte wasn't there either. I stood on the corner for a while, and then, during a lull in the traffic, I heard my phone ringing. I took the phone out of my pants pocket and flipped it open.

"Hello?"

"Where are you?" Rebecca asked.

Damn it, why didn't I check the caller ID?

"On my way home," I said.

"It's almost six-thirty."

"I know."

I thought I saw Charlotte, waiting to cross Third, but then the woman turned toward me and I saw that she was young and very good-looking.

"So when're you coming home?" Rebecca asked.

"What difference does it make?"

"Why are you yelling at me?" Rebecca said, acting hurt. I remembered how she'd threatened to kill me last night and how I definitely didn't have to explain my whereabouts to her.

"I hope you started packing," I said, and clicked off.

I waited awhile longer, then went back to the other Starbucks, to see if Charlotte was there. She wasn't. I stayed until past seven o'clock, then gave up. I bought a slice of pizza on Eighth Street and ate it walking toward the subway on Christopher.

* * *

Trying to ignore the schizophrenic sitting across from me who was engaged in a conversation with his imaginary friend, "Wally," and the woman next to me whose pocketbook kept jabbing into my ribs, I hoped that Charlotte's standing me up was a good sign. Maybe she wasn't involved in Kenny's blackmailing scheme after all, and she'd talked him into leaving me alone. I couldn't think of any other reason why she didn't show.

Now if I could only get rid of one more person.

Because of a track fire at Seventy-second Street, the train went out of service at Columbus Circle, and I decided to walk home rather than wait for a bus. As I opened the door to my apartment, I braced myself for another attack from Rebecca. Sure enough, it came.

"Why'd you fucking hang up on me?"

She was standing in the foyer, several feet in front of me, looking like hell. Her hair was a mess, hanging over her face, and she looked exhausted. The glassy look in her eyes told me that she was drunk, on something, or both.

"I hope you found someplace to live," I said.

I tried to go around her, but she wouldn't budge out of my path.

"You can't treat me this way," she said.

"Excuse me," I said as she continued to block me.

"Where were you?" Her breath smelled like alcohol. I glanced beyond her, at the kitchen counter, and saw the open bottle of whiskey that had been in the closet above the refrigerator.

"That's none of your business," I said.

"Were you cheating on me with Angie?" She smiled ambiguously, as if maybe she didn't believe that Angie existed.

"Maybe I was."

"You're full of fucking shit," she said, giving my face a nice shower of saliva.

I tried to get by her again; this time she grabbed my arms, above the elbows.

"If you don't let go of me I'll—"

"You'll what?"

I backed away, freeing myself, then said, "I want you out of here tonight."

"I'm not going anywhere," she said.

"Yes, you are," I said.

She tried to kick me, but I reacted quickly, avoiding her skinny leg. I pushed past her and headed toward the bedroom, figuring I'd lock myself in for a while, when I felt the blow on the back of my head. I stopped and covered my head instinctively, not sure what had happened. I straightened up and turned around just in time to receive a hard punch to my chin. My head jerked back and my body followed. I landed on my back, and, before I could react, Rebecca was crouching on top of me, looking rabid, slapping me in the face. If she were in a zoo they would've shot her with a sedative dart.

Rebecca's face had turned dark pink and she was shrieking at me; her voice was so loud and shrill I couldn't understand a word she was saying. She continued to slap me in the face—I blocked a few of the blows, but some connected—and then she leaned forward and started to bite me, just below my left cheekbone. I grabbed a fistful of her hair and yanked her off me. But she wasn't through. Still shrieking, she started slapping me harder in the face, and I knew I had to do *something*. I couldn't just lie there and let a hundred-pound woman beat the living shit out of me.

Like a wrestler escaping the three-count, I raised my legs off the floor, brought them down, then raised them again swiftly. The action was enough to catapult Rebecca and her slight frame off my chest, and my hands did the rest. Grabbing her hips, I continued her momentum and she flipped over my head. I heard her bang against the hallway wall, but I didn't wait to see if she was okay. I rolled onto my side and got onto my knees, then turned to face her head-on. Sure enough, she was coming after me again, her hands spread open like claws, closing in on my face. This time I was ready, lowering my head and grabbing her by the waist. It wasn't hard to force her onto the floor and pin her down. She was still shrieking, spitting at me, acting like a mental patient, and I just wanted the noise to end. My hands moved off her shoulders to around her neck and I started squeezing. The sudden silence was a big relief, and I was barely aware of the shade of blue her face was turning. If I just squeezed a little harder …

I let go just in time. Rebecca was coughing, trying to catch her breath, and I backed away, trying not to believe that I'd almost strangled her.

I became aware of someone banging on the front door. Then I heard Carmen, the old Italian woman from next door, saying, "Will you stop with all the noise in there? You two are fighting and screaming all the time, I can't even hear my television. Hello? Hello?" She continued to bang on the door.

Rebecca was still coughing, rubbing her neck where my hands had been. I looked down at my hands, which were still curled into the shape of her throat.

"I know you're in there," Carmen said. "Open this door right this instant!"

"Shut the hell up!" I screamed, and then I stood up and marched into the bedroom. I went into one of the closets Rebecca had taken over, grabbed a big armful of her clothes, and stormed back through the hallway. Rebecca, still kneeling on the floor, saw me pass, but didn't say anything.

I opened the front door and saw Carmen standing there. She was a squat, hunched-over old biddy with a big bun of black hair.

"I hope that wasn't me you were speaking to that way," she said. "There's so much screaming coming from your apartment every day I can't hear what the people on TV are saying."

"I'm sorry, all right?" I said.

"This better stop right now or I'm gonna call the police," she said.

I sidestepped around her and went toward the vestibule and then outside. From the top of the stoop, I tossed

Rebecca's clothes toward the sidewalk. Carmen was gone from in front of my apartment, but Rebecca was still in the hallway, trying to grab my leg as I went back toward the bedroom.

"I'm so sorry, David," she said. "Please forgive me. You have to forgive me."

Ignoring her, I grabbed more of her clothes from the bedroom closet, then went by her again.

"Don't do this to me, David," Rebecca said. "I'm warning you."

I dumped the clothes onto the sidewalk, then returned to the apartment. This time Rebecca clung to my legs as I attempted to pass.

"Please don't leave me," she said desperately. "I can't lose you again—I can't go through that again."

She was making no sense. I decided I just needed to get away from her as soon as possible.

I wriggled free, then said, "If you're not out of here by the time I get back, I'm tossing the rest of your shit onto the street."

I grabbed a jacket and left the apartment. The annoying homeless guy who always panhandled to the curbside diners on Amsterdam and Columbus by singing "What a Wonderful World" had started collecting Rebecca's dresses. I walked right by him and headed down the block.

I didn't have a destination, but when I approached Dublin House, a bar on Seventy-ninth and Broadway, I decided to go in. It was a dark, dank, narrow bar that

Barbara and I had gone to a few times. I sat on a stool near the front and ordered a Bud. The bottle arrived, and when I put my hand around it I remembered how I'd had my hands around Rebecca's neck. With a gulp of beer I tried to wipe that image from my mind, and then I saw myself holding Ricky in a headlock, ramming his head against the steel door. I told myself that none of it was my fault, that in both situations I'd acted in self-defense, but I wasn't sure I believed it.

I took another swig of beer, then looked down the bar and saw Barbara. She was with a guy, laughing at something he was saying. I looked closer and realized the woman looked nothing like Barbara. She had the same wavy brown hair, but her nose had a bump on it that Barbara's didn't, and Barbara had been much better-looking.

The woman was looking at me, and I shifted my attention straight ahead, not wanting her to think I'd been staring. I took another sip of beer, then took out my wallet and slid out the picture of Barbara. I stared at the picture, drinking my beer, remembering when it was taken—on the night of her junior prom. She blew off all the parties and her friends to stay at home with me, and we spent the whole night just hanging out, listening to music and laughing.

"Why do you still have that?" she asked.

We were at her apartment on Eighty-fourth Street, watching some TV movie, when I took out the picture and showed it to her.

"I don't know," I said.

"Rip it up."

"No way," I said, keeping it away as she reached for it.

Thinking about Barbara made my eyes start to tear. I put the beer bottle down with too much force and it slid out of my hand and smashed behind the bar. The bartender came over and offered me another.

"It's okay," I said, suddenly feeling very hot. "It was almost empty anyway."

I left a dollar tip and exited the bar quickly. As I wandered onto Broadway I decided that it was stupid to leave Rebecca in the apartment alone. She was probably so pissed off at me for dumping her clothes on the street that she'd started tossing out my stuff in revenge. I jogged toward Eighty-first Street, and then, as I imagined all of my personal things on the street, being rummaged through by that homeless guy, I started to run.

Approaching my building I was relieved to see that the homeless guy wasn't there and that Rebecca hadn't tossed out any of my things; only a few of her tops and dresses were strewn on the sidewalk.

I entered my apartment, expecting to encounter Rebecca either crying hysterically, begging for my forgiveness, or attacking me again, but none of this happened. The apartment looked pretty much the same as when I'd left. I glanced down the hallway, seeing that the bathroom door was shut, and then I went into the kitchen. Scavenging in the fridge and freezer, I found a couple of pieces of hardened, week-or-so old pita bread and a half a box of frozen soy chicken wings. I cooked the wings and warmed the pita on the George Foreman Grill, and about five minutes later I was eating a very shitty dinner.

I cleaned up the kitchen, then went down the hallway, passing the still-closed bathroom door, and went into the bedroom. I changed into sweats, deciding that if Rebecca started acting psycho again, I'd just ignore her until she settled down. I definitely wasn't going to let her drag me into another fight.

Rebecca was still in the bathroom when I headed back along the hallway into the living room. With nothing else to do, I logged on to the Internet. I checked my e-mail— just a spam message from a porn site featuring horny coed sluts—and my 401(k) account, which seemed to lose value no matter how I allocated my money. Then I surfed the Web for a while, reading news stories on Yahoo! I had to pee badly, and I got up and saw that Rebecca was still in the bathroom. I decided that she was staying in there on purpose, to punish me for dumping her clothes on the street.

I knocked on the door. She didn't answer, so I knocked again, three times. She still didn't answer.

"Come on, come out," I said. "I have to use the bathroom."

Nothing. Listening closely, I heard water running; it sounded like it was coming from the faucet in the bathtub. I pictured Rebecca relaxing, a Zen-like smile on her face, enjoying my discomfort.

"I'm serious," I said. "Open up."

There was still no sound except for the steadily running water. Getting really pissed off, I was about to say something else when I noticed some water leaking out under the bathroom door. I was confused for a few seconds; then the panic set in. I don't know exactly what I did next, but I remember screaming and banging on the door, then ramming against it with my shoulder. I'm not sure how long it took for the door to open, but I'll never forget the sight of Rebecca's naked body bobbing in the overflowing bathwater.

10

IDIALED 911 and explained to the operator that there had been a suicide. The operator took my address, and then she asked me how the victim had killed herself. I said I had no idea but that her body was still in the bathtub.

Since I'd discovered the body I'd been surprisingly calm, and I remained calm as I sat on the armchair in the living room, waiting for the police and EMS workers to arrive. Of course, I was upset that Rebecca was dead, but I was in shock and didn't have any real emotion about it yet.

A few minutes after I made the 911 call, the buzzer rang. Without bothering to find out who it was I pressed the door button on the intercom. Leaning out into the hallway, I saw two cops—a squat white guy with a walrus mustache and a tall, younger black guy—approaching my apartment. I had a moment of panic, remembering leaving Ricky's body against the garbage can. I told myself that this had nothing to do with Ricky, but I still didn't feel comfortable having cops in my apartment.

"She's dead," I said, and I stood to the side and let the cops pass.

"Where is she?" the walrus cop asked.

"Bathroom," I said. "First door on the left."

As the cops approached the bathroom I realized I hadn't shut the water off in the tub. I noticed that more water had flowed into the hallway.

The walrus cop glanced into the bathroom, then started talking into his radio, describing the scene in an official, monotone voice. The other cop, wearing rubber gloves, went into the bathroom, and, a few seconds later, I heard the water shut off.

The buzzer rang again and I let the two EMS workers into the apartment. They were carrying a stretcher. I returned to the living room and sat in the chair, waiting, as the men did whatever they were doing in the bathroom.

After a couple of minutes, the walrus cop came into the living room. His name tag read *Robert Fitch*.

"Excuse me," he said, "Mr ...?"

"Miller. David Miller."

Fitch took out a small pad and wrote down my name. I just wanted him out of my apartment as fast as possible.

"We're very sorry about your loss," he said, trying his best to sound sympathetic.

"Thank you," I said.

"Do you have a mop?" he asked.

"Yes," I said.

I went into the tall kitchen cabinet and gave him the mop. He took it into the bathroom then returned to talk to me in the kitchen.

"So was she your wife?" he asked, getting ready to write in his pad again.

"No," I said.

He looked up, waiting for me to elaborate.

"She was my girlfriend, I guess," I said.

"You guess?"

"She was my girlfriend," I said, more definitively.

"What was her name?"

"Rebecca. Rebecca Daniels."

He wrote this down.

"Did she live here?" he asked.

"Yes," I said.

"Does she have family?"

Rebecca had told me that she hadn't talked to her mother, or any other close family members, in years.

"Her mother lives in Texas," I said.

"Will you contact her?"

"Yes."

He jotted something in the pad. "When did you discover the body?"

"Right before I called nine-one-one. I saw the water coming out under the bathroom door, so I knew something was wrong. I broke down the door and saw her there. Then I went and called for help."

"Did you touch the body or anything else in the room?" he asked.

"No," I said, wondering why he was asking me this. Did he consider this a possible criminal investigation? "I mean, I don't think I … No—definitely no."

The buzzer rang and I went to answer it. When I opened the front door Carmen was standing there with the young bearded guy who'd recently moved into the apartment across the hall.

"What's going on?" Carmen said, trying to see into the apartment.

"Nothing," I said. I didn't want Carmen to tell the police about how Rebecca and I had been fighting earlier, but I didn't see any way to avoid it.

"What do you mean, nothing?" she said. "There're police cars and an ambulance out there."

"Was somebody hurt?" the bearded guy asked. He spoke in an uppity, pretentious way; he was probably a self-important grad student or a college professor.

A squat, dark-but-graying middle-aged guy, wearing a black sport jacket, came up behind the bearded guy.

"Do you live at this address?" the man asked me.

"Yes," I said.

"Detective Romero." He flashed a badge. "Can I come in?"

"Yes, please, of course," I said. I was trying not to act nervous. Then I thought, Why shouldn't I be acting nervous? After all, my girlfriend had just killed herself.

226

As Romero entered the apartment, Carmen said, "Why won't you tell me what's going on?"

Romero was looking back, and there was no way I couldn't answer.

"My girlfriend committed suicide," I said.

"Oh, my God," Carmen said, looking truly horrified. "But she was okay just an hour ago, when you two were fighting."

Romero suddenly seemed interested.

"It happened when I was gone," I said to Carmen. "Remember, you saw me leaving before. When I came back Rebecca had locked herself in the bathroom."

"All I know is you were throwing her clothes out on the street," Carmen said. She turned to Romero and said, "You can go look—some of her things are still out there. You should hear them fighting all the time. It's like I'm living in a flophouse."

"Excuse me," Romero said to Carmen, and he continued into the apartment ahead of me. I glared at Carmen as I shut the door.

Romero went over to Fitch and got an update on the situation. I wasn't sure what to do, so I just stood there, waiting in the living room.

I watched Romero and Fitch go toward the bathroom. They spoke with the black officer, who was standing in the hallway, and then Romero went into the bathroom by himself.

Romero stayed in the bathroom for what seemed like a long time. It might've been ten minutes, but that still seemed like a long time to view the body of a suicide victim.

The buzzer rang again. When I opened the door a young Asian guy with a camera around his neck was standing next to a red-haired guy with a beard.

"Police photographer," the Asian guy said.

"Medical examiner," the red-haired guy said.

I directed the men toward the bathroom, trying to stay calm. I didn't know why a crime-scene photographer and a medical examiner had been called to the scene of a suicide.

Several more minutes passed, and then Romero exited the bathroom. He exchanged some more words with the officers, then approached me.

"Mr. Miller, I want to give you my condolences," he said. "It must've been pretty rough, finding her in there."

"It was."

"Can we sit down?" he said. "I need to ask you a few questions."

"Sure," I said.

I sat on the couch and Romero sat across from me in the chair. I'd thought he was older when he arrived, but now I could tell that the gray in his hair was premature, and he looked like he was about my age, maybe younger.

"So do you have any idea why she would kill herself?" Romero asked. He had taken out a pad.

"No, not really."

"You have no idea at all?"

Figuring that, thanks to Carmen, he was going to ask

me about the fight Rebecca and I had had, I decided to beat him to the punch.

"I mean, there'd been some tension between us lately," I said, "but I don't think she'd kill herself over it."

"Yeah, the old lady was saying, you two were having some kind of fight?"

"It wasn't a *fight*," I said. "We were in the process of breaking up."

"Is that why you tossed her clothes out on the street?"

"I really don't see what this has to do with anything," I said. "Like I said, we were breaking up. I admit it wasn't the most cordial breakup in the world. Maybe that was why she killed herself—that was your question, wasn't it?"

"Yeah, that was my question," Romero said, looking down as he wrote in the pad.

"I don't get this," I said. "Isn't it obvious she OD'd?"

"Why is that obvious?"

I looked beyond Romero as I saw the EMS workers carrying Rebecca's body, covered by a white sheet. Everyone left the apartment except Fitch and Romero.

"We mopped up a little for you in there," Fitch said.

"Thanks," I said.

"The body will be taken to Bellevue for the autopsy." Fitch handed me a card. "You can call this number for any information you might need." Then Fitch turned to Romero and said, "Should we stick around, Tony?"

"Yeah," Romero said, "I'll be done in a few."

Fitch left, and Romero and I were alone. I felt

uncomfortable, suddenly remembering the pictures Kenny had taken.

"Are you okay?" Romero asked.

"Yeah," I said. "Fine."

He squinted at my face. "How'd you get that?"

"I fell the other day," I said, touching my lower lip, "leaving a bank."

"It looks like teeth marks."

Remembering how Rebecca had bitten into my face, I realized he wasn't referring to the healing fat lip from my struggle with Ricky.

"Oh, *that*," I said. "Yeah, they're teeth marks."

"Where did they come from?"

I shook my head, fed up, then said, "Rebecca bit me, all right? Like Carmen told you, we had an argument and it got a little out of control. Rebecca was crazy—she flipped out sometimes. I told her she had to move out and she basically attacked me. I was trying to get her off me, and she started biting me. Then I got angry and dumped some of her stuff on the street. I took a walk, and when I came back she'd locked herself in the bathroom. I saw the water coming out into the hallway, so I broke down the door and called nine-one-one."

"The medical examiner noticed trauma to the victim's throat. Do you know how that happened?"

"I might've grabbed her throat," I said, "trying to get her off me."

Romero had turned his head, looking back toward the kitchen counter at, I noticed, the empty bottle of whiskey.

"Were you drinking today?" he asked.

"Rebecca was," I said. "When I came home from work she was drunk and acting crazier than usual. That's when I told her I'd had it, and she came after me. Are you done with the questions?"

"Not yet," Romero said. "You said you suspected an overdose. Do you know what kind of drugs she might've been taking?"

"Rebecca was into the club scene," I said. "I know she took a lot of Ecstasy."

"Anything else?"

"Pot, coke, some meth."

"That it?"

"Far as I know."

Romero wrote in his pad.

"Was she depressed lately?" he asked.

"No, not really," I said.

"Did she ever try to kill herself before?"

"Not that I know of."

Romero was about to ask another question when the buzzer rang. Figuring it was officers coming back into the apartment, I pressed the buzzer, and, about a minute later, I opened the door, surprised to see Rebecca's friend Ray standing there. He looked like he'd been crying, and I knew the officers outside must've told him about Rebecca.

"Say it ain't true," Ray said. "Please say it ain't true."

Romero and I just looked at him.

"Fuck!" Ray shouted. "Why? Why'd she have to go do that shit? Why?"

Ray started crying.

"What's your name?" Romero said to Ray.

"His name's Ray—he was a friend of Rebecca's," I said.

"I'm Romero, NYPD. Did you happen to speak with Ms. Daniels recently?"

"She called me up before," Ray said, still crying, "like at nine o'clock. She sounded whacked, know what I mean? Started talkin' some crazy shit—said she was gonna kill herself."

"Did she say why she wanted to end her life?" Romero asked.

"She was sayin' all this shit," Ray said. "Said she was a horrible person and all this shit made no sense. She was talkin' about him a lot too." Ray jutted his chin toward me.

"What about him?" Romero said to Ray.

"I don't remember all of it," Ray said. "She just said he'd been takin' a lot of shit out on her lately, and said he was bonin' some other bitch too."

"*What*?" I said.

"That's what she said," Ray went on. "Said it was some bitch, Angie."

"That's a total lie," I said.

"I ain't lyin', man," Ray said to Romero. "She was real mad about it too. I was like, 'Take it easy, yo, chill,' but she said she was gonna take pills and shit. I didn't believe her, man, but I told her I'd come by later anyway, just to hang out with her."

"Who's Angie?" Romero asked me.

"I work with a woman named Angie, but we're just

friends," I explained. "I have no idea why Rebecca would've said that."

"Yo, you think I'm lyin'?" Ray said to me, as if challenging me to a fight.

"No," I said, "I believe Rebecca *told* you that, but it's not true."

"Why would she lie?" Ray said.

"I don't know," I said. "She was always making up stories, getting paranoid. Come on, you knew Rebecca. You knew she was crazy, right?"

"Becky wasn't crazy, yo," Ray said. "She was a little wild, that's all."

"Did Rebecca tell you anything else on the phone this evening?" Romero said to Ray. "Did she say something else was bothering her?"

"Yeah," Ray said, "she said she was afraid David was gonna dump her ass on the street."

"Thank you," Romero said. "Can you wait outside, please, Mr ...?"

"Ramirez," Ray said. "Yeah, I'll wait." Then he left the apartment, pulling on the door handle to make the door slam.

"I guess I'll get out of your way now too," Romero said to me, "give you some time alone. But about this Angie he mentioned. What's her last name?"

"Nothing was going on between Angie and me," I said. "I have no idea why Rebecca told Ray that."

"I believe you, but can I have her last name anyway?"

"What does she have to do with anything?" I said. "I

mean, I don't want to drag her into—"

"Can I just have her last name please?" He sounded frustrated.

"Lerner," I said.

"Thank you," he said as he wrote in his pad. Then he said, "Phone number?"

"Don't know it," I lied. I had her home number programmed into my cell phone.

He looked at me suspiciously, then said, "How about a work number?"

I gave him the main number at *Manhattan Business*, figuring it would be easy for him to get it anyway, then said, "But please don't drag her into this if you don't really have to."

Romero put his pad away in his jacket pocket.

"I'll be in touch with you after the autopsy results," he said. "You'll be around, right?"

"Yes," I said.

"Good."

After the door shut I went into the foyer and listened. Sure enough, I heard the doorbell to the apartment across the hall ring, and then Romero started talking to Carmen. Their voices were so muffled that, even with my ear against the door, I couldn't make out exactly what they were saying. Their conversation lasted only a few minutes; then the door closed and there was silence. I walked away, deciding that I should call Angie at home and warn her that Romero might call her. I reached into my pocket and took out my cell phone, then decided that

I wasn't in the mood to talk to her. But while I had my phone out I decided I might as well get it over with and call Rebecca's mother. I went to the hallway where Rebecca's pocketbook was hanging on the knob of the closet door. I found Rebecca's cell phone, but her mother's phone number wasn't programmed in. I didn't know why I expected the number to be there, since Rebecca had barely been in touch with her mother. I remembered Rebecca telling me her mother's name was Edna, and that she'd never remarried after her husband took off. Rebecca had said that her mother had moved from Duncanville to another part of Texas—I couldn't remember if it was Houston or San Antonio. After striking out in San Antonio, I tried Houston, and sure enough the operator had a listing for an Edna Daniels. I dialed the number.

"Edna Daniels?"

"Who's this?" the woman asked with a Southern drawl. A TV was blasting in the background.

"My name's David Miller," I said. "I'm sorry to call so late, but are you Rebecca Daniels's mother?"

There was a long pause, and all I heard was the TV noise; it sounded like the Home Shopping Network.

"Are you still there?" I asked.

"Yeah, I'm still here."

"Are you Rebecca Daniels's mother or not?"

"I used to have a daughter named Rebecca, but, far as I'm concerned, she's been dead a long, long time."

"So she is your daughter," I said.

"Was," she said. "What's this all about anyway? Becky's

in some kinda trouble, I'm sure."

"I'm afraid I have some very bad news," I said. "Rebecca and I have been living together for about a year, and she … well, she committed suicide today."

For several seconds all I heard was TV noise. Then Edna said, "That's all you called to tell me?"

"Yes," I said. "Are you okay?"

"I'm fine," she said. "Never been finer, if you wanna know the truth. Is that all you want to say?"

"Maybe you didn't hear me," I said. "Rebecca killed herself today."

"I heard you."

"I just thought you'd want to know."

"I told you, my daughter's dead to me before you called, so what difference does it make, you call me up and tell me she's dead?"

"None, I guess."

"You know how much humiliation that girl caused me? You know how much pain she caused? Good, I'm glad she's dead. She's better off dead. Now when I tell people she's dead it'll be the truth. Can I hang up now?"

"Sure," I said, and the call clicked off.

I held the phone up to my ear for several seconds before shutting it off. Although Rebecca had never given me many details, she'd always made out as if her mother was extremely overbearing and controlling, and I knew they'd had serious problems when Rebecca was a teenager. Still, I couldn't imagine what had happened between them that had made her mother become so cold and heartless that she didn't care that her own daughter had died.

I hadn't peed since I'd come home from the bar, and I had to go badly. About to enter the bathroom, I hesitated, then went in, trying to avoid looking toward the bathtub. I had to stand over the bowl for a long time, feeling like an old man, waiting for my urine to start coming out. Finally it started to dribble out, but it took a few minutes for my bladder to drain completely. After I flushed I accidentally glanced toward the bathtub, which looked perfectly normal, as if nothing had happened. Then my legs started buckling and I had to rush out of the bathroom and catch my breath.

In the hallway I started breathing semi-normally, but then the tears started coming and then the momentum-crying kicked in. Finally I pulled myself together, reminding myself how crazy Rebecca was, and how she'd attacked me earlier and could've seriously hurt me.

I went into the kitchen and poured myself a glass of water from the Brita pitcher. I drank it quickly and poured another and drank that too. I felt better for a while, and then I remembered the sight of Rebecca's naked body bobbing in the bathtub—how white she'd looked—and I decided that spending the night someplace else could be a good idea. I thought about where to go, and the first idea that came to me was Barbara's; then I had to actually remind myself that she was dead. I laughed, shaking my head, then considered taking a train out to the Island and spending the night at Aunt Helen's. She'd definitely let me stay for as long as I liked, but did I really want to deal with her nagging? When she found out about Rebecca, she'd start hounding me to see her friend Alice's son, the grief counselor, and that was the last thing I needed.

Maybe I could stay at a friend's. Keith lived right across town, on Seventy-fifth and Second, but since the failed intervention over Rebecca I'd fallen out of touch with him and the rest of my friends. A few months ago, he'd called me at work and asked if I wanted to meet up for lunch sometime. I was on another line and told him I'd call him right back, but I never did. It would have been awkward to call him now and say, "Sorry I've been such a dick lately, man, but my girlfriend's dead, so could I crash at your place for a couple of nights?"

Without realizing it, I'd picked up the phone and started dialing.

"Angie?"

"Yeah." She sounded half-asleep.

"David. Sorry to call so late."

There was a pause, and then she said, "It's okay, I wasn't asleep yet. What's up?"

"Nothing much," I said, wondering why I'd called.

"Oh," she said.

"It sounds like I woke you," I said.

"You didn't."

"I'll call you tomorrow."

"No, it's okay."

"It's no big deal," I said. "Get some rest."

"Is something wrong?" she asked.

"No, of course not," I said. "Good night."

"Good night," she said, sounding confused.

I had to do something to keep my mind occupied, so I started playing stock-car racing on my PlayStation. Barbara had bought me the console and a few games for my thirtieth birthday. Whenever she came over we'd play, getting loud and competitive, like kids.

"I'm gonna lap you," I said.

"No, you're not," she said, hitting the brakes, causing me to rear-end her, lose control, and crash into a brick wall.

"Cheater," I said, steering my car back on the road. "I'm gonna get you." I accelerated at top speed, getting back into the race. "Okay, here we go, baby."

"So you want to go on a date Friday night?" she asked.

Making a hairpin turn at top speed, I said, "With you?"

"With my friend Stacy at work."

"Not interested."

"She's really cute."

"Okay, ready? Watch this."

"Don't you want to meet somebody?"

"There you are ..."

"I think you'll really like Stacy."

"... and here I come."

"Won't you just call her?"

"Ha! Lapped you!"

I continued playing the game for a while longer, but I was too distracted to focus on it and I kept crashing into things, exploding.

At one point I thought about Charlotte and Kenny. It was strange, but with everything that had happened this evening, I'd almost forgotten that I was being blackmailed. As I drove my car off a bridge in a fiery crash, I decided that they had given up. They must've realized I was broke and couldn't give them any money, or one of them would've contacted me by now.

When I glanced at the time on the cable box I was surprised to see that it was one-fifteen, meaning I'd been playing the video game for almost an hour. I decided that a good night's sleep would do me a lot of good, so I shut off the lights in the living room, foyer, and kitchen, and went down the hallway into the bedroom. I stripped to my underwear and realized I had to pee again. I dreaded having to return to the bathroom, but unless I wanted to pee in the kitchen sink or into a milk carton, I didn't have a choice. Finally I decided to just grow some balls and go in there.

As I urinated, I made a point of looking at the bathtub, and the strategy worked. I wasn't sad or horrified anymore—I was just angry. Rebecca was crazy—there was no doubt about that—but why'd she have to kill herself?

I got into bed and tried to fall asleep. After about an hour of stirring, I returned to the living room and resumed playing the stock-car racing game, getting into a four-car pileup on the first bend.

11

SATURDAY MORNING, I decided I needed to get the hell out of my apartment. Without shaving or showering, I put on my Rollerblades and glided along Eighty-first Street. I hadn't bladed in a long time; I felt awkward for a block or so, stumbling a few times, and then I got back into the groove. At a deli on Broadway, I bought a chocolate chip muffin and a cup of coffee, and then I bladed into Riverside Park.

It was a perfect day—the sun blazing, the sky deep blue and cloudless, and it felt like it would definitely hit eighty later on. I headed downtown along the promenade adjacent to the Hudson, going at a pretty good clip by the time I reached the West Fifties. I'd been planning to blade all the way to Battery Park, but I tired out near the Chelsea

Piers and had to sit on a bench to rest.

A young woman with long, dark hair in a ponytail was sitting at the other end of the bench. She was wearing black yoga pants and a black sports bra and looked like she'd just finished a run.

I stared at her until she noticed me, and then I said, "Great day, huh?"

"Yeah," she said. She smiled politely and looked away again. She had a plain-looking face, but she was still very good-looking.

"So do you run here often?" I asked.

She turned back toward me suddenly, as if my lame pickup line had jolted her.

"Once in a while," she said.

"Me too." I squinted. "Have we met somewhere before?"

"I don't think so."

"You really look familiar. Have you been on TV?"

"No."

"Radio?"

"You recognize me from radio?"

I laughed, then said, "I know I've seen you somewhere. Do you live uptown?"

"No."

"Oh, well. We must've crossed paths somewhere. By the way, I'm David."

"Ellen," she said.

I held out my hand and we shook. I hadn't done anything to hide the fact that I was blatantly hitting on her, but she seemed amused anyway. She acted like she wasn't used to guys trying to pick her up.

"So what do you do?" I asked. "Maybe that's how we know each other."

"I'm a speech therapist," she said.

"Really?" I said, trying to sound truly interested. "Where do you work?"

"St. Vincent's Hospital."

"Cool. I mean, that's a great hospital."

"What do you do?" she asked.

"I'm the associate editor of *Manhattan Business* magazine." It was strange, saying my new title aloud for the first time.

"I subscribe to *Manhattan Business*," she said, her voice brightening.

"Really?" I said. "I don't think I've ever met an actual subscriber. Or at least not a subscriber who's a speech therapist."

She laughed at my attempt at a joke. We started talking about the magazine for a while, and then I asked her a few questions about her job. We were making a lot of eye contact and she seemed to have warmed up to me.

"Do you want to get something to eat?" I asked.

She hesitated, caught off guard.

"Come on, I know we're not dressed for anything fancy," I said. "We could just go to a diner or something and talk some more. What do you say?"

"I have to be home for something at noon," she said. "What time is it now?"

"Just after eleven," I said. "Come on, there must be something nearby."

"All right," she said.

She stood up and I was pleasantly surprised—she had a much better body than I expected. She was thin and toned all over.

We exited the promenade, talking about Chelsea Piers. She said she used to be a member of the health club there, but had quit because it was too expensive. Then we started talking about restaurants in the area, recent movies we had seen, and how nice the weather had been so far this spring. The conversation was dull but pleasant.

We walked over a few blocks to Eighth Avenue and decided to go into a bagel store. I bought us bagels with low-fat lox spread and coffees and we sat at a table by the window and continued to get to know each other. She told me about how she'd grown up in Manhattan, in Stuyvesant Town, and gone to Hunter College. When it was my turn to give a personal history, I intentionally omitted that my girlfriend had committed suicide yesterday.

I noticed it was a few minutes past noon and I said, "Didn't you have to get back?"

"It's okay," she said. "I just had to do some laundry and shopping—I can do it later."

We continued chatting until long after our food was gone. During our conversation, she mentioned that she sometimes went to the weekend antiques flea market on Sixth Avenue and Twenty-sixth Street. I suggested going there, and she said that was a great idea. At the flea market we strolled around, browsing the junk and furniture. She said she needed a lamp for her night table and I helped her pick out a green-and-red stained-glass one.

"You'll have to see how it looks with the rest of my stuff sometime," she said.

We left the flea market, holding hands. I told her that my ankles were sore from blading and that I was going to take the subway home. She walked me to the subway station at Twenty-third and Seventh. We chatted for a while longer by the entrance to the station, and then I said, "So we'll have to go out sometime."

"Definitely," she said.

At a nearby news kiosk, the worker lent us a pen and gave us a small piece of paper. She jotted down her number on the paper and gave it to me.

"I'll call you early next week," I said.

"Great," she said.

I could've kissed her good-bye, but I didn't. I went down the stairs to the subway. On the platform, I ripped up the paper into little pieces and dropped the shreds onto the tracks.

* * *

Back home, I showered. It was surprisingly easy, standing where Rebecca had died. I barely even thought about it.

Fully dressed in slacks and a button-down shirt, I went into the living room. The answering machine was flashing, indicating a new message. I hadn't noticed the message when I came home before, so the person must've called while I was in the shower. I pressed play and listened to Angie's voice, asking me to call her back. She sounded normal, so I didn't think the police had talked to her. I deleted the message, figuring I'd call her back later or tomorrow, or just see her on Monday.

Deciding that I was in the mood for Japanese, I went to Haru on Amsterdam. As I settled into a chair at the end of the sushi bar, I noticed, three spots down from me, a woman reading an Anne Rice novel. She had reddish-brown hair and appeared to be about twenty pounds overweight. Her face was average-looking, but she had light blue eyes and there was something sexy about her. We started talking. She was an aspiring stand-up comic, and going by her dry, biting sense of humor that had me cracking up several times, I told her I thought she was going to make it big someday. As I finished my sashimi, I continued chatting with her, enjoying her company. I knew I could've gotten her number and gone out with her sometime, if I wanted to. After paying for the sushi by breaking one of the hundreds Aunt Helen had lent me, I told the woman, "I hope we run into each other again sometime," and I left.

At a deli on Amsterdam, I bought a six-pack of Heineken and went to the video store on Columbus and rented *Pretty Woman* on DVD. Back in my apartment, I was drinking beer and watching the movie when I sensed Barbara's presence on the couch next to me.

I paused the movie and tried to concentrate on Barbara, attempting to somehow communicate with her. After a few minutes, I realized I was being ridiculous. Naturally, I'd felt a connection to Barbara while watching *Pretty Woman*, because we'd watched the movie so many times together. The fact that I'd downed a couple of beers might've been a factor too.

"I must be losing it," I said out loud.

I watched a few more minutes of the movie, and then the phone rang. I pressed pause again and let the machine answer. When I heard Angie's voice I went to the phone and picked up.

"Hi," I said.

"Oh … David," she said, as though she'd been mentally prepared to leave a message.

"Sorry, I just walked in," I said.

"Oh, okay," she said. "Hey, I just got this really weird phone call from this police detective. He said your girlfriend died yesterday."

Romero must've gotten Angie's number from Information.

"Actually, she committed suicide," I said. "Did the detective say died?"

"Yeah."

"Well, it was definitely a suicide. They think she OD'd."

"God, that's so awful, David. Why didn't you tell me about it last night?"

"I don't know."

"You poor thing. Did you ... I mean did you like ... discover the ..."

"Yeah."

"Oh, my God."

I didn't say anything.

"I'm so sorry," Angie said. "I mean, that's so awful. Jesus ... This detective guy said something weird, though."

"Weird?"

"Yeah," Angie said. "He said something about how your girlfriend thought you and I were dating."

"I know," I said. "I have no idea where she got that. She knew we were friendly at work—I mean, I mentioned your name to her a few times, so she must've just made up stories to herself. Rebecca was very paranoid. She had a lot of problems ... obviously. I guess I should've listened to you."

"Stop it," Angie said. "You had no way of knowing ... You can't blame yourself when something like this happens."

"I know," I said.

"That's good," Angie said. "Anyway, I was just calling because this detective guy called me, you know, saying your girlfriend was dead, and then he said she thought you and I were ... So I just wanted to call you and see if—"

"I'm really sorry about all of this."

"Oh, that's okay," she said. "So how're you doing? I

mean handling everything."

"I'm fine," I said, glancing at the paused scene from *Pretty Woman* and then at the spot on the couch where I'd imagined Barbara was sitting. "I mean, I'm a little shaken up, of course, but all in all ..."

"If you need a place to stay," Angie said. "I mean, to get out of your apartment for a while. I mean, you know you're welcome to come to my place."

"I appreciate that," I said, "and thanks for calling, but I'm fine—really. I'll see you at work on Monday, okay?"

"Okay," she said.

I hung up with Angie and watched the rest of the movie. Toward the end, I had an unsettling feeling. I thought it might have to do with Rebecca, and then I remembered about Charlotte and Kenny. At least they hadn't called me, or tried to get in touch, but I wasn't sure if this was necessarily good news.

* * *

Sunday morning I decided I couldn't procrastinate any longer—I had to call the hospital morgue and start making arrangements for Rebecca's funeral.

"Hello," I said to the woman I'd been transferred to. "My name's David Miller. I believe you're holding the body of my girlfriend, Rebecca Daniels."

"Hold on," the bored-sounding woman said. When she

returned she said, "Rebecca Daniels's boyfriend already made arrangements for those remains."

"That's impossible."

"Are you Raymond Ramirez?"

"*Ray* called you?"

"A Raymond Ramirez called yesterday and made arrangements for those remains. Is there a problem?"

"No, there's no problem," I said. "Thanks."

I was relieved that I didn't have to plan—or pay for—Rebecca's funeral. I doubted Ray would invite me, but I wouldn't have gone anyway. Thanks to Ray, all of Rebecca's friends probably blamed me for her death and not having to go would help me to avoid an uncomfortable situation. But it was funny that Ray had claimed to be Rebecca Daniels's boyfriend. For all I knew, he wasn't lying. My suspicions could have been right all along—Ray wasn't gay, and he and Rebecca had been screwing since I'd known her.

It was a beautiful day—warmer and less breezy than yesterday. I went out and bought bagels, tofu cream cheese, and the Sunday *Times*, then returned to my living room and made a fresh pot of decaf and turned on the stereo to a light jazz station. As I was relaxing, I realized that if Rebecca hadn't killed herself, we'd probably be having one of our violent fights this morning.

As I was skimming an article in the magazine section on the baby's brain, I sensed Barbara next to me.

"How's it going, Barb?" I said to the empty space to my left. I waited, as if giving her time to answer, then said,

"Yeah, I'm pretty good, thanks. Recovering, anyway. These past few days have been out of control." I waited again, then said, "So are you really here or what?" I was hoping she'd give me a sign, but there was nothing. I said, "Okay, if you're really here, prove it to me—do something. Move the Arts and Leisure section." I stared at the Arts & Leisure on top of the pile of papers on the floor, waiting for it to rustle. I thought it moved a little, but I was probably just imagining it.

After breakfast, I went out to a moving supply store and bought ten cardboard boxes. Back at home I put the boxes together, and then I started packing Rebecca's clothes, CDs, shoes, and other belongings. One thing for sure—with Rebecca gone, I'd have a lot less damage on my credit cards. I was so excited about having the bedroom to myself again that the couple of hours or so that it took to pack all of Rebecca's crap passed by quickly. I stacked the boxes in an out-of-the-way spot, in a small alcove in the living room. Although I was anxious to get the boxes out of the apartment, I figured I'd wait a couple of weeks and then call Ray and give him a chance to pick them up; if he didn't want them, I'd just have to get a thrift shop to come.

I spent the rest of the afternoon relaxing, reading more of the *Times*, and watching TV.

"Nothing's on," I said. Then, turning to golf on ESPN, I said, "I know, you hate golf," and switched to something else.

I realized that, semiconsciously, I'd been making occasional comments to Barbara all day. While I knew that to an outsider I might've seemed slightly insane, I enjoyed talking to Barbara, and didn't see any reason to stop. I'd just have to be careful not to do it in public.

I decided I'd go out to dinner again.

"How about Italian?" I said.

Barbara always hated going for Italian food, claiming it was too fattening. She always wanted to go for Japanese or Vietnamese, and whenever I won and we went to an Italian place she'd order the spaghetti carbonara or the eggplant parm, then tell me how she was going to gain five pounds, thanks to me.

"Tough," I said, "we're having Italian."

I was about to go into the bathroom to shower when the buzzer on the intercom rang. I headed toward the door, wondering if it was Ray. I was about to press the talk button on the intercom when I shuddered, thinking that it could be Kenny or Charlotte. Of course they hadn't forgotten about me.

The buzzer rang again. I was going to ignore it; then there was another, longer buzz, and I decided to at least ask who was out there. If it was Kenny or Charlotte, or both of them, I couldn't avoid a confrontation forever. I was better off trying to reason with them.

"Yes?" I said into the intercom.

"Police," the male voice responded.

It sounded like Detective Romero.

"Who is it?" I asked, to make sure.

"Romero—NYPD."

Relieved, I buzzed Romero in. Then, as I waited by the

door, I started to get pissed off. For all he knew I was devastated by Rebecca's death and in the midst of intense mourning. This was a major violation of my privacy. I didn't want to talk to him, and I didn't know why I had to.

I opened the door, ready to tell Romero I couldn't talk right now, when I saw him standing there with three other men—one gray-haired guy in a suit and two uniformed cops.

"We have a warrant to search the apartment," Romero said, flashing a piece of paper.

I glanced at the men's serious, determined faces and I knew this wasn't just a routine follow up to a suicide investigation.

"A warrant for what?" I said. "My girlfriend committed suicide."

"Not your girlfriend," Romero said. "Another woman was killed early Friday morning."

"Who?" I asked.

"Charlotte O'Dougal," Romero said. "Now can you step aside, please, Mr. Miller?"

12

AS THE OFFICERS started searching the apartment, I tried to make out like I was confused and completely innocent, asking Romero all the logical questions—Who's Charlotte O'Dougal? What does this have to do with me? Can you just tell me what the hell's going on here?—all the time hoping, although I knew I was kidding myself, that maybe Charlotte O'Dougal wasn't the Charlotte I knew. It didn't matter what I said, though, because, for some reason, Romero barely seemed interested in me. He just kept telling me to sit down and relax and that he'd fill me in later.

So I sat in the armchair and watched as the officers spread out around the apartment, searching through drawers, cabinets, closets, and just about everywhere else.

Romero asked me what was in the boxes, and I explained that I had packed up all of Rebecca's belongings earlier in the day. Romero immediately ordered the cops to start searching the boxes, and they came into the living room and started opening them, spreading the contents out all over the living room floor, making a total mess. As the search continued, Romero had a hushed conversation with the tall, gray-haired man who I assumed was another detective.

The idea that Charlotte was dead hadn't fully set in yet. I wondered if she'd died of natural causes, or OD'd, or if someone had killed her. The first idea that came to me was that Kenny had done it. Maybe they'd had some fight about money or drugs or whatever, and Kenny had snapped. That would explain why Charlotte hadn't shown up at Starbucks the other day, and why Kenny hadn't tried to blackmail me again. If Kenny had been arrested he could have made a deal with the cops— turning over the pictures of me dumping Ricky's body in exchange for a lighter sentence. But none of this explained why Romero had gotten a warrant to search my apartment, but hadn't bothered to arrest me or even question me.

I watched as the officers continued their search. Finally, Romero and the gray-haired man came over and sat down on the couch across from me.

"This is Frank Glazer from the Ninth Precinct downtown," Romero said. "Frank, this is David Miller, Rebecca Daniels's boyfriend."

"Good to meet you," Glazer said. "Can you tell us where Rebecca Daniels was Thursday night and early Friday morning?"

"I have no idea," I said. I felt frazzled and it was hard to concentrate.

"Come on, it was only a few days ago," Glazer said. "Think."

"I don't know," I said. "Let's see—Thursday night. Um, she was home, I guess."

"You guess?"

I remembered that Thursday night was the night I'd gone to meet Charlotte at the Holiday Cocktail Lounge.

I looked over at the cops, who were now meticulously examining each pair of Rebecca's shoes.

"Why does it matter where Rebecca was?"

"We're talking about after midnight, up till around three A.M. Friday morning."

I'd been with Charlotte until about two A.M.

"Can you please explain what's going on?" I said.

"Have you noticed a steel sharpener missing from your apartment?"

"What's a steel sharpener?"

"It's about ten inches long—kind of shaped like a screwdriver."

"I don't own a steel sharpener," I said.

"Well, Rebecca Daniels did," Romero said.

"Can you just tell me what the hell's going on?" I said.

"We believe that Rebecca Daniels stabbed Charlotte O'Dougal to death with a steel sharpener between two and three A.M. on Friday morning," Glazer said. "The incident took place in the vestibule of Ms. O'Dougal's apartment on East Sixth Street."

It was a good thing I was sitting down, because I was suddenly so dizzy I probably would've passed out. Even sitting, Romero and Glazer's faces became fuzzy.

"You okay?" Romero asked.

"Yeah, fine," I said, although I clearly wasn't.

"You want something to drink? Some water or something?"

"No, that's okay," I said.

"This is a photo of Ms. O'Dougal," Glazer said. "It's an old one, but it's the only one we could find."

I glanced at the crinkled snapshot of Charlotte that looked almost nothing like her. It must've been taken in high school, in Bloomfield Hills, Michigan. She had waist-length brown hair and was smiling, leaning against a red sports car. She looked sexy in a slutty kind of way.

"Have you ever seen her before?" Glazer asked.

"Never," I said. My voice was still unsteady.

"So do you know how Rebecca could've known Charlotte O'Dougal?" Romero asked.

"No idea," I said. "So why do you think Rebecca killed this—what was her name?"

"Charlotte O'Dougal," Romero said.

"Yeah, Charlotte O'Dougal," I said.

"We had no idea at first," Glazer explained. "There were no witnesses to the murder and no fingerprints or other physical evidence. All we had to go on was a price sticker on the murder weapon."

"A price sticker?" I said.

"The steel sharpener had been purchased at Bed Bath and Beyond," Glazer explained. "On the chance the purchase had been made recently, we contacted the Bed Bath and Beyond stores in the New York area and created a list of the people who had purchased this particular steel sharpener and who'd paid by credit card. Rebecca Daniels was on this list. She'd purchased the steel sharpener at the Sixth Avenue store on Thursday afternoon with a Discover card."

"What the hell are you talking about?" I said. "Just because she bought a steel sharpener, what makes you think she killed somebody?"

"I guess you don't know about Rebecca Daniels's history," Romero said.

"History?" I asked.

Romero and Glazer exchanged looks again.

"Three years ago Rebecca Daniels was living in L.A.," Romero said.

"Yeah, so?" I said.

"Did you know she was married to a man named David Hardle?"

So Rebecca hadn't been lying about her former husband, the other David.

"Yeah, she did tell me a little about that, just recently, as a matter of fact," I said. "She said they got divorced."

Romero and Glazer looked at each other, smirking.

"What's so funny?" I said.

"It wasn't a divorce," Romero said. "What your girlfriend might've forgotten to tell you is that one night she stabbed her husband to death in the chest with a steel sharpener. She claimed somebody broke into the house and did it, but the case was pretty much open-and-shut. Her prints were on the murder weapon, and she had motive. The victim's friends said Hardle had been having an affair and wanted out of the marriage, and Daniels was giving him a hard time about it."

Feeling dazed, wondering if this was really happening, I said, "So if Rebecca killed her husband, why didn't she go to jail?"

"Thank the American legal system," Romero said. "Evidence was mishandled, witnesses lied, and, apparently, Daniels was good on the stand. She claimed her prints got on the weapon when she tried to pull it out of her husband's chest. The jury bought it and she got off and moved to New York."

One of the cops searching through Rebecca's things said, "Hey, Frank, check this out."

Glazer and Romero went over and the cop showed them a pair of Rebecca's shoes. Glazer examined the shoes closely, then said, "Looks good." The cop put the shoes in a plastic bag, and then another cop showed the detectives one of Rebecca's jackets.

As the detectives and the cops continued to talk, I tried to absorb the fact that for over a year I'd been living with a cold-blooded killer. Rebecca had told me that I didn't really know her, and now I knew what she meant. Then I started to imagine what could've happened on Thursday night. I'd thought Rebecca had been asleep when I left to meet Charlotte at the bar, but she could've been awake. She could've followed me downtown, maybe in another cab, and seen me with Charlotte. She could've assumed that Charlotte was Angie, then followed her home and killed her.

Romero and Glazer returned to their seats on the couch.

"So you really had no idea about what happened in L.A.?" Romero said to me.

"If I knew, why would I stay with her?"

"Unfortunately we might have some more bad news for you," Romero said, and then he turned to Glazer.

"Charlotte O'Dougal," Glazer said to me, "the woman who was killed, was a junkie and a prostitute. She lived with a guy named Ricardo Alvarado."

Glazer showed me a picture of Ricky. This photo looked much more recent than the one of Charlotte. Ricky's scruffy face and dark, wolflike eyes looked painfully familiar. Somehow I managed to stay calm.

"Alvarado and O'Dougal had a history of domestic abuse," Glazer said. "On Thursday morning he was found dead from severe head injuries in front of the building where he and O'Dougal lived. It was just a few feet away from where we discovered O'Dougal's body."

"Jesus," I said, still looking at the photo. I realized that my hands were tensing, and I had to consciously try to keep them still.

"Initially we thought Alvarado's murder had been

drug-related, or maybe a botched robbery attempt," Glazer said, "but now that his girlfriend's dead it looks like there could be more to it. Do you have any idea what Rebecca's connection to these people was?"

"Nope," I said, shaking my head.

"Are you sure?" Glazer asked.

"Positive."

"Look at the pictures again," Romero said.

I glanced at them, then said, "Sorry, I've never seen these people before. I'm absolutely positive."

They seemed to believe me.

"Do you have any idea at all how Rebecca Daniels could've come into contact with them?" Glazer asked.

"Nope," I said, shaking my head. "I mean, Rebecca used to go out a lot—I mean, dancing at clubs downtown. She also went to raves sometimes in the East Village and Alphabet City. Maybe she met them at a club or something."

"You know which clubs she went to?" Glazer asked.

I gave him the names of several clubs I knew Rebecca had gone to—Vivid, Carbon, Chaos, Twirl. The way Glazer was writing in his pad I could tell he thought he had a serious lead.

"You told Detective Romero that Rebecca took various drugs," Glazer said. "What about heroin?"

"What about it?"

"Alvarado and O'Dougal were hard-core addicts," Glazer said. "Did your girlfriend shoot up?"

"Not that I know of."

"Where were you Thursday night?" Romero asked.

"Thursday, lemme think," I said, as if I had to remember. "I think I was home."

"You think?"

"I'm positive. What difference does it make where I was?"

"We got Rebecca Daniels's autopsy results in yesterday. She had Ketamine in her system as well as extremely high levels of GHB, otherwise known as liquid Ecstasy. She could've OD'd, or somebody could've slipped the drugs into a drink."

"Hold up," I said. "If you think I had anything to do with Rebecca's death—"

"You admitted having your hands around her throat, and we got two witnesses, Raymond Ramirez and Carmen Stappini, who say you and Daniels had been fighting a lot lately."

"I want a lawyer," I said.

"You're not under arrest," Romero said.

"I don't care," I said.

"Look, if you want to know the truth, I don't think you killed your girlfriend," Romero said. "But until we're sure who killed Charlotte O'Dougal and Ricardo Alvarado, all options are open."

"I'm telling you," I said, "I don't know anything about any of this, and that's the God's honest truth."

"Did Rebecca mention anything unusual happening in her life lately?" Glazer asked.

"Unusual?" I said.

"Maybe someone had threatened her or tried to blackmail her?"

I had to catch my breath, but I coughed into my hand to cover it up.

"No," I said.

"Did Rebecca ever mention a guy by the name of Kenny Farrini?"

"Who?" I asked.

Glazer repeated the name.

"Nope, never heard of him," I said believably. "Why? Is he dead too?" I prayed the answer would be yes.

"Farrini's alive and well," Glazer said. "He was I guess what you'd call an associate of Ricky's. They were small-time con artists, and they both have long rap sheets. We've been questioning Farrini, but so far he hasn't given us much."

"I have absolutely no idea who he is," I said.

The cops seemed to be finishing up searching the apartment. I breathed deeply, hoping this would signal to the detectives that it was time to wrap things up, but Glazer and Romero didn't budge.

"There's another theory we're toying with," Romero said. "As I'm sure you recall, Rebecca's friend Raymond Ramirez claimed that Rebecca had told him she thought you were having an affair with that girl—Angie Lerner."

"So what does that have to do with anything?" I said.

"I already spoke with Ms. Lerner, and she confirmed she wasn't having an affair with you," Romero said, "but maybe Rebecca somehow mistook this Charlotte for Angie and killed her in a jealous rage."

"I guess it's a possibility," I said.

"But the questions remain," Romero said. "Why did she go down to the East Village to kill this woman? How did she get the idea she was Angie? And how does Ricardo Alvarado figure into all of this?"

"Maybe you're better off with your drug theory," I said.

"Maybe," Romero said. "But Charlotte O'Dougal wasn't a dealer—she was a heroin addict, and there wasn't any evidence of heroin in Rebecca Daniels's system. It's hard to see how drugs could connect them."

I shook my head, as if stumped. Romero and Glazer exchanged *I guess we should go now* looks, and then they both stood up.

"Sorry if we interrupted your grieving," Romero said, maybe sarcastically. "We'll definitely be in touch."

After the cops left I bolted the door and remained in the foyer, listening to hear if they were going to talk to Carmen again. I didn't hear a bell ringing or any voices, and I was satisfied that the detectives had left the building.

The apartment was a mess. Drawers and closest doors had been left open, and some of Rebecca's stuff was still strewn on the floor. I figured I'd clean later. I'd sweated a lot during the past hour and needed a shower desperately.

I turned on the water as hot as I could stand it, and I used the shower's massage mechanism, but I couldn't relax. There had definitely been sarcasm in Romero's voice—he knew I wasn't grieving as much as I should be after my girlfriend's suicide, and he suspected I was somehow involved. I imagined the detectives going to talk to Kenny again and accusing him of killing Ricky. If they put enough pressure on him, or even took him in and started beating the crap out of him, he'd turn over the pictures of me, and that would be it.

Then I started replaying the events of Thursday night. I remembered how Charlotte's phone call had awakened me on the couch. Rebecca could've listened in on the conversation on the bedroom extension. Then Rebecca wouldn't have needed to follow me downtown, because she'd have known I was going to the Holiday Cocktail Lounge. When I came home, I'd seen Rebecca in bed, but I recalled how after I left the bar I'd walked for a while in the rain. Rebecca would've had time to kill Charlotte, then return home before I did.

Other details that had confused me were suddenly clear. Rebecca's motive for suicide was more understandable now, since she was probably reeling from killing Charlotte the night before. Rebecca's mother's nonreaction to her daughter's death also made sense, given the humiliation that Rebecca's trial had probably brought her.

As the water beat down against my head, I imagined Rebecca stalking Charlotte in the rain. Rebecca was gripping the steel sharpener, maybe concealed inside her coat. As Charlotte approached her building, Rebecca had probably rushed up behind her and forced her way inside. I pictured the steel sharpener going into Charlotte's bony back and her body crumpling onto the floor. Then I imagined Rebecca standing over the body with a gleeful, crazed expression before walking away in the rain.

The shower water was still very hot, but I got chills anyway, thinking about how Rebecca could've easily killed me during one of our fights, or while I was asleep.

I turned the dial on the shower massage to its strongest level. The firm, single stream of hot water kneading into my back and neck muscles still couldn't relax me.

"Everything's gonna be okay," Barbara said.

"Yeah, sure it is," I said.

I was getting dressed in the bedroom when the buzzer on the intercom sounded again. Now what the hell did the police want?

Deciding that this time I'd definitely refuse to let them into the apartment, even if it meant getting arrested, I said into the intercom, "What is it?"

"*New York Post*," a man's voice said.

Shit, I should've realized that the media was going to be all over this story.

"No comment," I said.

As I walked away, the buzzer sounded again. I ignored it and went back into the bedroom and put on jeans and a sweatshirt. That *Post* reporter was still ringing the buzzer, and I realized he wouldn't give up until I gave him some kind of statement. I put on sneakers with no socks and left my apartment. Approaching the vestibule, I saw a young blond guy with his finger on the buzzer to my apartment. Beyond this guy, behind the other door leading to the outside, there seemed to be about ten other people.

I opened the inside door and the small crowd rushed into the vestibule through the other door. They all seemed to be speaking at once, pointing mikes in my direction, shouting questions.

"All right, all right," I said. When they quieted down I said, "Just go back outside and I'll make a statement."

The reporters started to move back outside when I heard someone approaching behind me. I turned around and saw it was Carmen. She was hunched over with her chin tilted up, glaring at me.

"What's going on now?" she said.

"Nothing," I said.

"What do you mean, nothing?" she said. "The cops were here before, and now all these reporters are here, causing a racket."

"Please just go back into your apartment," I said.

"Why do I have to go back into my apartment? This is my hallway as much as it is yours. I've been living here thirty-seven years. I can stand wherever I want to stand."

I realized it didn't make a difference whether Carmen heard my comment in person or read about it in tomorrow's papers.

I went outside and Carmen followed behind me. I was surprised to see a few news cameras aimed at me, in addition to all the microphones. Photographers were there too, and I squinted as the flashes went off.

"This has all come as a shock to me," I said. "All I ask is that you please have some respect for my privacy during this very difficult time. Thank you."

As I headed back into the building, stepping around Carmen, the reporters shouted questions at my back. I made out a few of the questions—"Did you know about Rebecca Daniels's past?" "How does it feel to know your girlfriend was a psychotic murderer?"—then the voices merged into loud noise.

Following me to my apartment, Carmen said, "What's this about your girlfriend murdering people? What happened now?"

I went into my apartment and bolted the door and put the chain on. Then I went into the hallway closet and took the Phillips screwdriver out from the toolbox in the closet. I unscrewed the cover to the buzzer and yanked out several of the wires. Hopefully the reporters wouldn't harass me anymore, but just in case I wanted to make sure I didn't have to listen to the buzzer all night.

Going out to dinner was out of the question now, with all the reporters out there.

"How about we eat in instead?" I asked Barbara.

I didn't sense her presence the way I had earlier.

"Barb, are you here?"

I waited, but I still didn't sense anything. I figured I wouldn't push it; I'd just try again later.

I decided that ordering food in was a bad idea. For all I knew there were even more reporters outside now, and they'd rush the door when I let the delivery guy in.

There wasn't much in the house to eat: a packet of Cup-a-Soup and a jar of marshmallow fluff in the cupboard, and a package of frozen peas that I used as an ice pack in the freezer. After I had the Cup-a-Soup, I turned on the TV to the Cartoon Network and ate fluff on a spoon as Tom chased Jerry.

"God, you're so immature," Barbara said.

"Are you here?" I said.

"You know what your problem is? Your problem is you never grew up. You can't let go."

"Barb?" I said. "Barb?"

There was no answer.

During "Popeye," I found myself nodding off. I left the dirty dishes on the coffee table and went into the bedroom and lay down.

I fell asleep and quickly began to dream. Barbara and I were in a split ranch-style house, decorated like Aunt Helen's house, but it wasn't, in someplace suburban that looked like Dix Hills, Long Island, except there were mountains. Then the scene switched to Manhattan and we were in Barbara's old apartment on Eighty-fourth Street. The apartment looked exactly like her old apartment, except the ceilings were much higher and the furniture was different—Danish modern, like the furniture in Aunt Helen's house. Then Barbara became Charlotte and the dream turned horrifying. Charlotte was sitting on my lap, playing with my hair and kissing me. I tried to get her off me, but she was too heavy; then I stood up, trying to walk, but she was still attached to my thighs. Then Charlotte turned into Kenny and I tried to get away from him, but we were stuck like Siamese twins, and he was laughing in his sick, demented way.

I woke up sweating, convinced that Kenny was attached to me. After a few seconds, I realized I'd been dreaming, but I couldn't calm down.

The room was empty and very quiet. I still didn't sense Barbara anywhere.

13

THE NEXT MORNING there were only a few reporters camped in front of the building. As I went down the block they followed me, shouting questions at my back as if I were Princess Di.

Finally I turned around and shouted, "Leave me the hell alone!"

They followed me for another half a block, but gave up as I turned onto Amsterdam. Walking along Seventy-ninth Street, I looked behind me, thankful that the reporters weren't there.

Crossing Broadway, I stepped off the curb while the light was still yellow, and then I heard the loud, screeching brakes. Thanks to quick reflexes, I managed to jerk backward out of the way, just avoiding getting hit by an

SUV. The driver—a young Asian guy—gave me a long, mean stare before he continued on, shaking his head.

I continued down to the subway, feeling shaken up and out of it. Several people on the packed platform seemed to be staring at me, and I wondered if it was because they recognized me from the news last night or if they just thought there was something wrong with me.

I didn't remember that today was my first day at my new job as associate editor until I entered my office building. It was too bad that a blackmailer had pictures of me leaving the body of the man I'd killed against a trash can, and that the world had just found out that my dead girlfriend was a psychotic killer, or I might've had something to look forward to today.

When I got off the elevator, I went right to my new office and tried to get involved in my routine. On my calendar, I had scheduled two early phone interviews with analysts familiar with the operations of PrimeNet Solutions, the DSL company I was doing a story on. I called the analysts who had some doubts about the company. Due to severe competition, unreliable customer service, and a mixed balance sheet, the future of PrimeNet was uncertain. I began writing my article:

Odds are you've never heard of PrimeNet Solutions, but that's about to change. Thanks to a flood of new subscribers and an already satisfied customer base, this resurgent DSL company is about to take charge of Manhattan's high-speed Internet industry.

Writing the positive opening paragraph improved my mood. I outlined the rest of the article and started pulling out the most positive portions of the analysts' quotes. I also came up with a title for the article: "PrimeNet: Primed for Greatness." By later in the morning I was able to block out most of my worries, and I felt almost normal again.

"You're here," Angie said.

I swiveled away from the computer monitor and saw her standing at the entrance to my office with a baffled expression.

"Yeah, I decided to come in," I said. "You know, it being my first day at the new job and all."

"Oh," she said. "I just figured you'd be taking some time off. So how are you?"

"Okay," I said. "I mean, considering."

Angie pulled up a chair and sat across from me. In the fluorescent light I noticed her bleached mustache hairs.

"I was going to call you today anyway," she said. "That Detective Romero talked to me again. This time he came to my apartment."

I felt a surge of panic, wondering why Romero wouldn't leave Angie alone.

"So I guess you heard everything," I said.

"I couldn't believe it," she said. "So is it all true?"

"I guess so."

"Detective Romero told me she might've made a mistake. She might've really meant to kill me."

"I doubt that. Rebecca had a lot of strange friends, and she was probably mixed up in some kind of

275

drug thing downtown."

By the look Angie was giving me, I wasn't sure she believed me.

"It was just really scary," Angie said. "I mean, to even hear something like that."

"They're just following up leads," I said. "They get all kinds of crazy leads they have to explore in cases like these. But I'm telling you, I really doubt it had anything to do with you."

"It's just all so freaky," she said. "I mean, I know it's even freakier for you, but still … So you're really okay?"

"I'm just trying to go on with my life," I said. "Hopefully, in a day or two, everybody'll forget all about this."

Angie looked at me as if she thought I was joking. She left my office and returned with a copy of the *Daily News*. She held the newspaper up and I saw the headline, "MANIAC," with what looked like an old mug shot of Rebecca.

"The *Post* has the same picture except they went with 'PSYCHO' as their headline," Angie said.

I remembered how, months ago, my friends had warned me that Rebecca was psycho and how I'd refused to believe them. I was going to ask Angie to hand me the copy of the *News* so I could read the article, but I decided against it.

"Hopefully it'll all die down by tomorrow," I said, but I knew it wouldn't. This was the type of story that grew and grew. The tabloids would have a field day with it.

"I still can't believe you came in at all today," Angie said. "You should go on vacation to Mexico or someplace. Just lie on the beach for a couple weeks and veg."

"Maybe we could go together."

Angie seemed surprised for a couple of moments, not sure how to react, and then she played along. "Okay, where do you want to go? Puerto Vallarta? Cancun?"

"How about Cozumel?"

"Cool, let's do it," she said. "How long do you want to stay?"

"How about a week?"

"A week it is," she said. "I better go bikini shopping. I better go on a diet too, if I want to fit into it."

"You kidding? You look perfect just the way you are." There was awkward silence, and then I added, "Well, better get back to work."

"Me too," Angie said. "Hey, you up for going to lunch later? Or maybe we could order in?"

"Jeff and I talked about doing lunch today," I said.

"Ooh, an editorial lunch," Angie said jokingly.

I smiled. I could tell she was waiting for me to suggest another time to go to lunch or to do something else, but I didn't say anything.

"Anyway," she said. "Maybe we could do something tomorrow?"

"Yeah, tomorrow," I said, leaving it vague.

Angie left and I tried to lose myself in my work again, but people kept stopping by, interrupting me, to offer their condolences about Rebecca. I thanked everyone graciously, although I really wanted to be left alone.

After Kevin and Amy from Payroll came in together to offer their support, Jeff stopped by.

"I heard what happened," he said. "I'm really sorry."

"Thanks," I said.

"You know, you could've taken some time off, just to rest or—"

"I wanted to get back into the swing of things," I said.

"You sure? Because if you want someone to cover your stories for you, that's no problem. And we don't have to discuss your new editorial duties until later in the week."

"Aren't we having lunch today?"

"I thought you'd want to take a rain check on that."

"No, I really want to go," I said.

"Okay," he said. "I didn't cancel the reservation yet, so I guess I'll come by to pick you up around noon?"

"Sounds great," I said.

As the morning went on the flow of people stopping by my office dwindled, but I kept getting interrupted by phone calls. The media had found out that I worked for *Manhattan Business*, and reporters from all over the country were harassing me, trying to get me to comment about Rebecca. After I hung up on reporters from the *Miami Herald*, the *L.A. Daily News*, the *Minneapolis Star Tribune*, and the *Hartford Current*, I turned on my voice mail. I wrote a rough version of the entire PrimeNet article, in which I described the company's twenty-seven-year-old CEO as "a young Lee Iacocca" and concluded that the company's stock price—it was currently trading at about two bucks a share on the Nasdaq—was a bargain at current levels. When I checked my voice mail there were about a dozen new messages from newspapers and radio stations around the country. There was also a message from Aunt Helen. She said she'd read about me in the newspaper and was very concerned that she couldn't reach me at home. She told me to please call her as soon as I got her message.

I was deleting all the messages when Jeff came into my office and said, "Ready?"

I didn't see how it could possibly be noon already, but it was.

"Let's do it," I said.

Jeff and I went to a steakhouse on Forty-ninth Street. The maitre'd seated us at a table upstairs, and a waiter automatically arrived with a mixed drink and a plate of fried calamari. The waiter asked me what I wanted to drink, and before I could answer Jeff said, "Another Manhattan."

Several minutes later, my drink arrived; then Jeff lifted his—it was already half-gone—and said, "To better days."

"To better days," I said.

We drank. The alcohol was relaxing me, and, for a while, I managed to forget all of my problems. It helped that Jeff was avoiding talking about Rebecca. He went on about his daughter Gretchen, who was the star of her high school soccer team and had just had a small role in her school's production of *Our Town*. I told him about how my sister, Barbara, had played Emily in *Our Town* in our high school production. As he went on, telling me about his daughter, I remembered how Barbara had looked so pretty and confident onstage and how proud I'd been that she was my sister.

"I was so proud of you," I said.

"What?" Jeff said.

"What?" I said.

"You said you're proud of me. Why are you proud of me?"

"Oh, not you, I ... I mean I was just thinking, *Our Town*'s a really great play, isn't it?"

Jeff was looking at me in a confused yet concerned way when the waiter arrived at the table. Jeff ordered another round of drinks, and then the waiter asked me for my lunch order. I said I'd have the Caesar salad with grilled chicken. The waiter didn't bother to ask Jeff for his order; when the waiter was gone, Jeff told me he'd be having the sirloin.

Jeff started telling me all about his country club near his house in Upper Westchester, and I was zoning out, thinking about Barbara onstage again. I stared at Jeff's mouth and concentrated on the words he was saying, but I kept seeing Barbara in the outfit she wore during the play's third act—a white blouse tucked into a knee-length navy skirt. Jeff invited me to come play golf with him sometime. I warned him that I was an awful golfer, and he said that was fine with him; he loved playing with bad golfers because it made him feel better about his own game. I smiled, remembering how, at the end of the play,

Barbara had smiled at me in the front row while the audience applauded.

We ordered another round. I was feeling pleasantly buzzed, but the alcohol was having a noticeably opposite effect on Jeff. As he told me about my new duties at the magazine—in addition to editing I'd have the authority to assign stories to the reporters—I noticed that he was starting to slur. Then, as he went on about how the magazine needed to start covering more provocative local stories to differentiate itself from the national competition, he started cursing and speaking in a louder voice. I declined a fourth drink, but as Jeff had his he suddenly started telling me a joke about a priest who had sex with a gorilla. He said the punch line in a booming voice, and two women at a nearby table who seemed to be having a business lunch kept glaring in our direction.

When Jeff stopped laughing, he said, "I got another one for you—a guy goes into a proctologist's office," and I suddenly started feeling nauseous. I was hoping it was just indigestion, but then the discomfort started moving higher, from my stomach toward my throat, and I knew I was about to get sick.

"Excuse me," I managed to say as Jeff was still telling the joke.

Keeling over, holding my stomach, I headed toward the bathroom. I was feeling even sicker, and I didn't think I'd make it to the toilet. I thought about solid things—wood, cement, bricks—and I reached the bowl just as I was starting to yak. After a few minutes I thought I was through, but the sour taste lingering in my mouth reminded me of the last time I threw up—in Charlotte's bathroom—and I threw up again.

I was sweating badly, and then my knees buckled as I started to stand and I had to grab onto the toilet paper roll to steady myself. Finally I made it to my feet and over to the sink. I stared at the mirror. My eyes were bloodshot and my mouth was sagging open. Splashing a few handfuls of cold water against my face didn't make me look or feel any better. I gargled a few times, and then I left the bathroom and headed back toward my table.

Jeff was arguing with the waiter, but I couldn't hear what they were saying. The waiter had his back to me, and Jeff's face was pink as he spoke in an animated way, gesticulating with his arms. As I got closer to the table, I heard Jeff saying, "… and you're telling me this meat is rare? There's no blood in it. Show me the blood. Show me the fuckin' blood!"

The waiter, a young blond guy, said calmly, "Would you like me to bring the dish back, sir?"

"For what?" Jeff's thin salt-and-pepper hair was usually combed straight back, but now loose strands were hanging over his eyes. "What're you gonna do, *un*cook it?"

The waiter was acting as if he'd seen outbursts like this from Jeff many times before. "We can cook you a new order, sir."

"Yeah, and I'll have to wait another twenty fucking

minutes to eat. Did you tell the chef I wanted rare? Did you tell him or did you forget?"

"I told him, sir."

"Sure you did." Jeff looked toward me, but didn't make eye contact. "See? This is what happens when they don't hire professional waiters and they hire fucking actors instead."

"Would you like me to take your dish back, sir?"

"Do whatever the fuck you want," Jeff said. "I'm not eating that shit."

Jeff was shaking his head and cursing to himself; he didn't seem to notice me as I joined him at the table. My salad had arrived, but just looking at food brought back memories of the toilet bowl and I had to cover the dish with my napkin.

"What?" Jeff said. "Something wrong with your food too?"

"I'm just not feeling very well," I said.

"It was probably the calamari," Jeff said, and then he downed the rest of his drink. As he signaled to the waiter for another, he said, "Take a good look at me in this shithole. This is the last time I'm coming here. Four, maybe five years ago the food was great. The last couple of years it started going downhill. Now they should serve it in a fucking feedbag."

Another drink was brought to Jeff. As he drank it he quickly deteriorated into full-blown drunkenness. He was cursing, spraying spit, talking too loud. When he got back to the office he'd probably fire an intern or two.

As another wave of nausea overcame me I said, "Maybe we should just go."

"Good idea," Jeff said. "What do you say to some Japanese?" He pulled on the sides of his face with his index fingers, slitting his eyes.

"I think I'm just gonna get back to the office," I said.

"Come on, don't be a wimp," he said. "The afternoon's young."

I felt like I was at some college frat party and a guy was trying to peer-pressure me into drinking. I got up and went outside. Breathing in the fresh air—if you'd consider the air in midtown fresh—didn't help much. I still felt sick, and I wondered if I had a virus or if maybe Jeff had been right about the calamari.

Jeff came out of the restaurant, mumbling to himself, and we headed up the block; he was walking half a stride ahead of me, as if I weren't there.

At the corner, I said, "Jeff, I don't want to hold you back. If you want to go someplace else—"

He grunted, then said, "It's all right. I'll just order a sandwich or something."

We didn't say anything else to each other until we were back in the office and I said, "See you later," and he said, "Yeah, later." Then I branched off along a different corridor and went into my office.

I had gotten about ten more messages from reporters and one message from Aunt Helen. She sounded even more concerned than before and told me to please call her back as soon as possible.

I still felt zonked out and really didn't feel like talking to her, but I didn't want her to worry about me.

"Hi, Helen."

"David, where are you?"

"Work."

"I was calling you at home too—I thought you'd be there today. So is it all true?"

"Looks that way."

"You poor thing—I'm so sorry."

"It's okay—thanks."

"So you had no idea? I mean, about her husband in Los Angeles."

"No," I said, suddenly feeling clammy.

"It's so awful," Aunt Helen said. "All of it. I'm just glad to hear you're safe."

"You don't have to worry about me."

"Tell me something, David. Does this have anything to do with the money you borrowed?"

"No, of course not," I said.

"Oh, because I was just wondering," she said, "because you were so secretive about it, and then I heard about this and ... I just thought I'd ask, that's all."

It was hard to think clearly with the way I felt, but I realized that Helen's trying to make a connection about the money could be a potential problem. If, for some reason, the police started investigating me, they could talk to Helen. She'd tell them about the thousand dollars I'd borrowed, and they'd wonder if I'd given Rebecca money for drugs, or if I were involved some other way.

"That money was for a class at the Princeton Review," I said.

"The Princeton Review?" Aunt Helen said.

"Yeah," I said. "I wanted to see how I did on the test before I told you about it, but I'm studying to take the GMATs. You know, so I can get into an MBA program."

"That's wonderful!" Aunt Helen said. Then her voice became distant as she said to someone else in the office, "My nephew's going to get an MBA." I heard a woman's voice say, "Mazel tov."

I knew the MBA lie would make Aunt Helen happy. After college, before I got my job at the *Journal*, she used to nag me to apply to grad school every time I saw her.

"So what're you going to do with your MBA?" she asked.

"I don't know, probably get a job as a stock analyst," I said. "You know how much those guys make? Mid six figures or more."

"I think that's great, David." Then, as if suddenly remembering why she'd called, she said, "I just wanted to tell you—if you want to come stay with me, you know you're always—"

"That's all right," I said.

"Are you sure?" she said. "Because I know how—"

"Positive," I said.

I heard her breathe deeply, as if she were frustrated with my stubbornness.

"I know you're going to put up a stink about this, David, but I'm going to say it anyway. I really think you should see my friend Alice's son Benjamin, the grief counselor. Even if you only have one session with him—"

"It's not necessary," I said.

"Are you sure, David? Because now I think you have even more reason to—"

"It's okay—"

"—discuss what you're feeling—"

"It's okay—"

"—with a professional—"

"I said it's okay," I snapped. Then, in a calmer voice, I said, "I'm sorry, Helen. I really appreciate all your concern, but I can handle this myself—I really can."

"I want you to call me tonight," she said.

"I will," I lied.

"Promise."

"Yes."

"I love you."

"I love you, too."

Hanging up was a huge relief. I made sure the voice mail was still on, and then I locked the door to my office and started working again. I still felt weak, but not as bad as I'd felt inside the restaurant; in a few hours I'd probably be fine.

I worked on another draft of my PrimeNet article, and then Matt Stern, a young reporter at the magazine, sent me his article to edit. It was a well-written piece about a chain of watch stores that were expanding around the tri-state area. If Peter Lyons were still associate editor he would've decimated the article, extending the sentences into run-ons and adding adverbs and Britishisms. But I edited with a light hand, enhancing Matt's own style, rather than imposing my own. When I was through I read the article over and was very pleased. I was a damn good editor.

Toward five o'clock, the effects of whatever had gotten me sick earlier had almost completely worn off. On my way home, I picked up some safe food to eat—bread, yogurt, ginger ale, and bananas. I was relieved to see only a few reporters camped out in front of my building, and I ignored the questions they shouted at me as I went inside. When I opened the door to my apartment, the phone started ringing. Figuring it was another reporter, I let the machine pick up, then heard Detective Romero saying, "Yeah, it's Romero, NYPD again. When you get home can you please—"

I picked up and said, "Hello?"

"Mr. Miller?"

"Yes, hi."

"I tried you a couple times today."

"I was at work."

"Really?" he said. "I'm surprised you didn't take some time off."

"What's going on?" I asked.

Although I detected some suspicion in his voice, I wasn't very concerned. I figured if there had been a really important development he wouldn't be contacting me by telephone.

"Well, we've been continuing our investigation, but unfortunately we haven't made much progress. We're still not sure why Rebecca Daniels killed Charlotte O'Dougal, but it's this other murder—Ricardo Alvarado—that's getting at us. Alvarado was a strong guy. We just don't buy that Rebecca Daniels was able to kill him, causing those kind of head injuries. On the other hand, when a guy and his girlfriend are killed less than a couple days apart we gotta think there's some connection."

"I don't know what to tell you," I said.

"I was hoping you might've thought of something you didn't tell us yesterday," Romero said. "We checked out those clubs you mentioned, but that didn't get us anywhere. You have any other ideas how your girlfriend might've come into contact with Alvarado?"

"If I did, I would've called you."

"Sometimes people forget things, or they think something's not important so they don't bother—"

"I didn't forget anything."

"I understand that, Mr. Miller, but I'm conducting an investigation—"

"There's nothing to investigate," I said, nearly screaming. "You know Rebecca killed that woman, and it's obvious she had nothing to do with killing Alvarado."

"Why is that obvious?"

I realized I was talking too much and I'd better shut up.

"Because," I said, "like you said, he was a strong guy and—I don't know, okay? Maybe Rebecca did kill him, but I told you everything I know."

"Very well," Romero said. "But if anything else comes up I'm going to contact you again. I'm sure you won't hesitate to do the same."

A few minutes later I was putting the groceries away, wishing I hadn't lost my cool. Rather than saying it was obvious that Rebecca hadn't killed Ricky, I should've tried to convince Romero that Rebecca had done it, suddenly remembering some story about a drug dealer she was in debt to. I feared that the longer Romero dug around, trying to figure out what had happened to Ricky, the more likely he'd stumble on the truth.

I had other messages on my machine and I played all of them. Aside from the messages from Romero and Aunt Helen, a few of my old friends had called, saying that they'd read about Rebecca in the papers and wanted to check on how I was doing.

I ate half a banana and a spoonful of yogurt, but I was too aggravated to eat anything else. I imagined Romero questioning Kenny, and Kenny turning me in or holding out to blackmail me—either way I'd lose. I considered beating Kenny to the punch and calling Romero back. I could swear that Ricky's death had been an accident, but why would Romero believe me now? It wouldn't help my case that Charlotte, the only person who could back up my story, was dead.

I was short of breath and starting to sweat.

"I need some space," Barbara said.

"Oh, stop," I said.

"I'm serious," she said. "I think one of us should move—leave New York."

"What're you talking about?"

"I applied to some firms in San Francisco."

"What?"

"And if I get a good offer, I'm leaving."

"Why the hell're you gonna do that?"

"To get away from you."

"Is this more crap from Dr. Kellerman?"

"No, this is what I think."

"Yeah, right. What else did Kellerman say about me?"

"Listen to me—this'll be good for you too. You'd be better off with me gone. You could meet somebody, have a normal relationship—"

"You just need a vacation. Maybe we should go someplace, the Berkshires or Vermont, or how about Europe? I saw an ad in the paper for cheap tickets to Paris."

"You have to be your own person, David. You have to be a leader, not a follower—"

"What're you talking about?"

"You can't depend on me so much—you can't follow me everywhere."

"You're not leaving me."

"Yes I am."

"If you go to San Francisco I'm going with you."

"You can't do that."

"Oh, yes I can."

* * *

When I left for work in the morning all the reporters were gone, and I decided this was a sign that things might work out for me after all. Some new story had probably broken that was more interesting than Rebecca's, and pretty soon Rebecca's story would fade completely. As for Kenny, now that he was being questioned and maybe watched by the police he'd probably decide that trying to blackmail me was too much trouble. If I was lucky, I'd never hear from him again.

At work, I remained in my office most of the day, editing several articles. I also worked on my PrimeNet article, which was getting even more positive. A few newspaper and TV reporters had left messages on my voice mail, but the Rebecca murder/suicide story definitely seemed to be petering out. Around lunchtime Angie dropped by, suggesting we go out, but I told her I was too busy. Later in the day I saw her talking to another reporter in the corridor outside my office, and I went in a different direction to avoid her.

On my way home, I said to Barbara, "Okay, you want me to become my own person—I'll become my own person."

I stopped at a wine store on Amsterdam and decided I'd become a wine expert. I usually never spent more than ten bucks on wine, but I asked the owner to suggest a cabernet in the thirty-dollar range. At home, I sipped the Chateau Montelena with my eyes closed, trying to appreciate its nuances, and then I decided I'd have to make other changes in my life. I'd throw out my rock CDs and replace them with a collection of light jazz and classical. I'd redecorate my apartment, get classier furniture from Restoration Hardware or Ethan Allen. And I'd take a class at the Culinary Institute, learn how to cook French food.

Wednesday morning I was still feeling upbeat about myself and the future when I entered my office building and got the shit kicked out of me. It happened so fast I didn't realize what was happening until I was on my back in front of the revolving door and punches were landing against my face. Finally, a security guard pulled Robert Lipton off of me.

Lipton looked like a wreck—his thin gray hair hanging over his scruffy face, his eyes swollen and puffy, as if he hadn't gotten any sleep in days. I realized that the edition of *Manhattan Business* with the negative article I'd written about Lipton's company had hit the newsstands.

"Son of a bitch!" he screamed at me as the guard held him back. "I'll kill you! I'll fuckin' kill you!"

He continued yelling, telling me that, thanks to my article, he'd lost three of his biggest clients. Two cops showed up. After the security guard explained what had happened, one of the cops asked me if I wanted to press charges. I declined. I didn't want any unnecessary involvement with the police, but I also felt bad about what I'd done to Lipton and I didn't want to screw up his life more than I already had.

The injuries to my face from Ricky and Rebecca had almost disappeared, but now I had a fresh welt on my left cheekbone and my upper lip was swollen and bleeding.

The security guard had given me a first-aid ice pack, but Lipton had gotten a few good whacks in and it didn't help much. I was hoping to lock myself in my office and stay there all day to avoid any attention, but Mike, the guy Angie had dated, had been downstairs in the lobby while the cops were talking to me, and when I arrived in the office he had already told everyone what had happened. Holding the icepack up to my face, I had to hold court in the office's reception area, giving my account of the incident. Everyone expressed their sympathy, and then Jeff took me aside and tried to persuade me to press charges.

"It's okay," I said. "I'd rather just forget about it."

"You sure?" Jeff said. "Because we could send that prick to jail."

I explained to Jeff that, given everything I'd been through lately, I didn't want any more turmoil in my life. Jeff said he understood, but he still thought I was making a mistake.

In my office, I tried to block out what had happened with Lipton and focus on work. A few articles had been e-mailed to me for editing, including one of Angie's. Since I'd been at *Manhattan Business* I'd always written my articles as quickly as possible, treating my work simply as a job, a means of making money. Now, as an editor, I worked much more diligently, laboring over every word, making sure each sentence was as good as it could possibly be. The only break I took from work all day was during my lunch hour, when I browsed the Net for information about upcoming wine tastings in the New York area.

Thursday was a repeat of Wednesday, minus the attack by Lipton. I was enjoying working late and spending a lot of time alone. For months I'd been so absorbed in Rebecca and our problems that I'd barely had time to myself, and now I enjoyed coming home to a quiet apartment.

Friday morning I was waiting for the elevator in the lobby when Angie appeared behind me. We exchanged hellos, and then the elevator arrived. Other people got on with us, so we didn't talk during the ride up. When we got out on our floor I said, "See ya later," and headed toward my office. Several minutes later I was settling in to start my workday when Angie entered and said, "Can I come in?"

"Sure," I said.

She came farther into my office, but remained standing.

"Look," she said, "I know awful things happened this week and I totally understand that, but I still don't understand why you have to treat me this way."

"What do you mean?"

"Come on, all week you've been blowing me off, pretending that I don't exist. Didn't you even notice we've barely been talking to each other?"

"I've been busy," I said.

"I can't do this anymore," she said. "I mean, if you just need some space I totally understand that, and if you want me to back off I will. But if there's more to it—I mean, if you're angry at me for something, or if I did something wrong—"

"Have dinner with me tonight."

She waited, then said, "Really?"

"I'll come by your place at eight o'clock. Come on, what do you say?"

"Okay," she said, "but if you wanted to go out, why have you been blowing me off?"

"Because I was a jerk, that's why. I really want to take you out tonight. What do you say?"

She stared at me for a few seconds; then the corners of her lips curled into a slight smile.

"All right," she said.

"Great," I said.

She gave me her address on East Seventy-fourth, and I told her how much I was looking forward to tonight.

Later in the morning, I went downtown to interview the CFO of PrimeNet Solutions. During the interview I kept zoning out, thinking about Angie and getting excited about our first date. Back at my office, I conducted a few phone interviews for the PrimeNet article and had to edit the text for next week's Company Report section. I was going to stop by Angie's cubicle to say hi; then I had a better idea. I sent her a bouquet of virtual flowers with a message that read, *Thanks for being so patient.* After she received the bouquet she IM'd me, telling me how sweet I was.

I'd been staying at the office until seven-thirty, eight o'clock the past couple of days, but today I figured I'd leave at around six, which would give me plenty of time to go home, shower, and change before I went to Angie's.

Around five forty-five, I finished up my work and went to the bathroom. At the urinal, Kyle from Sales told me a long story about his misadventures of trying to sell his East Side co-op. I continued chatting with him for a while outside the bathroom, then headed back toward my office, deciding that I'd take Angie out to a restaurant near her apartment, maybe to one of those little romantic Italian places off Second. It was going to be perfect, I thought, and then I entered my office and saw Kenny, reclining in my chair with his feet resting on my desk.

14

H E LOOKED THE same as the last time I'd seen him, at the bar the night I was pickpocketed. His long hair was messy and greasy, and he had about a week's worth of beard growth. He was wearing a light blue short-sleeved button down shirt, but he'd missed a couple of buttons and I could see his wife-beater tank top and sweaty chest hair. His body odor—a combination of sweat and Old Spice—had permeated my office.

"How'd you get in here?" I asked, although this was the last thing I cared about.

"I told the girl up front you were doing an article about me," he said. "This is a business magazine, right? So how 'bout you do a thing about the blackmailing business? Come in, interview me, I'll tell you exactly how it's done."

"What do you want?"

He laughed, then said, "Besides all your money?" and continued laughing. Finally he calmed down and said, "What do I want? That's a good one. Please, man. If you make me laugh any more I'm gonna pull something." He stared at me seriously, then said, "If I really wanted you to put me in your magazine you'd have to do it. If I wanted you to run around this office screaming, 'Suck my hairy cock! Suck my hairy cock!' you'd have to do that too!"

Kenny's voice tended to boom, and I was afraid other people in the office might overhear what he was saying.

"But I gotta admit, you had me scared there for a while," he said. "When the cops came to me and told me about Charlotte, I thought you did her. I mean, it woulda made sense. She comes to you with the pictures, asks you for the money, then you whack her. Actually, you should thank me for saving your ass. That first night the cops were coming down heavy on me, they thought I did Charlotte *and* Ricky. They had me in lockup overnight. I was almost gonna finger you for both raps, but then the cops came to me and said they found out your little girlfriend did Charlotte. At first I didn't know what to think; then I was glad 'cause I knew you were still my butt boy for Ricky's murder."

"I didn't murder him," I said.

"And I'm Mother fuckin' Teresa," Kenny said. "Tell me, was this a hobby for you and your psycho bitch girlfriend? You went around town killing people for kicks?"

"I think you should get out of here," I said.

"Excuse me?"

"You heard me."

"I don't think you understand what's going on here," he said. "I control you now, not the other way around, you fuckin' prick. I tell you what to do and you do it. Maybe I *should* make you take your pants down and run around here—that'd be a fuckin' riot." Kenny laughed. "You gotta give me credit—I was pretty swift, wasn't I? I mean taking them pictures in the first place. I knew something was going on that night, the way Charlotte was acting, all fucked up, but I didn't know what. Then, when I got her outside, I got her to spill it. You shoulda seen her, shittin' bricks. She thought I was gonna take you both down; then I told her I was just gonna go after you—'cause you killed Ricky. I told her we could take you for everything you're worth, and look what happened—I am!" Kenny laughed. "I told her, 'Just make sure he takes the body down alone and I'll take care of the rest.' Of course, she went along with it when she realized she could make a few bucks. Holding money in front of her was like putting a dick in front of Linda Lovelace's mouth. Yeah, Charlotte was a sweet little whore, all right, I'll give her that much. I'll miss her; I really will miss her. She knew how to suck cock like a pro, and you don't see that in a lot of whores these days. Most whores use their teeth and start biting on you like you're a fuckin' hot dog. But Charlotte knew how to deep-throat it, all right. She took it up the ass, too. You gotta respect a whore for that. A lot of whores these days won't let you anywhere near their assholes."

Kenny laughed again, then said, "Charlotte tell you about my will?"

I didn't bother answering.

"I made up a will," he went on. "I paid a lawyer to do it, so it's real official and everything. When I die an envelope gets opened. I wrote out the whole thing—how I saw you kill Ricky, how you said you'd kill me if I went to the cops. I got copies of the pictures in there too, with your name and everything. So you see how you can't win, Davey boy. You better hope I live a long life, because when I die you go to jail. Until then, you gotta do whatever the fuck I tell you to do. I don't know if you knew this, but there's no statute of limitations on murder. I could die thirty years from now and they'd still put you away."

I looked at Kenny deadpan for several seconds, then said, "I don't have any money." I let this sink in, then added, "I gave everything I had to Charlotte that night, and I don't know what happened to it, if she spent it on drugs or whatever, but I don't have any more. That's the God's honest truth."

Kenny's eyes narrowed. "Listen to me, you fuckin' dick. I don't think you understand what's going on here. I'm the one calling the shots, not you. You think I don't know you're full of shit? I know more than you think I know, and don't you worry, I'm gonna make you pay for what you did. Charlotte was a nice little whore and I'll miss her, but Ricky was my homeboy. We dropped out of high school together—I knew him twenty years and loved him like a brother. You took my brother away from me, you scumbag, and I'm gonna make you pay for it."

"It was an accident," I said. "He was coming after me—"

"I did some research," Kenny went on, ignoring me. "I called here the other day, and my friend the receptionist told me you're the associate editor—just got promoted. Congratulations, by the way. So then I went to the library—you know, the big one on Fortieth—and they got this book there. You look up somebody's job; they tell you how much they make. The book says an associate editor takes in thirty-five to seventy-five a year. So I figure you're probably making fifty a year now, give or take. After Uncle Sam, you probably take home about two grand a month. I don't want you to go broke—that won't help me any. What I'm gonna do is take half. I figure if I leave you with a thousand a month you'll be able to pay your bills, buy some food, and I'll get the rest."

"My rent's sixteen-fifty a month," I said.

"That's your problem, not mine," Kenny said. "If you can't get by, you'll have to get a night job, scrub floors or some shit. But you'll get by somehow, and as long as you get by, I get by. See how this is gonna work?"

"What if I lose my job?" I said.

"I guess you'll have to find another one. But first—just to get us started—I want that twenty grand."

"I don't have twenty grand."

"Get it."

"I can't get it. I have nowhere to get it from."

"You must got retirement money, a 401(k) or some shit like that."

Last time I checked, I had about fifty thousand dollars in my 401(k), and I also had a Roth IRA with about fifteen grand.

"Sorry," I said. "I got wiped out when the market crashed."

"You must got something in it."

"Maybe a couple grand."

"Take it out and give it to me."

"I can't. There're forms to fill out—paperwork. It could take a few days to get the money, and I'll have penalties and—"

"Look, I don't wanna hear any more of your bullshit," Kenny said. "I want at least two grand tonight. If you don't bring it, I'm gonna go to the cops. You think I'm fucking around?"

Kenny stood up. I couldn't tell if his gut was bigger than I'd remembered or if he just had bad posture.

"Tonight," he said, "ten o'clock—Tompkins Square Park."

"I can't tonight," I said.

"Yes, you can," he said. "You know, it's kind of—I don't know the word—funny. Not funny, but you know what I mean. That's where Charlotte said you were gonna dump Ricky's body and now that's where you're gonna be making your payoffs. Hopefully every time you go there it'll remind you what you did, you piece of shit. The last Friday of every month you're gonna be there with my thousand bucks, but tonight it's gonna be two grand or I'm going to the cops. Ironical. That's the word I was looking for. It's ironical."

Kenny explained which bench in the park he'd be waiting on, and then he left my office, leaving his odor of Old Spice and BO behind. Gradually it set in that my life was ruined.

I didn't move for a while, and then I called Angie at home and left a message on her machine, canceling our date tonight. I told her that there had been an emergency with my aunt and I had to go to Long Island for the weekend. I didn't know how I'd come up with Kenny's payments. With the rest of the money Aunt Helen had lent me and the paycheck that had been direct-deposited into my bank account this morning, I could scrape up the money for the first two grand. After that, unless I drained my retirement accounts, I was in trouble. I'd have to live on Kraft macaroni and cheese and Ramen noodles, and I'd probably have to work nights and weekends.

Since I didn't have to meet Kenny until ten and I had no reason to go home, I stayed late at work. When Jeff left for the day, at around six-thirty, he poked his head into my office and said, "I love your work ethic, David. You're showing true commitment to this job. See ya tomorrow."

A couple of people in Production stayed until around seven, and then I had the office to myself; the only sounds were the hum of the air-conditioning system and an occasional horn or siren from Broadway. I didn't feel like sitting around doing nothing, so I wrote a final draft of my article on PrimeNet Solutions. Earlier in the article I'd mentioned how PrimeNet had been the major sponsor of a sailing competition, so, continuing with the metaphor, I wrote:

> PrimeNet has weathered a great storm, and if the company stays on its current course, and market winds remain steady, the future for this DSL firm will be full of blue skies and clear sailing.

When I finished the article, I did some editing, then left my office at about nine-fifteen.

The businessmen who cluttered the midtown streets during the day had been replaced by tourists and teenagers. I went to an ATM, withdrew the rest of the money I needed from my bank account and by taking a cash advance on my Discover card, and then I took the subway downtown.

I arrived at the Avenue A entrance to Tompkins Square Park at five to ten. The park at night didn't seem nearly as spruced up as it did during the day. As I headed along the path toward the middle of the park, I passed groups of seedy-looking guys, obviously drug dealers, huddled around trees or benches. One skinny black guy rushed up to me, walking alongside me, and asked if I was buying. I shrugged him off without saying anything and continued straight ahead.

I passed the circular, courtyard-like area in the middle of the park, and kept going. On the bench where Kenny had said I should meet him, a big, bearded homeless guy was sprawled out with an old baby carriage filled with bottles, cans, and other junk parked in front of him. The guy's head was hanging to the side and his eyes were half-open; he looked dead, but he was probably just sleeping. I sat on the opposite end of the bench and checked the time on my cell phone—two minutes to ten.

Two minutes later, Kenny arrived. He was walking along the path, coming from the direction of the Avenue B entrance. I waited until he reached me before I stood up.

"On time, I like that," he said. "This is how I want it to go every time, you get my drift? None of that waiting-around-for-you-to-show-up bullshit."

I'd been planning to give him the money and leave without doing or saying anything, but I hesitated, asking myself if I really wanted to give in to this scumbag. Maybe he was lying about having a will and other pictures put away. Maybe there was another way out.

"What're you waiting for?" he said. "Dig."

I continued staring at him.

"Come on, stop bullshitting around," Kenny said. "I got a whore to fuck tonight and she doesn't like it when I keep her waiting. Come on, just give me the fuckin' money."

"Maybe we should go someplace else," I said, glancing toward the homeless guy.

"What, that fuckin' bum?" Kenny said. "He probably doesn't know what year it is. Just gimme the money so I can get outta here."

The homeless guy stirred, his head jerking a couple of times.

"All right, all right," Kenny said.

He walked along the path, back toward Avenue B, and I followed him. The path was well lit by a small lamppost.

"This way," I said.

I veered off the path, through an opening in the short fence, onto an area of dirt and grass.

"What the fuck?" Kenny said.

I kept walking. Looking over my shoulder slightly, I saw that Kenny was following me. I stopped in a dark area between two trees.

"Are we done walkin' now, Moses?" Kenny said. He was two or three feet away from me. "You better have that fuckin' money, because if you're shittin' me around, I swear, I'm goin' to the cops."

"Who's that?" I said.

When Kenny turned his head I grabbed his throat. I was in an awkward position, too far away to strangle him effectively, but I'd surprised him, which gave me an advantage. I squeezed harder and his neck seemed to be shrinking between my hands, and then he reached up and grabbed my wrists and my grip loosened.

"You fuckin' crazy?" he said in a gargled, muffled voice. "I got the pictures, I got the—"

I forced him back against a tree and squeezed harder. I wasn't letting go this time; I'd keep squeezing for as long as I had to. My nails were digging into his throat, and I figured it couldn't take much longer, maybe five or ten more seconds. Then Kenny forced me backward and I stumbled. I tried to grab his throat again, but he tackled me hard to the ground. He tried to pin me down, but I fought back and managed to get up again. He came after me and I grabbed him around the shoulders and got him in a headlock. I remembered ramming Ricky's head against the door, and I wanted to ram Kenny's head into the tree. But the tree was behind me somewhere, and Kenny was fighting hard and wouldn't let me turn him around, so I started twisting his head, trying to break his neck.

"Let go," Kenny said. "You stupid piece of shit. Let—"

I twisted his head further, waiting for his neck to break, and then I heard the shot and felt the excruciating pain in my stomach. Kenny was kneeling over me, holding a gun.

"Fuckin' moron," he said. "What the fuck's wrong with you, you dick?" He reached into my pocket and took the money out of my wallet, and then he stood up all the way and ran.

I tried to go after him, but when I got up onto my knees, I crumpled right back down onto my side. My stomach killed, as if the bullet were still working its way inside me. I felt the warm, wet area where the pain was centered; then I looked at my bloody hands.

I lay still, with my face pressed against the dirt, waiting to die. It was hard to breathe and I was too weak to get up, so I knew it would happen soon. I was very dizzy and I was having flashbacks. I was five years old and Barbara was seven, but she looked younger. We were playing in the snow in Aunt Helen's backyard. We were laughing, running around, throwing snowballs at each other. Then the images started coming faster. We were in Helen's finished basement, thumb-wrestling. We were adults, walking up Broadway and laughing. We were kids, playing on a slide in a park as our parents watched. We were lying in the sun in the Sheep Meadow. We were on campus at Syracuse. We were at our parents' funeral. We were Rollerblading down the steep hill near the Met. We were watching *Pretty Woman*. We were shopping at Banana Republic. We were walking in the rain along West Eighty-first Street. We were fighting about Jay. We were throwing snowballs at trees. We were laughing in Aunt Helen's basement. We were listening to the Police. We were running around Aunt Helen's backyard. We were thumb-wrestling. We were in a snowstorm. We were—

My body tingled and there was sudden pressure in my head and throat. I felt numb and weightless, and then, an instant later, I was dead.

15

A MAN WITH a thick gray mustache and cigarette-stained teeth said, "I saw his eyes open; I saw 'em open."

A woman next to the man was doing something to my stomach. Something was over my face, and my throat killed.

* * *

I didn't know where I was. I tried to scream, but I couldn't. I was fucking freezing.

* * *

I woke up, still very weak. I turned my head to the right and saw the tubes or IVs or whatever was connected to my body.

A nurse appeared over me and said, smiling, "Look who's awake."

I couldn't speak.

"This'll make you feel better," she said. A few minutes later I was dreaming again.

* * *

The next time I opened my eyes I was angry because my throat still killed. I pressed the call button on the string next to my bed, and a Haitian or West Indian nurse came. I lifted my hand toward my mouth, as if lifting a cup to drink.

"Sorry, you won't be able to drink for a while longer. Let me check your stitches."

The nurse lifted my gown and examined my stomach area.

"Looking good," she said.

She said that a doctor was going to see me soon, and she left the room. I stared at the TV hanging over my bed, which was blasting CNN. About an hour later, a skinny, balding doctor who looked about five years younger than me came into my room. He looked at my chart, then said to me, "I know you can't talk, so just nod yes or no. Can you do that?"

I didn't feel like having to talk to this asshole, but I figured if I answered his questions he'd leave me alone sooner. I nodded slowly.

"You're a very lucky man," he said. "Do you remember what happened to you?"

I nodded again.

"That's good," he said, "that's very good. Do you remember how it happened?"

I changed my mind—I didn't feel like cooperating. I shook my head.

"You don't know how it happened?"

I nodded.

"Ah, so you know how it happened, you just don't know who did it to you."

I looked away, shaking my head.

"Well, your injury was quite severe," the doctor went on. "You lost quite a bit of blood, and the EMS workers said you didn't have a pulse when they arrived at the scene. You had two transfusions and seem to have stabilized, although your spleen was ruptured and you sustained a serious stomach injury. Physically, you're doing much better, but you suffered a period of anoxia, a cutoff of blood flow to the brain, the effects of which we'll need to monitor. But, I have to say, you're a lucky man, Mr. Miller. If that homeless man didn't find you and call for

313

help, you probably—no, you definitely wouldn't've made it."

I remembered seeing the homeless man lifting me up and dragging me out of the park. I'd been standing off to the side with Barbara, watching it all happen.

"By the way," the doctor continued, "there're quite a large number of reporters downstairs. I had to comment on your condition, but I'm trying to respect your privacy as much as possible. There's also a Detective Romero who wants to speak with you, but I told him that wouldn't be possible until we remove you from the respirator, which should be later today."

I tried to ask the doctor if I'd been legally dead, but with the tube in my mouth I couldn't speak.

"Don't waste your energy," the doctor said. "Just get some rest."

* * *

That night, after I was taken off the respirator, Detective Romero insisted on questioning me. He pulled up a chair next to my bed, but I looked away, refusing to make eye contact.

"How you feeling?" he asked.

I continued staring away.

"Take this," he said. "I know it's hard for you to talk, so I figured you could write down answers to my questions."

I looked over and saw he was holding a pad and a pen out to me. I hesitated before taking them from him.

"Who shot you?" he asked.

I wrote on the pad, *I don't remember.*

"What were you doing in the park?" he asked.

I underlined what I had already written.

"Were you going to meet somebody? Maybe a friend, a drug dealer?"

I underlined the words two more times and added, *Leave me the fuck alone.*

Romero continued to question me, but I stuck to my story that I didn't remember anything that had happened after I left my office. Romero finally got frustrated and said he'd come talk to me again in a couple of days, and then he left.

I knew Romero hadn't bought my amnesia story, but I was going to stick with it anyway. The idea had come to me earlier in the day—if I kept my mouth shut about who had shot me, Kenny wouldn't be able to blackmail me anymore. Now we had something on each other—if he tried to blackmail me, I could have him arrested for attempted murder. As for the police, I'd just continue to play dumb about everything and eventually they'd leave me alone.

I slept miserably. I woke up every few minutes with a dry, irritated throat, and they must not've been giving me enough Percocet, because my entire body killed. In the morning, after my first solid food in nearly three days, my strength started to return. Around noon, a short-haired, very thin, dykey-looking woman came into my room. She said she was a neuropsychologist. After she asked me to say my name, my age, what city and state I was in, the date, and a bunch of other things, she made me repeat numbers and words back to her.

"Okay," she said. "Now turn over the paper, hand me the pen, and point to your nose."

I handed her the pen, pointed to my nose, then turned over the paper, but I only screwed up because I was bored stiff and just wanted her to leave me alone. After asking me some more dumb questions and having me identify pictures and shapes, the woman explained that I was suffering from the aftereffects of anoxia. She said my memory would probably improve over time, but that I'd continue to exhibit on-going symptoms, such as irritability, impulsiveness, and disinhibition. As she spoke to me, I just stared at her, half smiling, thinking, Who the hell did she think she was kidding? She wanted to bill my insurance company for as much as she could, so she was making it out like I had brain damage. There was nothing wrong with my brain. My brain was perfect.

Later, a doctor examined me and checked my charts and told me that, assuming there were no complications, I'd be discharged from the hospital in a few weeks. I'd have to do about a month of rehab, and then I'd be back home, as good as new.

In the afternoon Aunt Helen visited. When I saw her wrinkled face and maroon hair, I remembered what an annoying old bitch she was. I didn't feel like getting her sympathy or listening to her nagging me to see psychiatrists and grief counselors so I lied and told her I was too exhausted to see her. Thank God she left quickly.

A few minutes later I started to panic when I realized I didn't know where my wallet was. My pants had been taken off and I feared that my wallet had been lost or stolen.

"Where's my wallet?" I screamed. "Where the fuck's my wallet!"

An aide, an old Chinese woman, came into the room and said, "What's wrong?"

"My wallet," I said. "Where the hell is it?"

"Your personal items are in this drawer," she said.

She opened the night table drawer and handed me the wallet. I immediately opened it and checked behind my driver's license and, thank God, the picture was still there. I kissed it twice; then I propped it up against the phone on the night table so I could look at it all the time.

After the dinner trays were collected, the fat, ugly nurse entered my room to give me my medication.

"Hey, where the hell's my juice?" I said. "I asked for more apple juice an hour ago."

"I'll bring it right away," she said.

A few minutes later Angie arrived. I immediately noticed the weight she had gained in her face and that her mustache looked darker than ever. I wasn't in the mood to see her.

"How're you feeling?" she asked.

"Exhausted," I said, hoping she'd get the message.

"I'm sorry," she said, "I'll let you rest. I just wanted to say hi and see how you were doing, and I wanted to give you this."

She handed me a large envelope. I slid out the card and opened it. It read, *Get well soon!* with some other crap below it, and was signed by people from the office. I looked at a few of the signatures, noticing Jeff's, larger than anyone else's, and then I tossed the card onto the floor.

Angie gave me a funny look, as if I'd done something to insult her.

"So," she said, "how are you?"

"Can't you shave that fucking thing?"

She saw that I was staring at the area above her upper lip. She backed away a couple of steps, looking hurt.

"What?" I said. "You know you have a mustache, don't you? And what did you do, gain ten pounds? You really need to hit the gym big-time."

"I should go now," she said. "I mean, I just came by to see how you were doing, but I ... I really better ... What's *that*?"

She was looking toward the night table with a shocked, disgusted expression.

"What does it look like?" I said. "It's a picture."

"But who is it?"

"My sister."

"Come on, that isn't really—"

"Sure is. Can't you see the resemblance?"

"But ... but she's naked."

"So?"

Angie leaned closer toward the night table and looked back and forth at me and at the picture a few times.

"Oh, my God," she said.

"Nice rack, huh?" I said. "And look at those legs—not an ounce of flab on 'em. Yeah, Barb had a great bod and she knew how to use it too."

Angie backed away farther, stumbling on her heels; then she turned and rushed out of the room. I shook my head, wondering what was wrong with her, when I noticed the empty cup on the tray. I pushed the call button until somebody answered on the intercom, and then I screamed, "Hey, where the hell's that fat bitch with my apple juice?"

Jason Starr

The following titles by Jason Starr are available from:

No Exit Press,
P O Box 394
Harpenden
AL5 1XJ

ISBN Code	Title	Author	Price
1901982459	Cold Caller	Jason Starr	£4.99
1901982998	Nothing Personal	Jason Starr	£6.99
1909182831	Fake ID	Jason Starr	£6.99
1842430475	Hard Feelings	Jason Starr	£6.99
1842430955	Tough Luck	Jason Starr	£6.99

Please add, ten per cent in the UK and twenty per cent elsewhere, of the order value for postage and packing. Cheques should be made payable to **Oldcastle Books Ltd**

We accept Switch, Mastercard and Visa Please enclose expiry date with Mastercard/Visa and issue number with Switch plus card number and full name on card